BLURB

Georgia Donnelley is determined to be the boss of her own life by doing the things she never got to do while growing up. That and a few extra adventures added in. The only problem? She is broke, homeless, and hiding from an abusive ex. So instead, she heads back home to Darling, Tennessee.

Who knew life would take her back home to the man who awakened her Little eight years ago? Hutch hasn't thought about Georgia since the night she left Darling eight years before. At least, that's what he told himself until she crashed, literally, back into his life. It turns out the girl who sparked the Daddy inside him is his one and only. He'll spend forever with her if only he can protect her from her crazy adventures.

Oh yeah, and make sure her ex, who is determined to get her back, doesn't make her dead instead.

HUTCH

SABRE SECURITY DADDIES

BOOK ONE

CAMI CARLISLE

WRITEWAY PRESS

Writing a book is such a huge project. This would not have been possible without the help and support of so many people.

Thank you to Kate Oliver. Your advice, encouragement and support truly made this all possible.

Thank you Cheryl Maddox, editor extraordinaire. I appreciate the love you showed for Hutch and Georgia and your commitment to helping me bring them to the page.

Thank you to all my beta and ARC readers. Your willingness to spend time reading and honing this story with me were so very necessary.

Thank you most of all to my husband, who spent countless hours helping me figure out the business side of things and gave his unwavering support and motivation to make this all happen. I love you!

There are so many more, so thank you to everyone I didn't mention who helped me on this journey. You made it all worthwhile.

NOTE FROM THE AUTHOR ABOUT TRIGGERS

This book is a Daddy Dom, little girl, age play romance. Age play falls under the BDSM umbrella. The MMC in this book is a Daddy Dom and the MFC identifies as a Little. This is an act of role-playing between the characters. This is a consensual power exchange relationship between adults. In this story there are spankings and discussions of other forms of discipline including writing lines, corner time, mouth soaping, and anal play. This story also deals with the themes of narcissistic parental abuse and domestic violence.

Please consider your own well-being before reading.
Love, Cami

CHAPTER 1

*G*eorgia opened one eye and surveyed her surroundings. Between the skidding tires, the shrieking brakes, and the out-of-control spinning, her truck was toast. At least she had avoided plunging off the side of the winding mountain road.

Even though her truck had stopped spinning, her head was another matter. She sucked in a steadying breath to keep from throwing up. Now what?

She flinched when yet another drop of water splatted against the plastic bag bonneting her head. Better than having it soak her hair.

She added repairing the truck's roof to the growing list of things to fix.

Having things to fix on the truck didn't matter. Her new truck was fabulous.

As soon as she'd squirreled away four thousand dollars, she'd thrown the cash and a few clothes in her suitcase and run.

A salesman had headed straight for her and before long, she was driving off in a hot pink 1954 Chevy truck with giant flowers painted all over it, twenty-five hundred dollars lighter. It was awesome! She'd promptly named her new truck Petals.

Most people would call her gullible, but she wasn't. She wasn't stupid, either, though many people from her past called her that, too. They were wrong.

Her truck made her happy. For eight, miserable years, she'd searched for her joy. Petals gave her more joy than her soon-to-be ex, Jarrod the Jerkface, ever had.

At least it had until a few hours ago when the rain hit. In hindsight, when the salesman said the truck needed a little work, she should have asked more questions. But her truck was special. And if her truck could be special, maybe she could be special, too. She hadn't felt special in a long time. Ever, really.

She had spent twenty-six years living her life to please others and it had never worked. It was time to live her life for herself. From now on, she was going to please her true self. As soon as she figured out who her true self was. She'd already learned one thing. Her true self liked big pink trucks, even if they broke down in the middle of the road.

She tapped her head with her fingers to relieve her growing headache. Unfortunately, the plastic bag she wore crackled in her ears with each tap.

Petals couldn't stay in the middle of the road. She should get out and evaluate the situation. When she twisted her door handle, however, nothing happened.

Right. Another item for the 'Fix-It' list.

A glance at her watch told her to hurry. All the beds at Darling's only shelter would be gone by five o'clock. That was another sign her luck was changing. Darling hadn't had a shelter when she lived there before.

She hadn't needed the shelter until her conversation with her sister. Why had she thought her sister would help? She should never have come home, but she had no choice.

She straightened her imaginary crown. The old Georgia let adversity stop her. She was a new person, focusing on her next adventure.

Which right now meant fixing her truck, driving to Darling, and spending the night in a shelter. She squeezed her eyes shut and tried not to hyperventilate.

It wouldn't be so bad. A shelter was better than sleeping in her truck at all those rest stops. Rest stops were dark and scary. She hadn't gotten much sleep, but she had made it, thanks to Petals. Her truck had taken good care of her. Now, she needed to take care of her truck.

Since she couldn't open her door, she might as well try to crank Petals one more time. She had never driven a stick shift truck before. Never driven anything at all, actually. The salesman had given her instructions, which she probably should have written down.

He'd said to turn the key to the on position. Step on the starter pedal. Pump the gas twice. To be safe, she pumped it six extra times. Then step on the starter and head on your way.

Only, she couldn't head on her way. Petals just whirred at her. She tried again and got the same result.

Sweat stung her eyes. Petals had no air conditioning, and the vent didn't work unless the truck was moving. She would have let the windows down, but the handles kept falling off. She'd added those to her list.

The ominous clouds chose that moment to open their floodgates, battering her truck loud enough to block out the thunder.

Then, out of nowhere, tires squealed, and a dark shape flashed past the back of her truck, almost hitting her. It hadn't been big enough to be a car. Maybe a motorcycle? It stopped, and she could vaguely make out movement. The driver headed toward her truck.

"You have got to be kidding me!" Georgia groaned. She had

made it across the country unscathed, only to be axe murdered by a biker.

She dropped her head to the steering wheel of her truck with a thunk and winced as pain flared across her forehead. Tears joined the sweat burning her eyes, but she blinked them back. She would not cry. She was pursuing joy, darn it!

Cranking the truck would have to wait. Right now, she had to deal with whoever had almost hit her. To be fair, her truck spanned both lanes. Hopefully, they weren't too mad. When people were mad at her, it made her heart race and her tummy hurt. Like it was doing now.

Good thing she was now a lucky person who wasn't afraid of adventure and the great unknown. There were nice bikers, right? He would be kind, understanding, and helpful. The new Georgia was lucky that way.

A sharp rap on her window made her jump. The wavey, unfocused shape of a man stood by her truck. Thanks to the broken defroster, she couldn't see out her side windows any better than she could see through her windshield.

"Let… down… make… alright," a muffled voice asked.

Georgia couldn't catch most of his words because it was still raining so hard, but the voice was rich and deep. She shivered, and not in fear this time.

"Just a second," she called out, scouring the seat for the window handle. Where was it?

It only needed a screw to reattach it to the door, but she hadn't stopped to fix it. It hadn't been an issue until the bottom had fallen from the slate-gray clouds overhead earlier. That's when she discovered the defrost didn't work.

The man tapped on her window again and leaned closer. "… name… Hutchinson… window."

Georgia's efforts to remain calm flew right out the foggy

window. Holy Moly! It had been eight years, but she would never forget that name. That voice.

Jedidiah "Hutch" Hutchinson stood outside her door. Hutch was her former best friend Tazzy's cousin, but he acted like her brother. Georgia had crushed on him throughout her childhood. He was still as bossy as he had been back then.

"Just a second," she called out. "I'm trying."

Why was he here? He had joined the military and intended to make it his career. Of course, that had been eight years ago. He must have changed as much as she had.

By the tone of his voice, he was less than happy. His mood wasn't going to improve, though, because she couldn't let down the window or open the door.

She searched again, but the handle wasn't there. Even if she found it, her hands shook too hard to fit it back in place.

Breathe. She had to breathe.

Something had sucked all the oxygen out of the truck. She grabbed for Penny, her stuffed unicorn, lying on the seat beside her. She squeezed and released Penny's soft fur and concentrated on how it felt in her hand. Slowly, her pulse returned to normal.

"… can't… saying… just… window."

He needed to stop talking. Something about his voice gave her tummy serious butterflies.

The rain had slacked off again, so maybe she could hear him better.

"I'm only going to ask one more time. Let down the window right now."

Yep, he was definitely irritated. His irritation consumed all her energy. Not that she blamed him. He was getting soaked. But it wasn't like she wanted to sit here, stranded across both lanes of the road, entombed in her admittedly awesome truck. Suddenly, she was irritated, too. So there.

Giving up on the handle, she opened the vent window. The slit was only large enough for one finger to stick out through the thin crack. She imagined her finger poking his chest. He was going to listen to her by golly.

"Listen, you. I'm trying. I can't hear you over the rain. Nothing on this door is working right now. Go around and get in the truck so we can talk." She tugged at the vent window, but her conscience wouldn't allow her to be rude. Before she could stop herself, she called out, "Thank you!"

With that, she snapped the window shut. He had her so flustered she hadn't even told him who she was. If only she could drive away.

At least he'd stopped to check on her. He could have driven by and left her stranded. And why had she invited him to get into her truck? The knot of nerves in her stomach tightened.

He took his time walking around the truck. Penny's soft white fur underneath her hand calmed her while she waited. She yelped as it dawned on her that her stuffie was beside her on the seat.

Grown women didn't carry around stuffed animals. If Hutch saw Penny, he would think Georgia was insane. With a whispered apology, she grabbed Penny, kneeled on the seat, and bent across the seat to hide her below.

Thank goodness her other belongings were under there so Penny wouldn't be afraid. She couldn't just put her precious stuffie on the floor of the truck. She pressed her chest into the seat to reach far enough to pull out her duffle bag. There might be just enough room inside to keep Penny safe and hidden.

Georgia unzipped her bag and pushed Penny into the most available spot, tugging the zipper back up just as the door opened, screaming in protest. Hutch had better not hurt Petals. Her 'Fix It' list was long enough.

And then he was leaning in through the door. So rugged. So handsome.

So angry.

Georgia couldn't look at him when he was angry, so she refocused on storing the bag holding Penny back under the seat.

"Do you have any idea how unsafe—"

He started ranting at her before she could even sit up. Did he lecture everyone he helped like this? In such a stern voice? She should have given him a piece of her mind, but when she looked up, he froze. Georgia got it. She couldn't move. Couldn't have spoken if her life depended on it.

Hutch had changed in the past eight years. He'd always been handsome, but now he took her breath away. Had his eyes always been that deep, ocean blue? If she stared too long, she might drown.

And he definitely hadn't had those muscular arms. Arms that would be perfect for warm cuddles or firm smacks to a misbehaving Little's bottom.

No, no. Nope. She was not having those thoughts now.

Hutch took a deep breath, and for one horrible moment, she thought she had spoken her last thoughts aloud. Her cheeks heated even as she attempted a smile.

He didn't say anything, merely raised one dark brow. Was he waiting for her to speak? She had to come up with something perfect. Something to wow him. "Hello, Hutch," she said. No, not said. It was more like she croaked like a frog.

Fan. Tastic.

CHAPTER 2

"Hello, Hutch." Georgia's words punched Hutch in the chest. It had been eight years since she had disappeared, and her last night in Darling had been extreme. He'd blamed himself for years. And she acted like it had been eight days rather than eight years?

Fuck that.

Tazzy had cried for weeks after Georgia ghosted. He'd taken her to Georgia's house to speak with the Donnelleys. Georgia's mother had explained that Georgia had moved to California after marrying. Planned for months, she'd said, and apologized for Georgia's unsurprising lack of manners.

Hutch hadn't believed her. Georgia's mother was a selfish bitch. Nevada, Georgia's sister, told Tazzy two days later that Georgia couldn't be bothered. She had a new life and was leaving small-town Darling behind her.

Maybe, but in his arms that night, there was no way she had been planning to marry another man. Georgia needed to pursue an acting career if her mother hadn't lied.

Tazzy hadn't believed them, either. She'd said Georgia wouldn't do something like that. They'd tried to track her down, but she'd disappeared. It had crushed Tazzy. Georgia had been her best friend.

And now, she was kneeling across the seat of a ridiculous pink truck older than dirt, smiling at him and throwing out a "Hello, Hutch." His shock gave way to anger. He wanted answers.

"Georgia Anne Donnelley," he said. "It's been a long time. But then, it's not Donnelley anymore." Her smile wobbled. "You want to sit up so I can get out of the rain?"

"Oh, sorry!" Pink stained her smooth cheeks as she scrambled backward.

Might as well start with the obvious. "What's with the plastic bag on your head?"

He hadn't thought her blush could get any deeper. She snatched the makeshift bonnet from her head. "I just… the roof leaks, and I was tired of it soaking my hair, so I— never mind. I…" She sighed. "It's good to see you, Hutch. How've you been?"

Oh, hell no. They were not making small talk. "What are you doing here, Georgia?"

She studied her lap. "Um, my truck won't start," she said, cringing as a drop of water smacked her head.

"I got that," he said. She jumped again when another drop of water splatted on her head.

Scowling, he snatched up the plastic bag, wedged it over the leak, and hooked it under the visor. "We'll get to your truck in a minute. That's not what I meant. What are you doing back in Darling? Does Tazzy know you're here?"

"No," she said, refusing to look at him.

Hutch swallowed his anger. She had to know how hurt Tazzy would be. Did she not care? The old Georgia would never have done something like that. Guess being married to big money changed people.

He locked down his temper. "Why not?"

Georgia glanced back up, her milk chocolate eyes sweeter than any candy on the planet, but she couldn't hold his gaze. He deepened his tone and said, "I asked you a question, Georgia Anne."

"I'm not staying so I didn't see the point. Nevada asked me to come."

She'd always crossed her fingers to cancel out lies. So, she was lying to him now. His hand itched to do something it had no right to do.

"Your sister asked you to come home for the first time in eight years?" He made sure the skepticism was evident in his voice.

Something flashed in her eyes. Hurt, maybe? Then she raised her chin a notch. "I can visit Nevada if I want to."

"You can," he said. "I just don't know why you'd want to." Nevada was a carbon copy of her mother. Those two had made Georgia believe she was unlovable. It worked. Georgia walked away and never looked back. She'd left everyone behind—even Tazzy. Even him. But his only concern was Tazzy.

How could she erase Tazzy from her life so easily? With that in mind, he demanded, "Why are you here? And don't lie to me. Need a break from the champagne and caviar lifestyle?"

Georgia's face paled. He was out of line, but he couldn't seem to rein it in.

Her eyes glistened with unshed tears. "Hutch, I didn't… I mean, it wasn't like that." Her lips parted as if to say more, but she didn't.

Hutch nodded. If she didn't want to explain, fine. He didn't care. He needed to get to Sabre Security anyway. His boss, Reid Nolan, was already going to be pissed as shit. This part of his day needed to be done. "It doesn't matter."

He ran his hand along the worn blanket draped over the seat. "Why didn't you fly home? Private jet not available?"

She seemed to panic for a moment, then said, "I don't like planes."

"Right," he said. "You'd rather drive in a dilapidated truck."

He had always been able to read her eyes. Right now, she was sorry and afraid. And he was being an ass. She didn't move, just stared up at him.

"Peaches, I'm soaking wet, and I've got somewhere to be. I'll look at your truck, and then I need to go."

She flinched when he used her old nickname. "I didn't know you were back in Darling," she said, wringing her shirt around her finger. "You said you were making the military your career."

"Plans change. More importantly, Tazzy's dad died four years ago. It hit her hard, so I came home to be with her and help Trev with their ranch."

She gasped and gave his arm a comforting squeeze. "I'm so sorry," she said, and he could tell she meant it.

Something hard poked his hip. Reaching behind him, he pulled out an old crank-style window handle from deep in the seam of the seat.

Her eyes brightened when she saw it. "My window crank thingy! No wonder I couldn't find it."

He scanned the interior of her truck. There were holes in the cushion, doors, and dash where the padding spilled out. The defrosters and other parts and handles were broken. A sopping wet piece of cardboard covered a hole in the floor under the brake pedal. He stifled a growl when he realized the mobile nightmare didn't even have a rearview mirror or seatbelts. She shouldn't drive this truck around the neighborhood, much less across the country.

She took the window handle from his hand and tried to shove it back into place. Jesus. He had never met a woman who needed a Daddy more than this woman. "How long have you been driving this heap?"

Her back snapped straight, and she glared at him. "Did you just insult Pet—my truck?"

Had she named her truck? His Daddy radar pinged, but lots of people named their rides. That didn't mean anything. She looked so affronted he almost grinned. He held back because this situation was serious.

"If that is what you call this motorized death trap. Now, how long have you been driving this truck? And I use that term loosely."

"I'll have you know I have had my incredible baby for over a week, and she has never had a problem." He held her stare until she mumbled, "Until now."

"Until now," he repeated.

She lifted her chin a notch. She did that whenever she knew she was standing on thin ice. Never one to back down, she added, "If you'd stop disrespecting my truck and help me, I'd appreciate it. I have an, um, important meeting at 5:00."

He was tired of the sass. "I should have reported this road hazard to the cops."

Her face paled. "Don't do that. Please?"

Oh, he wasn't going to like this one bit. "Why not?"

"Because," she said immediately. When he just stared at her, she sighed. "Fine," she said. Without another word, she took out her driver's license and handed it to him. What the hell?

He looked at the license. Yep, he didn't like it. It wasn't a license. "How in the hell have you been driving for the last eight years with a learner's permit? Hubby give you a personal chauffeur? Wait, how in the fuck did you buy this truck without a license?" Then it hit him. "You paid cash."

He cursed under his breath when he read the name on the card. Georgia Jemison. She was now Georgia Jemison. He wanted to rip the card in half. He hated her new name.

She lived in Los Alto, California. Well, shit. One of the wealthiest cities in the country. She traded to the top when she traded up, didn't she? Nothing but the best for Georgia Donnel—Jemison.

He needed to get back on his bike and pretend this delightful rendezvous had never happened. She had moved up and moved on. He hadn't crossed her mind once in eight years.

He gripped the armrest, and his finger punctured the thin leather. "How'd you wind up straddling the entire road?"

She started talking about foggy windows and sharp curves. His head almost exploded when she told him how fast she'd been driving.

He'd only thought he was angry before. He held up a hand to stop her mid-explanation and drew a deep breath through tight lips. "Let me get this straight. I almost wrecked my bike because you were driving so fast you almost ran off the mountain. What the ever-loving fuck, Georgia? You know better than that. You were raised—"

"You are not the boss of me, Jedidiah Hutchinson," she interrupted. "Maybe I had an emergency."

"Don't interrupt, little girl."

Damn it! That slipped out. He didn't know if she was a Little. But even if she were, she wasn't his, so he didn't need to use words like that.

"It's obvious someone needs to be the boss of you. You parked in the middle of the road instead of on the shoulder where you should have been."

She scowled at him, her hands finding her hips. "I wasn't parked. Petals cut off when she stopped spinning."

Hutch pinched the bridge of his nose. "You didn't mention any spinning."

"Because you butted in. I yanked the steering wheel back when I started off the road because the drop-off was so steep. Petals spun, and then I couldn't get her cranked."

Oh, he was going to spank her ass. He forced himself to refocus on what she was saying, following her gesture to the ignition switch. Wait. Was that a tiny penguin stuffie wearing a shark costume on her keychain? It was adorable. Just the sort of thing a

Little would have. Was Georgia a Little? He stopped that thought in its tracks. Lots of women had cute key chains. It didn't mean she was a Little. Right? He turned his attention back to what she was saying.

"—and she wouldn't start, even though I pushed the gas more than the salesman said I had to."

His head was definitely going to explode. They would find his remains in this flowery, hot pink truck with no head attached to his body. The itch in his palm grew stronger. He closed his eyes and counted to ten. "Is that everything?" he asked, striving to keep his voice level.

When he opened his eyes, she watched him with a wary expression. At least there was some sense of self-preservation in her.

She placed her soft hand back on his arm. "Are you alright? Your face is red, and there's a vein's jumping in your temple."

He counted to ten again. This time he pictured ten swats to her reckless, obstinate, lawbreaking backside.

Georgia was her husband's concern now. No matter what the Daddy inside him said. She stared at him, wrapping a strand of hair around her finger. Fuck it.

"Do you know how much trouble you are in?" he demanded.

She huffed at him. "Why? You're the one who almost ran into me." She must have heard his growl because her eyes widened and she stopped talking.

Smart girl. One more word and she would be over his knee getting the spanking she deserved, whether he had the right to do it or not.

"You're driving without a license, with no regard for your safety. Your truck is a ticking timebomb. You're going to kill yourself or someone else. You've been gone a long time, but not long enough not to know what I want to do."

CHAPTER 3

*G*eorgia squirmed in her seat, trying to stifle the tingles between her thighs. He wasn't talking about what it sounded like, right? "You can't do that!"

Hutch smirked. "Sure I can, Peaches."

He was hotter than in her dreams. Tazzy hadn't been the only person from Darling she'd missed. But he was scary when his brows met in that deep scowl.

"I couldn't move my truck out of the road. Petals wouldn't crank. I tried a bazillion times! What was I supposed to do, get out and push her off the road?"

" I could have killed you. Did you even think about that?"

She huffed and crossed her arms over her chest. "It's not like I planned it. I wasn't thinking at all. I just reacted."

"That's my point, little girl. If you drive, you have to think before anything happens. Especially if you are driving a truck that is hard to control on a wet mountain road."

He had to stop calling her little girl. But when the shoe fit and all.

He squeezed his thigh, which wouldn't have made her nervous

if he didn't keep glancing at her throat. He was over-stressed. She would ask as soon as he stopped talking.

He glared at her and demanded, "What if I had been driving my truck? I could have plowed right into you."

"How was I supposed to know you were coming around the curve? I couldn't hear you over the rain pounding on Petal's roof." He gave her a knowing look, and she narrowed her eyes. "Do not say anything to make me take out my pepper spray."

It was Hutch's turn to narrow his eyes, and she almost gulped. Now her bottom started tingling. She remembered more about that last night eight years ago and scooched back against her door.

"Good move, Peaches, but I can still reach you. Would you like to rephrase your last statement?"

Did he even know he was flexing his hand? If the tingling in her bottom got any stronger, her legs would start twitching—time to soothe the savage biker.

"I only meant I didn't think of someone coming around the curve. And I don't even own pepper spray, so I couldn't spray you even if I wanted to." At his raised brows, she quickly added, "Which I don't."

"Where's your roadside safety kit?" he asked. She slipped her hand behind her back but froze when he said, "Do not lie to me."

Darn it. He could be an over-protective, overbearing jerk. Her bottom lip trembled, so she caught it between her teeth.

"I didn't… I mean, I never… um, I never thought I'd need one." She lifted her chin, but she didn't think it made her look stronger the way it trembled. Darn it! She did not want to cry in front of him.

Hutch read her. "You can't go racing around on the mountain. Swear to god, you scared years off my life. Do I have any gray hairs?" He pulled his hair toward his face as if checking for silver strands.

She couldn't stop the giggle that escaped. "I'm sorry, Hutch. I was just in a hurry." He didn't need to know why.

He searched her eyes and then sighed. "Alright, but if I hear of it happening again…"

"I know. I'll be in for another lecture."

He leveled her with a severe gaze. "No, I'll make a much stronger impression than that."

And there came the tingles again. Hopefully, he couldn't tell.

"Tell you what, I'll crank your truck if you call Tazzy while you're home." He held out his hand for her to shake. "Deal?"

Could she reconnect with Tazzy? She had missed her best friend. If she reached out, Tazzy might say no, and why wouldn't she? Then Georgia's hope that one day they could be friends again would disappear.

It was a risk, but she'd never know if she didn't try. She grabbed Hutch's hand before she could change her mind. His large, firm hand gave her a funny feeling in her tummy. "Deal."

HUTCH

Georgia was all he remembered and so much more. He would bet everything he owned that she was a Little. She gave off all the vibes. Not that it mattered.

He wouldn't touch her. Too many things separated them, the most important being her husband. His jaw tightened at that thought. If she were his wife, she wouldn't be driving across the country in that junker. Especially all alone. But she wasn't his, and that was the point. He didn't steal from other men. Even if those men were apparently dicks.

So, no matter how adorable she was, she was off-limits. Besides, she wasn't staying. Hopefully, her contacting Tazzy wasn't a mistake.

"Swap places with me," he said. He pulled her onto his lap, and damn, she felt good there. But nothing could come from her time in Darling. He set her down to his right and slid behind the steering wheel.

"So, what did you shove under the seat earlier?" He kept his tone casual, noticing his question startled her.

"Nothing," she said. "I was making sure the bags hadn't spilled." Her hand disappeared between the seat and the door, and he knew her fingers were crossed.

"When your lies catch up to you, there is always a price to pay."

Her face went blank. "I know that better than you ever will."

"Maybe, maybe not. Now, what's under the seat?"

"It doesn't matter," she said with a flat voice he didn't like.

"I wouldn't have asked if it didn't matter. Answer me, or I'll look for myself."

She rolled her eyes. "Oh, for heaven's sake. I was tucking my st- stuff in place. Go ahead and look. All you'll find are blankets, water, and an old suitcase."

"Ready for my magic trick?" he asked with a wink. That earned him a smile.

"Dazzle me. I've tried everything."

"Everything, huh?" He went through all the steps, grinning when it cranked.

She glared at the starter as if it had betrayed her. "How did you do that?"

His grin broadened into a smile. She looked like an angry kitten, spitting mad and ready to scratch his eyes out. "I did the same thing you did, Peaches. The engine probably flooded when you spun out. You made it worse by pumping the gas. It usually takes a few minutes for the fuel to settle, and then it's fine."

"You knew it would crank! You tricked me into calling Tazzy."

He no longer felt like smiling.

"Tazzy was your best friend for years. I shouldn't have to trick you into calling her."

She deflated right in front of him. Leaning forward, she covered her face with her hands. He stayed still although everything inside him wanted to pull her into his lap.

When she sat back up, she looked lost. "What do I say to her? She probably hates me. I'm a horrible person and even worse friend."

The pain in her eyes almost gutted him. "You're not horrible. I just don't understand why you did the things you did. I want to, and so will Tazzy."

"I never wanted to hurt her, or you, or anyone. It just happened so fast. Everything changed overnight."

That didn't track. Her sister had said she'd been engaged for months. Still, even if it happened fast, she'd had eight years to explain. She hadn't.

Talking to Tazzy would give them both some closure if nothing else. Maybe it could be a new beginning.

"Just call her, Peaches. I'll give her a heads-up you're in town. That way, she'll be expecting your call."

Her face lit with relief. "You'd do that for me? Thank you."

"No problem," he said. "Give me your phone, and I'll put in Tazzy's number."

Her eyes widened, and she bit her lip. Now what? "Give me your phone, Georgia."

She sighed, then reached into her purse again. "I can give it to you, but it won't do you much good," she said, placing her dead phone in his hand.

And he was back to counting to ten. "How long has your phone been dead?"

She shrugged. "I'm not sure. A couple of days? Maybe more." She scrunched her nose at him.

Cuteness was not going to help her. "You drove alone, for over two days, without a way of contacting anyone in case of trouble?"

"There was no trouble. Well, until now. Then you came along and saved the day. Problem solved."

He forced his hand to loosen its grip on her phone. "Why is your phone dead?"

"I didn't have a way to charge it. Petals here is from the pre-cellular device era. She doesn't exactly come with charging ports."

He heard her unspoken *'duh.'* "Lose the attitude, little girl. That's no excuse. You could still have charged it in your hotel room overnight."

She stared out the window in silence. Tightness gripped Hutch's jaw. "Georgia, what hotels did you stay in on the way?"

Her chin notched up again, and Hutch braced. "I didn't stay in hotels. When I got tired, I pulled off at a rest stop. This seat is plenty comfortable."

"You're telling me you spent the night in your truck?"

She shook her head. "Not always night. Sometimes I was tired, so I stopped during the day. I always stopped when I was tired, even though it added more days to my trip."

He just stared at her. She shouldn't have had to stop that many times, even coming from California. Traveling on the interstate should have taken only three to four days.

"How long did it take you to get here?"

A guilty look flashed across her face, but she answered. "Eight in all. One day on the bus, and then seven in my truck."

"How did a four-day trip at most become eight?"

She shrugged, but she didn't meet his eyes. "I don't like driving on the interstate." When he didn't erupt, she quickly went on. "I need to get going. Slide this way. The driver's side door won't open." She gave him an apologetic smile and jumped down from the truck.

Hell, she needed a step ladder to get in and out of this monster. He couldn't think about her door not opening. She could have been trapped inside her truck by some thug at a rest stop.

Another growl escaped before he could stop it as he shoved himself across the seat.

"Thanks for your help. It was wonderful seeing you again. I wish we could talk longer, but I have that appointment."

That was it? She burst into his life and disappeared again, just like that? Not happening.

"Why don't I follow you? Make sure you get there in one piece? You headed home?"

She grimaced at his words, then smiled and shook her head.

"No, that's okay. I've already had a good visit at home. I'm... staying in town. At a, a hotel."

"A hotel? You drove all this way to stay in a hotel?" That settled it. Nevada was a bitch.

"Yes, well, I just showed up. There's a massive retreat booked this week at Graceview. I told Nevada I'd rather stay in town."

"I thought Nevada invited you to come to visit." When her hand edged behind her back, he changed course. "Never mind. I'll follow you to the hotel. Better yet, I'll follow you to Lowell's Garage. You remember Winnie, don't you? She can fix your truck in a day or two so driving back to California is safe."

"That isn't necessary." Georgia shook her head.

"I insist," Hutch answered back. "That truck is either going to the garage or the junkyard. Your choice, but you will not drive that truck in its current condition. It isn't safe."

"You can't do that." Georgia stomped her foot. Cute.

"You will discover I can do more than that, little girl." Dumb. This was so dumb. He should let her go. But not until he figured out what was going on.

He held up his cell phone. "What's it going to be? Am I calling the garage or a wrecker?"

"You... I... you're infuriating!" she shouted. Then she slumped against the side of her ridiculous truck as if all the air leaked out of her.

She looked utterly defeated. He couldn't have that. He wrapped his arms around her, holding her close. "I need you to be safe, little girl," he said, as he rested his chin atop her head.

She looked up at him, confused. And maybe hopeful. "Why?"

And if that wasn't the question of the century, he didn't know what was.

CHAPTER 4

Georgia sat behind the wheel in her cranked truck as instructed, waiting for Hutch to pull behind her to head toward Lowell's Garage. He was trying to look out for her like he always had. That didn't matter when she didn't have the money to pay for repairs. She would have taken Petals to the car doctor days ago if she did.

She had traveled to Darling for the sole purpose of asking her sister for a loan. It was a long shot. Her family didn't work that way. Not with her, anyway.

It didn't surprise her that Nevada was in charge now. She would have been the obvious choice in her mother's eyes. Even though they were twins, Nevada could do no wrong. Georgia never did anything right. She had never understood why. It didn't matter anymore.

With her mother gone, she had hoped her sister might help her at least a little in her current situation, especially since it was their mother's fault in the first place.

Georgia shook the thoughts away and forced her fingers to release their death grip on the steering wheel. She glanced in her side mirror. Yep, Hutch still followed her. At a safe distance, of course.

She sighed. He was a good man under his gruff exterior. Things might have turned out differently if her life hadn't taken such a nosedive on her eighteenth birthday. She had connected with him that night. She often looked back on his saving her from that awful party. And the lecture and punishment that followed. Her pussy clenched even now at the thought. He hadn't changed if some of the things he had said to her earlier were anything to go by.

She had forgotten what a sneaky sneak he could be when he wanted something. He had known her truck would crank after sitting for that long. Now she had to call Tazzy.

A wave of guilt washed over her, the same as it had for the past eight years. She should *want* to call Tazzy. She *did* want to.

Tazzy played a part in every happy childhood memory she had. The two of them had been inseparable. They had taken the same classes, joined the same clubs, and played the same sports. She smiled at the memory, even as her heart ached.

A cold knot formed in her stomach at the thought of calling her former best friend. What if Tazzy hated her now? Or worse, what if Tazzy didn't remember her, at least not as a best friend?

Her breath hitched at the thought, carried away with the tragic movie playing in her thoughts. Who could blame Tazzy for moving on and replacing her? Anyone would if their best friend had walked away without a word for eight years. Anyone would hate a person like that for life.

She hated to break her promise to Hutch, but there was no way she had the courage to make that call. Better to leave things as they are. Why stir things up when she wasn't even staying in Darling?

And she wasn't staying. She didn't deserve a life, safe and happy in Darling, reconnecting with all her friends. She had made her choices, sort of, and she had to live with the consequences.

She breathed in and let it out slowly, relaxing her grip on the steering wheel again. She didn't need another glance in the side mirror. Hutch would still be following her. He said he would follow her to Lowell's, even though it was in the opposite direction. And Jedidiah Hutchinson always did what he said he would.

Always.

That familiar sick feeling squeezing her chest grew tighter by the mile. The familiarity of the road allowed her to revisit that morning's conversation with Nevada.

She had crawled up the driveway to Graceview, expecting to meet with her mother. The ironic name of her childhood home did not escape her. Grace was the last thing she could expect there.

Nevada perched on a white wooden rocking chair on the front veranda, coming to her feet as Georgia parked. Her sister was the perfect picture of the cultured, warm-hearted, southern woman. In reality, Nevada was as cold and imposing as the manor house she stood before.

Georgia slid across the seat and opened the passenger door. Her heart had thundered so hard she wondered if she might pass out. She had held onto Penny, praying Nevada couldn't see her.

It was silly, she knew, how much comfort she drew from a stuffed animal. She should throw it away and find more adult ways to deal with her anxiety, but she couldn't do that. She shuddered and hugged Penny tighter in case her friend had heard her thoughts.

Penny had been with her since she was a child. The one thing her father had given her when he won the unicorn at the state fair. That trip had been just the two of them. Nevada had been competing in some beauty pageant or another.

Penny had been her comfort, her security, her everything. Her mother had thrown Penny away when Georgia was ten, telling Georgia she was much too old for baby toys. Georgia had rescued Penny from the trash bin and hidden her. After that, she pulled her out only when she was desperate.

27

Like eight years ago.

Like now.

She had pressed her stuffie to her chest as she slid across the seat. Just a quick hug, then Georgia could face her sister. The soft fur pressing against her palm calmed her. She would have cuddled Penny longer if she hadn't known Nevada was already staring.

Instead, she had straightened her shoulders and reluctantly inched toward what already felt like her doom.

Her sister leaned against one of the square columns that bracketed the long front steps. She hadn't spoken until Georgia placed a foot on the bottom step.

"I'm going to have to stop you right there, Georgia," her sister said as she stood. It was mid-July in Tennessee, and Nevada Donnelley stood, hair smoothed up in a chignon, makeup impeccable, in a bright pink power suit dress that barely covered the top of her thighs, complete with sparkling stiletto sandals.

Georgia had stared up at her, trying to come up with a way to break the ice. Before her brain had engaged, her mouth had spit out, "Nice dress. You match my truck. The feathers around the wrist are a nice touch."

Yep. That was what Georgia had said. Nevada had not been amused, so with a sigh, she had added, "Hello, Nevada. Is there a reason I can't come onto the porch?"

"There's no need, sister dear. You won't be staying, and we aren't interested in anything you have to say."

Georgia knew to keep a handle on her anger. She had learned that lesson in the eight years she'd been away. Painfully.

No, with people like Jarrod and Nevada, timing was everything. She tried damage control. "I'm sorry I didn't call before I came for a visit. I realize my arrival is unexpected. I've missed you."

Nevada's face had been a mask of indifference.

Georgia had kept going. She hadn't seen her sister in eight years, although they had spoken over the phone periodically.

28

Nevada kept her up to date on the latest Darling gossip. Although, she had neglected to mention Hutch returning to town.

After all this time, surely she should warrant at least a smile. She remembered the cold ache that had sparked in her chest and rubbed her chest as if it still hurt.

Standing in the yard before her childhood home like some unwanted cast-off, she had tried again. "Well, I know how important your schedule is. I will only take a minute of your time."

Her sister had drawn out an exasperated sigh. "I know why you're here, Georgie Porgie. You want money because you abandoned your husband. I knew you'd run eventually. I'm surprised it took you eight years."

Reality had slapped her in the face at that moment. She should have known what would happen. Of course, Jarrod would call her family when she hadn't come home and try to plant lies in her sister's head. That was his usual tactic. And, of course, her sister had taken his side.

She couldn't give up, though. She had driven all this way, so she'd forged ahead. "I see Jarrod called you. I can only imagine what he told you."

That got her a raised brow. "And what would that be, Georgie?"

"What would what be?"

"What he told me. I'm curious what you think he said."

Georgia's heart had sunk, realizing this conversation would not end well. Why had she thought it would? Mara had forced her to marry Jarrod. She had arranged the marriage without consulting her. Nevada wouldn't help her get out of it now. That would be admitting their mother had made a mistake.

I am so stupid.

She fooled herself into believing that once Nevada realized what Mara had done, her sister would welcome her back and help her get her life back. The only time her family helped her was when it benefited them. Of course, they took Jarrod's side.

The cold gleam in Nevada's eyes told Georgia all she needed to know.

Georgia stared through the windshield at the gorgeous Tennessee mountain surrounding her. She was so tired. Tired of being disappointed by the people who should be there for her. Tired of trying to make a marriage work all by herself. Tired of the lies. The cheating. The abuse.

Nevada's parting shot rang in her ears. "People are divided into two groups, Georgie, the superior and the inferior. You are inferior. I know it. You know it. And apparently, Jarrod knows it. People are only treating you accordingly."

Georgia's shoulders slumped. She hugged Penny to her chest. Why wouldn't they believe it? What had she ever done to prove them wrong? She was an embarrassment.

Her life was proof of it. What had she ever done but try to please the people in her life? But no matter what she did, it had never been good enough. *She* had never been good enough.

She should never have come back here. Darling wasn't her home anymore, and it never would be.

Georgia drove toward Darling, her mind racing. How in the world would she pay for repairs to her truck? Maybe she could get a temporary job at one of the shops. It was high tourist season.

And what had she been thinking when she told Hutch she was staying at a hotel? She wasn't thinking. She had panicked at the thought of his finding out that even her sister didn't want her.

She would have him take her to the first hotel they saw. She would pretend to go in and book a room. As soon as he drove away, she would thank them for their time and walk to the shelter.

Hopefully before 5:00 so she could have a bed.

CHAPTER 5

*W*hat was he doing?

Hutch followed Georgia back toward Darling, trying to explain it to himself. She had cut him and the entire town of Darling out of her life eight years ago.

That proved she neither wanted nor needed his help. Yet, here he was, following her to Lowell's to get the abomination she called a truck fixed. But he wouldn't sleep at night knowing she drove that thing.

There was something off with her story. He should dig into it and figure out exactly what she was hiding. But he didn't care. And if he kept telling himself that, he would eventually believe it.

He passed her when they got close to the garage so she would know where to turn.

He parked his bike and waited for her to park beside him. He tried to open her door, then stalked to the passenger side as she slid across the seat. Fucking heap of junk.

He helped her out of the truck so she wouldn't break her neck. And if he kept his hands on her hips longer than necessary, it was to make sure she had her footing. It had nothing to do with how perfectly her curves fit in his hands.

Billy Evans, the manager of Lowell's, walked out of the service bay area, wiping his hands on a grease-stained rag. "Hutch," he said, but he focused on Georgia.

Hutch didn't appreciate how Billy undressed her with his eyes. He threw his arm around her shoulder and pulled her close, ignoring her stiffness at his touch.

"Billy," he said, keeping his voice neutral. "You remember Georgia Anne Donnelley?"

Billy's eyes snapped to hers, his surprise evident on his face. "Sure do," he said. "I thought you ran off with some rich lawyer type. What brought you back to Darling?"

"Family," she said. "It's nice to see you again, Billy. How's Winnie doing?"

He grinned back at her. "She's good." Georgia jumped when he yelled, "Winnie, get your ass out here. We got company."

A voice called back from the bowels of the service bay, "Hold your horses. I'll be there in a minute."

The man glanced past them to Georgia's truck, then looked at Hutch in horror. "What the shit happened to that truck?"

Hutch just shook his head. At least it wasn't just him. "I would say Georgia, but she didn't do it. She just bought it and drove it all the way here from California. It needs a little work, and that's an understatement. I know Winnie can't fix it all, but I need it to meet safety standards so Peaches here doesn't get thrown in jail."

"There is nothing wrong with my truck. Petals is adorable. You're just jealous."

Hutch thought Billy's snort said it all, so he remained quiet. Georgia glared at him anyway before adding, "I need an estimate of the costs before you do anything. I'd appreciate it if you could put the most important repairs first."

Hutch could tell her it was going to cost a lot. Her truck didn't need repairs. It needed to be completely rebuilt and restored. When she saw how much it would cost, hopefully, she would sell it for scrap and get a newer car.

Not that he was going to tell her that. Nope. He was going to let Billy do the honors.

If she were his, he would have them restore it to mint condition just to see the smile it would bring to her face. But she wasn't his, and she wouldn't be his.

"Oh. My. Gosh!" Winnie's voice rang out from behind Billy. "Oh my gosh! Whose truck is that? It is awesome!"

Winnie stepped past Billy and saw Georgia. "Georgia Donnelley. It has been forever. How have you been?" She skipped forward and threw her arms around Georgia in a hug.

It was easy to see that Georgia hadn't expected the enthusiastic welcome. She froze solid, only hugging Winnie back when the girl didn't let her go.

Hutch hid his smile. His Peaches needed more people like Winnie in her life who would love her and show it.

When Winnie finally released her, Georgia grabbed Hutch's hand. He didn't think she even realized she'd done it. But damn if it didn't make him feel ten feet tall.

"Is that your truck?" Winnie asked. "Because it doesn't exactly look like Hutch's style." She grinned at him.

He liked Winnie. Her father died when she was young. Billy had stepped in to raise her. He only knew how to fix cars, so he taught Winnie that. It had not led to ideal friends.

She linked her arm with Georgia, saying, "Tell me what's been going on with you while you show me your truck."

As she led Georgia away, Winnie started doing a wide-stepped monkey walk. Georgia stumbled at first, and his heart lurched. But she caught on soon, and the girls traipsed across the parking lot, giggling and talking.

Hutch smiled. Yeah, if Georgia stayed in Darling, she would fit right in.

He talked with Billy while Winnie looked over the truck. Hutch didn't run into the mechanic often, but there was something off about the guy.

"You send that estimate to me, Billy," he told the mechanic. "I'll look over it and give it to Georgia."

It wasn't that he didn't trust Billy. All he knew was the mechanic could easily exploit Georgia's lack of knowledge.

Once Winnie saw what she needed to see, the girls skipped back. His heart warmed at the sight. Georgia was adorable. He could picture her coloring or playing with her stuffies in his cabin.

No. He was not going down that road. She had made it more than clear she was leaving. She would never be in his cabin. And damn if that didn't burn.

Once he made sure Billy had his cell phone number, he got Georgia's bags from her truck. It was the strangest mix he had ever seen. She had a polka dot Louis Vuitton suitcase that had to have cost thousands and two plastic bags filled with off-brand candy bars, ramen noodles, and juice boxes.

He might disapprove of the food selection, but the teddy bear stickers decorating the water bottle warmed his heart. Shaking his head, he threw the snacks into the saddlebag of his bike and strapped her suitcase onto the back.

"I did my best not to scratch your luggage, Peaches," he said as he strapped a spare helmet from the garage onto her head.

"Why do I have to wear this?" she demanded, face drawn into an adorable scowl. "You aren't wearing one."

"That is just one of the many perks of being the boss," he answered.

She stomped her foot and crossed her arms over her chest. "You're not the boss of me."

He just gave her a stern look, then climbed on his bike. "Get on behind me, Peaches."

She did as he said, with a little boost from him. He took her arms and wrapped them around his waist. She felt incredible. Her heat soaked through his shirt and warmed more than his skin. Thank goodness she was behind him and not in front.

"Hold on tight, and lean when I do. Ready?"

She nodded and pressed her helmet into his shoulder.

A few women had ridden behind him on his bike, but none affected him as Georgia did. She fit him perfectly. And her little body pressed so close to his had his cock throbbing.

He never considered Lowell's Garage to be that far outside of Darling. He was wrong. He would come in his pants like a teenager if he had to drive one more mile.

"What hotel?" he called back to her.

There was a long pause before she yelled, "The first one we come to."

What the hell?

"Are you telling me you booked a room at the Getaway Motel?"

"That's it."

She planned this trip. Why the fuck would she book a room in the skeeviest roach motel in Darling? She had to have known. It had been around since the 1960s.

Locals knew the place as the Getaway With It Motel. The police made regular sweeps because it was popular with drug dealers, though cheating partners were the primary clientele.

How did she find out about it? He didn't think they even had a website. Just inside the city limits, it was still a long way from the main thoroughfares. Out of the way, with no identification required. Those were the Getaway Motel's main attractions.

When he pulled into the motel parking lot, Georgia hopped off his bike and pulled off her helmet. She stared, eyes wide and mouth gaping, at the run-down building. Paint peeled from the walls in giant strips. Each room had an outside entrance to the parking lot, and he knew from experience that the chain locks inside the doors didn't protect worth shit against someone who wanted to get in.

She started to speak, but he got there first. "You are not staying here."

Her face was pale, but she notched up her chin at his words. "Still not the boss of me. I am staying here, and there is nothing you can do about it."

His temper had been smoldering, but her words set it on fire. "Georgia, this place is a shithole. There is nothing safe, or even clean, about it. Drug deals go down practically every night. There is no way in hell you're staying here. Does your husband know you have a room here?"

"He doesn't care," she said. "This is the closest place to Grace-view. It's fine."

He wanted to put her over his bike and spank some sense into her. He wouldn't allow his dog to stay here. She might be up in arms now, but she would be scared to death once she was alone.

He took a breath to calm his temper. "Georgia, this is not a safe place for you to stay. There was a shooting here just a few weeks ago. I forbid you to stay here."

He knew he had made a mistake the minute the words left his mouth. Her back snapped straight, and her eyes shot lightning bolts at him. She punched her fists onto her hips and leaned toward him. "You don't get a vote. It may have escaped your notice, but I managed to survive the past eight years without your oversight." She took a deep breath. "Look, I appreciate all you've done for me today. I'll only be here one night, two at the most. Will you call me when you get the estimate on the truck repairs? If you give me my things, you can get back to your day."

Her words slapped him in the face. She was right. He had no right or authority to tell her what to do. She was a grown woman who had been taking care of herself for a long time. She neither needed nor wanted his help.

There wasn't one damn thing he could do, so it was time he backed off.

It killed him to do it, but he unloaded her things from his bike. He put them down and looked at her. She drew up her mask, but not before he saw her. She was there. A Little girl, kicking and screaming, *'I can do it myself,'* all the while looking lost and afraid.

He brushed a strand of hair from her face and pressed a kiss to her forehead. "Be safe, Peaches, and call me if you need anything."

Georgia squared her shoulders, picked up her things, and walked into the motel's office to get the key to her room. Every Daddy in the county would kick his ass for leaving her there, but she had made herself crystal clear. So, he did the hardest thing he'd ever had to do. He got back on his bike and rode away.

CHAPTER 6

*G*eorgia started getting blisters on her heels and toes somewhere in mile one of her trek from the Getaway Motel to the Darling Shelter. The pain started in mile two when the blisters popped, and she was a hobbling mess by mile three. She refused to complain because she deserved every stab of pain she experienced from her now blister-ridden feet.

Lies were never okay, and she had lied to Hutch about where she was spending the night, insisting he leave her in motel hell. Of course, that was just the tip of the iceberg when it came to the lies she had spun through her silence.

To be honest, she couldn't believe he had let her get away with it. He had warned her, even trying to persuade her to stay somewhere else. But no, she had to book an imaginary reservation at the skankiest hotel in Darling. The next time she booked an imaginary stay in a hotel, she was imaginarily booking it at the Ritz Carlton.

The blisters were payback for how awful she'd been to Hutch. He had only been trying to look out for her, the same as always. She shouldn't have gotten so angry.

All her anger needed to be saved for Nevada. She was the one who had told Georgia that the Getaway Motel had gone through major renovations a few years before. How it was now a delightful little bed and breakfast with all the amenities. And how she had better hurry if she wanted a room because the rooms were always booked. Peaceful and quiet, she had said, because it was on the outskirts of town.

This hike was nothing like a stroll from the outskirts of Darling as her sister had described. This was a death march from outer east Mongolia in the sweltering heat of the Tennessee summer. Her heart sank when she looked at her watch. It was already past 5:00, but she couldn't hobble any faster.

She was never going to reach Darling alive. Why hadn't she brought her water bottle? She would kill for something to drink. Maybe Nevada would happen along. She could happily kill Nevada right about then. Georgia snorted at the thought of Nevada marching past in the heat in her neon power suit, sweating like a stuck pig. Nevada never sweated. She glistened. Well, if Georgia glistened anymore, she would pass out from dehydration.

She thought she'd cry when she finally saw the first signs of civilization again. Walking down the familiar streets of Darling in search of a drug store was bittersweet. Seeing all the usual places she remembered from childhood was marvelous, but so much had changed. She wanted to explore everything, old and new. However, it was too late to go inside most places.

She wouldn't have risked it anyway. What if they didn't want to talk to her? Worse still, what if they asked her about the past eight years? Her heart pounded at the thought. She could never admit what she had gone through.

That's why she was moving on. Jarrod the Jerkface was a best-forgotten memory. Much better to focus on the new adventures waiting for her. She was free now to figure out who she was, live life to the max, and do all the things she had never been allowed to do before.

She found a pharmacy that stayed open late and bought some mermaid bandages for her blisters and earplugs so she could sleep. She walked around town a little longer, then headed toward the shelter for a good night's sleep. It was probably too late for a bed but walking all the way back to the Getaway was not happening. She would sleep on a park bench first. Tomorrow morning, she would find a way to the garage, get her truck, and drive into her destiny.

Maybe she was rushing things. Perhaps she could get a temporary job. Save up until she could pay for the repairs to her truck. She might even splurge on more candy and ramen noodles.

The more she thought about it, the better she liked the idea. She'd get the latest copy of *The Daily Nugget*, go to the shelter, and scan the help-wanted ads for jobs. She would go job hunting tomorrow and hopefully get her first real job. Then she could check on Petals and work out a payment plan.

The negative voice of the old Georgia chimed up. Old Georgia didn't think she would ever get a job that paid enough to afford truck repairs. Who was she kidding? No one would want to hire a twenty-six-year-old with no job experience. She was useless.

She almost went in for a beer as she walked past The Salty Saloon. But she hated the taste of beer, and it made her whole body break out with giant, red, itchy bumps. One more proof of her inadequacy, according to Jarrod. He had expected a wife that could wine and dine his friends, not turn into a sunburned iguana.

She was so lost in her thoughts she lost track of where she was. Turning the corner, she found herself on the last street she should be on. And yet, she kept walking.

Her steps took her toward Books-N-Brews, her favorite place in the entire world. Mainly because Vivi was the most wonderful person Georgia had ever known, and she wasn't the only one who felt that way. The whole town loved Vivi.

One of the worst parts of leaving Darling was not saying goodbye to Vivi. It had broken her heart because Vivi was the closest thing to a grandmother she had ever had. Nevada had delivered messages to Vivi for the first few months but stopped when Vivi had said it was too painful to hear her name.

She should have called Vivi, but Georgia was too afraid after Nevada told her what Vivi said. Hearing the only woman who had ever shown her love refuse her call would have destroyed her.

With each step she took, she told herself to turn around. But her feet didn't listen. She needed to see if Vivi was still there.

She wouldn't go in. She'd stand to the side and look in through the front window. Just a quick peek, nothing more. That couldn't hurt anything. Then she would head to the shelter.

She plastered her stomach to the brick face of the shop and leaned around the corner to peer inside. The lights were on, and employees bustled around the shop, making drinks for customers and delivering them to tables. She didn't pay them any attention. There was only one person she wanted to see, and that was Vivi.

Georgia's shoulders dropped as low as her spirits when she didn't see her. But she wasn't ready to give up. Maybe Vivi was over in the bookstore section instead of the coffee shop.

That was what had first drawn her into Books-N-Brews. Georgia loved to read. Vivi would pick out a book for them both to read. When Georgia finished it, Vivi would fix them both a frappe, and they would talk about the story. Vivi never rushed her. She was always interested in what Georgia had to say. Vivi had made her feel smart.

Georgia checked behind her to make sure no one was sneaking up behind her. She tried to see over into the books, but someone's arm blocked her view. With a huff, she stepped over just a smidge, praying she'd be able to spot Vivi, but something still blocked her view. One more step to the right should do it.

Georgia's breath caught as she pressed her palm against the cool, glass window. Vivi was bent over a table, organizing a small stack of books. With her silver hair in a messy bun and a cardigan sweater tied around her shoulders, she was the loveliest sight Georgia had ever seen.

What sounded like a cannon boomed out behind her. She half turned to defend herself, for a moment thinking she'd been shot. She screamed before realizing the noise was only a truck backfiring.

Trying to steady her racing heart, Georgia returned her focus to the shop. Vivi now stood on the other side of the windowpane, her palm pressed to the glass opposite Georgia's, staring right at Georgia.

Georgia's skin flashed hot, then cold. She thought she might be sick. Vivi didn't move, just stared, her face void of expression. That wasn't good, right?

She needed to leave. How could she have let Vivi see her? Vivi didn't deserve the shock; she was obviously stunned, maybe even horrified. Georgia stepped back from the window and looked up and down the street. She had to get away from there. But which way should she run?

The door of the shop flew open, jingling the bell over the shop door. Before Georgia could move, warm arms enveloped her in softness. She breathed in deep and caught the vanilla and gardenia scent of Vivi's perfume. Suddenly, Georgia was eight years old again.

What was happening? Vivi's hug didn't feel like something given by a woman who wanted nothing more to do with her. Had Nevada been mistaken? A woman who'd refused to hear her name wouldn't hold her on the sidewalk as if loosening her arms might cause her to disappear.

Georgia gave up trying to figure it out. She didn't care anymore. Instead, she threw her arms around the plump woman and burst into tears. When her tears dried, she tried to pull back and look at Vivi. Vivi held her tight, refusing to loosen her hold. For a woman of seventy, she had a surprising amount of strength. Eventually, her arms relaxed.

Schooling her features, Georgia tried to appear stoic. It seemed a little like closing the barn door after the horses were gone. She'd already broken down in the arms of her fairy grandmother. That's what she called her because that's who she was. Half fairy godmother, half grandmother.

She needed to say something. Anything. She should smile and keep the conversation light. Nothing deep. Nothing personal. Then she would be on her way.

Back to no one and nothing.

Vivi cupped her cheek as concern creased her penciled brow. "It is so good to see you, Georgia. I have missed you. I can see in your eyes something is wrong, sweet child. Tell Vivi how she can help."

That was Vivi. No judgment for disappearing the way she had. No guilt trips. Only love was in her eyes, and her voice was as soft and melodious as Georgia remembered.

Georgia held her gaze briefly and then once again burst into tears.

CHAPTER 7

*G*eorgia could have stood in Vivi's warm embrace for hours. Vivi led her to one of the small tables on the patio area in front of the store.

"Vi-Vivi," she said with hitched breaths, "I'm sorry for leaving the way I did. I should have called, but—"

Vivi smiled gently and cut her off. "Hush, child. I know you had your reasons. One day you can tell me all about it. But right now, I want to hear about you. How have you been?"

There was no way Georgia was telling Vivi about her life in California. "I've been fine," she said, trying to make it sound true.

Vivi searched deep into her eyes. So deep, Georgia had no doubt Vivi saw to her soul. She braced herself for Vivi to call her on her lies. Instead, she patted Georgia's hand and said, "That's alright, child. You can tell me about it when you're ready. You know, someone with as many years as me under her belt is long on listening and short on judging. Can you at least tell me what finally brought you back to Darling?"

Georgia did. She told Vivi about everything that had happened. Vivi listened without interruption. Well, she didn't interrupt until

Georgia told her she was spending the night in the shelter and looking for a job the next day to earn money to pay for her truck's repairs.

Vivi said, "There is no need for that, darling child. You don't know it, but the good Lord has sent you to Darling in answer to my prayers."

What?

"What does that mean?" she asked when Vivi paused.

"You see, I find myself in need of some help in the shop."

Color heated her cheeks. Vivi felt sorry for her. "You don't have to do that. I don't know how long I'll be here."

"Now you just let me talk, child. I don't know how long I'll be needing help. But I do know I need it right now."

Georgia tried to control her hopes, but it was hard. "What is it you need?"

"I need someone to help me with the bookshop."

"Why?"

"Just let me talk, sweet girl," Vivi scolded, her tone gentle.

"Sorry," Georgia said. "Go ahead."

"I need someone to help keep up with reshelving and orders. It would be perfect for you. I know you love books, and that's what I need. Someone who will treat it as more than a job."

Georgia's hopes soared despite her best efforts. "That sounds amazing. I could start soon, but I might need some time tomorrow to find a place to stay."

In a real family, she would be able to stay at Graceview. She would be welcome in her childhood home. But Nevada had been more than clear she was not.

"That's the thing, dear. I can't pay above minimum wage, but the position comes with the studio apartment above the shop. It's not decorated in the latest fashions but has furniture."

Georgia could not have heard correctly. Her life didn't work out that way.

"Are you sure?" she asked.

"Well, it was there the last time I climbed the stairs, child. It has been a while since I took my old bones up there, but I don't think anyone has walked away with it." Her eyes twinkled as she spoke.

"I mean, are you sure you want to hire me? I don't have any experience." She wanted the job. She needed the job. But she wouldn't take advantage of Vivi, no matter what.

Vivi's eyes grew tender. She took Georgia's hands in her own. "Of course, I'm sure, Georgia Anne. It would mean the world to me to have you so close. I've missed you."

Darn it! There went the tears again. Georgia threw her arms around Vivi and hugged her as tight as she dared. "Thank you, Vivi. I'll take it. I think God was listening to my prayers more than yours. I promise I'll be the best employee you've ever had. You won't be sorry."

"I don't imagine I will, sweet girl," Vivi said.

Only the ringing of the bell on the Books-N-Brews door broke the spell. Releasing Vivi, Georgia stepped back, almost tripping over the suitcase and bags she had lugged all the way from the Getaway Motel.

"Well, well, well. Look what the storm blew in." Georgia knew that voice as well as she knew her own. Tazzy stood on the sidewalk in front of her. Her face was blank, but anger dripped from each word she spoke.

She stood and faced the woman who was once her best friend. "Hello, Tazzy," she said. "It's been a long time."

Tazzy snorted. "Yeah, I guess you could say that. So, what are you doing here?"

Georgia's heart sank. She had been right. If she had done as Hutch asked and called Tazzy, the conversation would not have gone well. Not only did Tazzy not want to see her, she wanted nothing to do with Georgia. And Georgia didn't blame her.

Her friend thought she'd walked away without a word or backward glance. That is what they all thought. She wrapped her arms around her middle and tried again. "I'm here visiting my sister. I was going to call you. I'm sorry about how I left Darling. I want to explain."

Tazzy snorted. "Don't worry. I figured it out on my own. Back then, I wanted your explanation, but not now." She turned to Vivi. "I just wanted to check on you. Make sure you were alright, taking a trip down memory lane. I didn't mean to interrupt. I'll go back inside."

Georgia had to stop her. "Tazzy, wait. I am sorry. There are things you don't know."

Tazzy shook her head, eyes cold. "It's not that I don't know. It's that I don't care. Fool me once, fool me twice and all that. I'll see you inside, Vivi." Without another glance in Georgia's direction, she left Georgia where she stood.

Vivi placed a hand on her shoulder. "Give her time, dear. It was hard for her, the way you left. She thought something bad had happened to you. She felt foolish, and maybe a bit betrayed, when she found out you were married and kept your engagement a secret. Be patient with her, and she will come around."

For once, Vivi was wrong. Tazzy had every right to be angry.

From what Hutch had said earlier, she had figured out no one knew what happened eight years ago. She would have to tell them, and hopefully, they would understand.

"We'll make the bed so you can sleep in your own room tonight. Tomorrow, I'll start your training."

Tomorrow would be better. It had to be. Georgia nodded and gathered the few belongings she had.

Walking into Books-N-Brews was more like coming home than arriving at Graceview would ever be. The worn wooden floors and paneled walls were warm and welcoming. Mismatched leather cushioned chairs surrounded the tables, and comfy sofas lined the walls. Mid-July was too early for a fire in the fireplace, but all manner of leafy green plants filled the space.

Georgia glanced through the arched brick doorway on the left at the shelves of books and reading nooks available to customers. Vivi never worried about whether a customer bought a book or just sat for a while and enjoyed a good read.

Tazzy stood behind the counter, but when she saw Georgia, she picked up her phone and walked out without giving her another glance. She spoke to the other person behind the counter, a man Georgia didn't recognize. "That's the new girl. Get her a drink. You might as well show her your mad frappe skills."

"Sure thing," he said with a grin. "Hi there, gorgeous lady. Welcome to the team."

Georgia walked to the counter and held out her hand. "Hi, my name's Georgia. It's nice to meet you."

His grin turned to a smile. "Gorgeous Georgias. Nice to meet you, too. My name's Memphis. What can I get for you?"

She stared at the menu, but it had been so long since she'd been to a coffee shop, she had no idea what to make of it. "I like almost anything. Why don't you surprise me?"

He studied her for a minute and then nodded. "One frozen Samoa frappe, coming right up."

As he worked, she asked, "So, how long have you been working at Books-N-Brews?"

"Going on six years. You'll love it here. What brought you to Darling?"

"I grew up here. I used to come here all the time as a teenager, but I haven't lived here in several years."

Banging pans from the back interrupted her. She couldn't hold back a sigh.

Memphis seemed to be used to it. "Don't mind her. I call her our little Tazmanian Devil for a reason." He threw a look over his shoulder. "Don't know what bee is in her bonnet now, though." He shrugged and poured her frappe into a clear plastic cup.

He handed it to her with an "Enjoy" and stood there. She wasn't sure what he was waiting for at first, but then realized he was waiting for her to pay him.

"Oh, sorry," she said, grabbing her purse. "How much?"

"No charge. Give it a taste and let me know what you think."

She sipped her drink, and an explosion of chocolate, caramel, and coconut flavors filled her senses. "Wow! This is delicious."

"Awesome," he said. "I'll let you drink in peace. Welcome to the Books-N-Brews family."

The couch in front of the fireplace called to her. She sank into the soft leather to wait, dropping her bags on the floor. It didn't take long for Vivi to join her. They spent a few minutes filling out the necessary paperwork and reviewing Georgia's responsibilities.

"I loved the frappe, by the way. Memphis is a maestro with a blender."

"Thank you," Vivi said. "But I will never understand the younger generation's compulsion to ruin an excellent cup of coffee. Coffee was meant to be strong and black."

Georgia wrinkled her nose at the thought. Coffee was simply the best way to get flavored creamers and sugar. Everyone knew that. Slurping down the final noisy sips of creamy goodness, Georgia stood. "Do you think I could look at the apartment now?"

Exhaustion swept over her like a thick, heavy fog. The stresses of the day had finally caught up with her. She barely contained a yawn.

Vivi jumped to her feet. "Of course, dear. What was I thinking, keeping you down here chewing the fat with an old biddy like me."

"You aren't an old biddy, and I love talking with you. I will never be able to tell you how much your kindness means to me. How much you mean to me."

Vivi patted her hand. "It is my heart's joy, sweet girl. Let's go see your new apartment."

As Georgia followed Vivi up the stairs, Vivi said, "I hope you don't mind my asking, child, because I could not be more thrilled that you will be here, but why are you not staying at Graceview?"

Georgia tripped on the steps before catching herself. She knew Vivi was the last person on earth to judge her, so she answered honestly. Sort of.

"They're hosting a retreat for some large religious group, so they didn't have time to fix up a room," she said. They did have a large event going on, not that it mattered. Nevada had made it clear she wouldn't be welcome anyway.

Vivi stopped mid-step. "Didn't have time? That's the most ridiculous thing I've ever heard. What kind of person makes her sister sleep in a shelter?" She stomped the rest of the way up the stairs.

Georgia smiled. She needed an attitude just like Vivi's. Straightening her shoulders, she remembered she was doing just that. Other people were no longer allowed to sit in the driver's seat of her life.

When she reached the top of the stair landing, she wrapped her arms around Vivi. "I love you," she whispered in her ear. "I promised I'll do a good job. You won't regret hiring me."

Tenderness warmed Vivi's expression. "For heaven's sake, child. Never thought I would. Now let me show you around your new home. I want you to get a good night's rest. Tomorrow is going to be a full day."

CHAPTER 8

*H*utch's phone jarred him awake at 2:00 in the damn morning. He'd been dead on his feet and blamed a little vixen with curves in all the right places, wounded and alone.

"This better be good," he growled, then shot upright. "Say again?"

"Police scanner reported a possible burglary at Books-N-Brews," Sawyer Dorsey, Sabre Security's tech wizard, repeated. The guys knew he kept an eye on the place.

"I'm on it." Hutch pulled on his jeans. "Thanks."

Who in their right mind would break into Books-N-Brews? Vivi was like a grandmother to half the town. If those asshat Taylor twins were at it again, he would kill them.

Last month, the twins had decided smashing windows in an abandoned building on the outskirts of town would be fun. No one would have cared, but they had interrupted a drug deal Sabre was watching to take down whoever was pushing fentanyl into the local high school. That had earned the twins a beating, and they'd get worse tonight if he dragged his ass out of bed because of them.

He slowed down when he closed in on Books-N-Brews. No one stood out front, and lights shone through the window. What kind of thief turned on the overhead lights?

He pulled behind the store. Nothing looked off there, either.

The back windows and door showed no sign of forced entry. Hutch walked along the side street to the front of the shop. One look through a large front window told him several things.

First, the Taylor twins were not involved. Lucky for them. Second, he would listen to that call to the police station to find out who made it.

And third, he was having a long discussion about personal safety with a certain little girl. Georgia Donnel—damn it, Jemison, stood behind the counter, clear as day, at 2:45 in the morning.

She danced from cupboard to cupboard, inspecting the contents of each one. Heat burned through him. Anything could've happened to her, alone and blissfully unaware.

The bright lights illuminated the entire shop, and Georgia was on display for all to see. Anyone could break a window and gain entrance.

Hutch edged toward the door, cursing when the knob twisted in his hand. The fire in his chest ramped up another ten degrees. How had she even gotten there? He'd left her at The Getaway without transportation. He walked in and strode to the counter.

Did she acknowledge his approach? No. Did she even hear his approach? No. She couldn't hear a damn thing because she wore earbuds with music playing so loud, he heard it from where he stood.

Was she listening to Disney tunes? She answered his question a second later when she belted out the chorus to *A Whole New World* at the top of her lungs. Her sterling rendition ended with a screech.

He grabbed her shoulder and spun her around to face him. The stack of paper cups she held flew in every direction. She stepped back on one foot, hands out in front like a caricature of a martial arts master.

Her fear morphed into anger the instant she realized it was him. She slapped his chest with both palms and yelled, "Don't do that! You scared the life out of me!" She bowed her head and put a hand to her chest.

"Do you want to tell me what in the hell you are doing here at 2:45 in the morning?"

A deep blush crept up her chest and blossomed as pretty as a rose on her cheeks. "None of your business," she said. "What are you doing here?"

"I'm here because I got dragged out of bed at the asscrack of dawn to check out a possible robbery. Now answer my question. Why aren't you where I left you?"

She crossed her arms and stared at him. Right.

"If you haven't picked up on it, Peaches, my patience is thin. You do not want me to waste what little I have left this early in our conversation. Now, I'll ask one more time. What are you doing, and how did you get here?"

Her whole body shook, probably from the scare he'd given her. He wanted nothing more than to take her in his arms and tell her she'd be fine. Strike that. He wanted to blister her backside for putting herself at such risk. Then he would hold and comfort her.

Jesus, this woman needed a keeper. She'd only been back in town one day, and he already remembered that much. And fuck it all if, despite himself, he didn't want to be that keeper.

But she wasn't staying so he wouldn't have that chance. Which sucked.

Georgia finally shrugged and said, "I didn't have a reservation at The Getaway. But you wouldn't have let me sleep in the local shelter. By the time I got to town, I needed bandages for the blisters on my feet. I ran into Vivi, and she offered me a job and a place to stay upstairs." She paused and took a deep breath. "Anything else you want to know?"

She stood there, arms crossed, uncertainty filling her eyes.

She had good reason to be uncertain. "You're telling me you walked to town?"

"Yes."

She infused an impressive amount of snark into that one word. It was dangerous for her ass, but he forced himself not to react. "The Getaway is three miles from here."

"I know," she said, rolling her eyes at him. "Blisters, remember?"

He was going to need a tube of ointment to calm his itching palm. Wait. Had she said she was staying? "So, you're not leaving?"

She shrugged. "I guess not, at least for a while. Vivi needs me right now, and I have to pay for truck repairs."

"So, you're staying."

"Yes, Hutch, I'm staying."

His mind spun. Georgia wasn't leaving. Not that it mattered to him. Nope. He wasn't excited about the possibility of her moving home and working in the shop.

Oh, shit. Georgia got a job at the shop. "Tazzy works here now as a barista. Did you see her?"

Georgia's face fell. She dropped her gaze, but he could swear he had seen tears in her eyes.

Fuck. "You saw Tazzy."

She rubbed a spot on the floor with her foot and nodded.

"What happened, Peaches? Did it not go well?"

"No," she wailed and threw herself at him. She clung to him and sobbed. "She hates me. I told you she would. She wouldn't even stay in the same room as me," she said.

He picked her up, and she wrapped her legs around his hips. Carrying her to the nearest sofa, he sat down with her straddling his lap, holding her as she cried. Rubbing her back, he promised it would be alright.

The Daddy in him needed to soothe her. When her pussy settled against his cock, the Dom in him needed to fuck her. He should put her across his knee and spank that heart-shaped ass, then fuck it all better.

She'd never had a Daddy. No way the dick she married was one. And she wasn't a cheater.

He should not think about how soft and sweet her lips looked or wonder how they would feel pressed against his. He absolutely should not imagine how those same lips would feel wrapped around his cock. He should steer clear.

Focus. He needed to focus on the current situation. "I'm glad you have a job and a place to stay, Peaches. I shouldn't have left yesterday afternoon."

He should have his ass kicked for leaving her to fend for herself. Vivi's actions didn't surprise him. Still, he would make a point to thank her. He hadn't heard she was looking to hire anyone, and that studio apartment hadn't had anyone living in it for years. Did it even have any furniture? He'd make a point to look into that, too.

"I would have made you," Georgia said.

"You would have tried." He injected steel into his voice.

Her past eight years hadn't been easy, but that part of her life was over now. No time like the present to start proving it to her. "If you're working and living here, a few things are going to change."

Her brows shot up. "Change how?"

"You're going to take better care of yourself, for one thing."

"I do take care of myself. I'm not a child."

She squirmed when he raised his brow.

"I didn't say you were. But let's review. You come back to

Darling in a truck that isn't safe with a dead cell phone. You drive too fast, almost running off the side of the mountain, then sit in the middle of the road, nearly causing an accident. That's strike one."

"Some of that wasn't my fault. And what do you mean, strike one?" She glared at him.

He ignored her glare. "Next, you lie about having a place to stay. Then walk along a busy highway for three miles hoping there's room in the shelter. Luckily, Vivi gave you a job and a place to stay."

He watched her face as he spoke. She didn't fight to get off his lap, but she couldn't meet his eyes. She wound a strand of her hair around her finger.

He pressed on. "Did Vivi tell you to work until 2:45 in the morning?"

He could tell she wanted to lie, but decided against it.

"No, but I wanted her to know I'll be a good employee."

Hutch nodded. "I get that. But you came downstairs, lights on, door unlocked, earphones blasting music, and not watching your surroundings. Do I have that right?"

"I guess," she said. "But I couldn't very well look around in the dark. And I didn't mean to leave the door unlocked. I just forgot. No one came in, so everything's fine. Well, just you, and you aren't going to hurt me."

He started his countdown again. It hadn't helped before, but it was all he had. "Little girl, you have no idea what I want to do right now, and I assure you it would hurt. You've had a hard day, and we are getting reacquainted. But that's strike two."

"You can't count strikes on me. I keep telling you that you're not the boss of me."

She could protest all she wanted, but his words were affecting her. Her voice had taken on that lilting Little quality, and she was squirming on his lap. A movement she needed to stop, or his dick was going to embarrass them both.

"Here's the point. You do not want to get to strike three."

"What happens at strike three?"

"I turn you over my knee and prove that I am absolutely the boss of you."

She gasped. "You can't spank me."

He couldn't hold back a smile. "We both know that isn't true, now don't we." Pink flooded her cheeks as her hands snuck behind her to cover her bottom. "I care about you, Peaches."

"You still care about me?" Her words came out almost a whisper, and the wonder in her voice damn near broke his heart.

"Of course, I do. It hurt when you left as you did, but I told myself you were happy. That wasn't true, was it?"

She pressed her forehead into his chest. "Not exactly."

His girl. Always honest, even when it was hard. He hugged her to him, and she relaxed in his arms. "Thank you for telling me the truth, Peaches." He held himself in check for her. "Now that you're back, you'll learn what being taken care of means."

She stared up at him but didn't speak.

"Peaches, do you understand me?"

Slowly, she nodded but said, "I don't think so."

He smiled. "We'll work on it." She was adorable. Giving up the fight, he brushed her lips softly with his own. Intending to go slow, he pulled back, but she followed, pressing her lips to his. That was all it took.

His fingers threaded through her hair. Pressing his tongue to the seam of her lips, which she parted eagerly, his tongue swept in, devouring her. She pressed her body closer, setting him on fire. He wanted to keep going, but she was going to need time. Reluctantly, he stopped the kiss.

She gazed up at him with glazed eyes and smiled. Beautiful. He kissed her forehead. She sighed with her eyes closed when he pulled away. "I need some sleep. Lock the door behind me, then go to bed."

"Okay, Hutch." Her dazed eyes were so damn cute he almost changed his mind. But she needed rest, too. Standing outside the shop, he waited for the lock to click.

Georgia had no idea what being taken care of meant, but she would. And soon.

CHAPTER 9

Georgia leaned over the shop counter and scowled at her latte art. After practicing for three weeks, she was starting to get the hang of it. Something was off with the floating creamy heart, though. She just wasn't sure how to fix it.

It would be helpful if Tazzy would give her pointers. Tazzy's latte art was incredible. People came to Books-N-Brews just to see her latest designs. So far, Tazzy only spoke to her in front of Vivi.

Georgia tried to break through the wall her friend had put up between them. Tazzy didn't want to hear it.

When Georgia went out of her way to be friendly, Tazzy called her a brown-noser. When she left her alone, Tazzy said she was just like every other stuck-up Donnelley. Georgia couldn't win.

Her heart broke each time she tried. It had gotten so bad she had thought about getting a job somewhere else, but she wasn't willing to repay Vivi's kindness by leaving her in the lurch.

She massaged her temples in an attempt to soothe her throbbing head. Something had to change because the stress was wearing on her. She ought to tell Hutch but didn't want to cause trouble. He would be angry if he found out how Tazzy treated her.

He'd be angry at her for lying when he asked how she was doing. She always told him fine. So far, he hadn't called her on it.

She couldn't escape the stress because she and Tazzy worked the same hours. The persistent ache in her stomach prevented her from sleeping. She had circles under her eyes. Her body needed rest, but her brain wouldn't shut up.

At least she made good use of the time by making a bucket list of everything she wanted to do. She was now an adventurer. At least, that was what she told herself. She worked on her list each night, adding things other people talked about that she had never been allowed to do.

Her first adventure had been getting her hair done at Zippity Doo Dahling. She had made a new friend, her stylist, Morgan Weston. Sure, she had gone intending to get a trim. But Morgan had been excited about a new technique she had learned, and somehow Georgia left the salon with sapphire blue hair.

Her mother would have disowned her. After all, nice girls did not have blue hair.

Georgia loved it. She felt beautiful when she caught her reflection in the shop windows as she headed back to Books-N-Brews.

Her joy lasted until she entered the shop, where Tazzy took one look at her, smirked, and said, "Nice hair."

The words were kind. The tone was not.

Georgia had wanted to cry. She probably would have, except when she looked back at Tazzy, tears filled her former friend's eyes, too. The first glimmer of hope shimmered through Georgia. Maybe Tazzy was finally coming around.

She smiled at the memory of Hutch first seeing the new Georgia. He had told her she was sexy and kissed her right in front of all the customers. That was all it had taken to restore her confidence.

Later, she caught Hutch talking to Tazzy in a back corner of the bookshop. She could tell from a distance he was unhappy with his cousin. Tazzy had glared at her the rest of the day, accusing her of tattling to Hutch. Georgia had insisted she had done no such thing, but Tazzy hadn't believed her.

Hutch had been fantastic since she'd started working at the shop. He stopped by every day to see her. And every night, he came by at closing to take her to dinner and make sure she locked the shop doors.

She didn't have to stress about anything when he was with her. He ordered for them both at the restaurant, which would have been annoying if she hadn't loved what he chose. Even the yucky vegetables.

With a sigh, Georgia returned her attention to the cup of coffee before her. She had already wasted an entire carafe of coffee trying to make a recognizable heart. Tazzy walked by, took one look at Georgia's efforts, and snorted.

Georgia waited for embarrassment and sorrow to fill her again, but they didn't. Instead, anger burned through her. How long was she supposed to pay for things from the past she couldn't change?

Yes, she had hurt Tazzy. And yes, she hadn't contacted her in the eight years she had been gone. But she had apologized a million times.

What angered her the most was that Tazzy wouldn't let her explain what had happened. If she had just listened, she would realize Georgia had not done what Tazzy thought.

But Tazzy wouldn't let her explain. And Georgia had had enough.

She pasted on a fake smile. "Thanks for the encouragement. I've made it this far because of all the help I have had."

CHAPTER 10

Georgia's cell phone rang as she walked back up front, but not with her regular ring. She had changed the ringtone of one particular contact to a ring she found on a list called 'Rings for Exes.' It thrilled her to hear *Goodbye, Earl*, by the Dixie Chicks. At least, it did until she remembered that tone was Jarrod on the other end of the call.

Not that she answered it. That was the point. She pushed the silence button.

Tazzy tipped a tiny pitcher of steamed milk over another mug as Georgia joined her behind the counter. As she did, her phone started ringing again.

"Cool ringtone," Tazzy said. "Someone seems to be calling more and more often."

Georgia stumbled at Tazzy's words. They were the most pleasant Tazzy had spoken to her since she returned home.

"Yeah," Georgia agreed. "If I keep ignoring it, he'll eventually get the message."

She hoped so, anyway. Jarrod could be obsessive when he didn't get his way, but she had no intention of talking to him ever again. The letter and divorce papers she had left on his desk said it all. When he signed them, he was to give them to her lawyer. There was no need for her ever to see him again.

The bell over the door jingled again, and when she looked up, her stomach dropped. Nevada. What was she doing here?

Nevada hadn't visited the shop once in the three weeks Georgia had been working there. She had hoped her sister would continue to ignore her, but apparently her luck had run out.

Nevada, dressed in some designer dress and high-heeled boots, came in carrying a large plant.

"Greetings," Nevada trilled as if she stopped by every day. As if she were welcome. "I gave up waiting for an invitation to visit your quaint little," she paused and scanned the area before adding, "shop."

Brilliant white teeth glowed from the fakest smile Georgia had ever seen, and she had seen her fair share of shark smiles in Los Altos. What was her sister doing here? There was no way she just stopped by for a chat.

"Why are you here, Nevada?" Georgia refused to pretend Nevada had stopped by for a friendly chat. Nevada always had an ulterior motive.

"Is that any way to treat a valued customer? With an attitude like that, it's no wonder your shop is empty."

Georgia gritted her teeth. "The shop is empty right now because it's mid-afternoon in the middle of summer break. The teenagers are either at work or the lake, and the after-work crowd won't be here for another half hour."

Tazzy giggled, drawing Nevada's attention. "You think that's funny? I didn't realize you worked here. Is it customary to let trash near the register?"

Tazzy snorted. "Don't take your foul temper out on me. You've had a stick up your butt since Hutch turned you down for a date years ago. Didn't mind my family being trash then, did you?"

Nevada sneered, but Georgia recognized the flush of color in her cheeks. What in the world had come over Tazzy? Georgia distracted her sister before things got nasty.

"What's with the plant? Are you a delivery girl for Magnolia's Gardens now?"

"I wish I hadn't bothered. It's no wonder your marriage is in trouble. You're a pain in the ass. Of course, that's nothing new. For your information, Jarrod called me because you won't answer your phone. For some reason, he is grief-stricken you abandoned him, and he desperately wants you back. He asked me to pick up the flowers he ordered and bring them so he would know you got them. I'll just put this here."

Nevada crossed to the fireplace and hefted the wide flat terra cotta dish filled with succulents and cacti onto the mantle. She turned it until it was how she wanted, then stepped back to admire her work.

Turning to Georgia, Nevada flashed a nasty smile. "I took the liberty of changing his order a little bit. He wanted five dozen long stem red roses. I thought, what with your inability to commit to anything and care for what you have, something that needed nothing from you would better suit you."

Before Georgia could react, a voice rang out behind her. "I'm surprised you can deliver flowers in the daytime, Nevada. I mean, what with sunlight turning blood-sucking vampires to ash. You must use one high-powered sunscreen. You should creep back to your skanky coffin before someone stakes you through your shriveled up heart." Tazzy stood beside Georgia and glared.

It took all Georgia could do not to cheer. That or collapse in shock. After weeks of snubbing, Tazzy was back by her side.

"Well, I wondered how long it would be before the two of you ganged up on me." Nevada looked like something had crawled up her nose and died. She refocused her attention on Georgia. "I see why you ran from a life of luxury. Living above a rundown coffee shop to socialize with the other dregs of society suits you. Good choice." With that, Nevada sauntered out the door.

Tazzy broke the silence by demanding, "Are you sure you two are related?"

Georgia sighed. "I'm afraid you can't get more related than being twins." Tazzy still held a cooled milk pitcher, reminding Georgia of what she had been doing before her sister blew in.

"Forget her royal bitchiness. Let me see your creation," Tazzy responded.

Georgia grabbed Tazzy's hand. "Hold on a minute. You can't just go from hating me to defending me in the blink of an eye. We need to talk."

Tazzy sighed. "Yeah, we do. But not right now. I never hated you, Georgia. Not ever. But when we talk, there will be angst and tears. That's not something I want to do in public. Can we work on your latte art for now? We can talk on our day off. Please?"

Georgia wasn't looking forward to their conversation, either. They would talk. Soon. But for now, she was going to enjoy having her friend back. "You got it," she said.

"Oh, I have something for you!" Tazzy yelled, then ran to the back of the shop.

A few minutes later, Tazzy raced back to Georgia. The light caught something sparkling in her hand. Before Georgia could ask, Tazzy held up a sparkling tiara. She ran forward and placed it on Georgia's head.

"Oh, my gosh!" Georgia ran her fingers along the points and dips of the rhinestone studded crown. "I can't believe you kept these!"

Tazzy grinned back at her, a matching tiara adorning her head. "I couldn't bring back the Musketiaras without these, could I? Now, let's see what we can do with your coffee art creation."

Before Tazzy could walk away, Georgia wrapped her arms around her friend. Nothing had ever felt more like home.

Tazzy leaned over the cup, ready to encourage her friend. She stared into the mug, sucked in a breath as if she were going to speak, but rolled her lips between her teeth and squinted at Georgia's design. Finally, she said, "What if we swirl this a little and pull this here? And maybe dot some sprinkles here and here. What do you think?"

Georgia looked at the mug and gasped. "Tazzy! That's incredible. It's the best fireworks rocket ever! And the sprinkles make it perfect."

Tazzy glowed at Georgia's praise. "Really? You think it's good?"

"Good, it's fantastic. No wonder people come from all over to see your art. Vivi was a genius to hire you!"

Tazzy laughed. "I was just playing around. I'll get back straightening the bookshelves now." Still smiling, she headed back over to the books area.

"Uh, hello! Don't you dare do my job. Vivi will have no reason to keep me on! You get back over here and perfect your latest creation."

Tazzy laughed and returned to the counter. "What's this?" she asked, picking up a large book. "*Adrenaline Adventures to Try Before You Die?*"

Tazzy's face lost its color. "No, Georgia! What's wrong? I didn't even know you were sick. How long do you have?" Tears gathered in her eyes.

Georgia wrapped her arms around her friend. "No, it's nothing like that! It's just, I'm twenty-six years old, and I've lived my whole life meeting everyone else's expectations. I'm tired of being that person. So, I'm making a bucket list of everything I missed out on growing up and anything else I want to do. I want to do all the things."

Tazzy cocked her head to the side. "The things?"

"Yeah, the things. You know, all the crazy things you do in high school or college. I never got to do any of that."

Tazzy's skepticism was evident on her face. "I'm not sure how I can help. Not sure I *want* to help." She opened the book and held it up to a picture of a man in an underwater cage with a ginormous shark barreling toward him. "What is this?"

Georgia swallowed hard at facing a shark in its natural habitat. "Well, maybe not that. At least, not at first."

"Does Hutch know about this list?"

"No, I don't see how it is any of his business. I can do whatever I want."

Tazzy smirked. "Uh-huh. You keep thinking that way. It's going to get you into a heap of trouble."

Georgia's heart rate kicked up a notch. She had to force herself not to squirm at the feeling between her thighs. She sniffed and gave a little humph. "I have no idea what you are talking about."

Tazzy's smirk blossomed into a laugh. "Sure, you don't. Hasn't Hutch been coming by every morning and evening for the last three weeks?"

"Yes, but I don't see what that has to do with anything."

"Has he made his intention of having a relationship clear?"

"Well, yes, but that hardly–"

"Oh yes, it does, and you know it. Remember how overprotective Hutch was back in high school? He hasn't changed. He still likes all the same things." Tazzy stared at Georgia knowingly, brows raised. "All. The things."

Memories of his actions on her eighteenth birthday flashed through her mind. She forced her hand not to cover her bottom. That evening hadn't ended like she thought it would.

Wished it had.

But that wasn't his usual way. That had been an exception. Nothing like that would happen again.

Right. And rain never made the flowers grow.

Her cheeks reddened at the memory of Hutch's three strikes warning.

"Ha," Tazzy burst out. "I don't even want to know what's going through your mind right now." She gave Georgia's arm a comforting squeeze. "I'm sorry your sister is so obnoxious."

"Me, too." She shook her head. She was not going down that road. "You know what? It doesn't matter. I'm making up for lost time. Now, are you going to help me with my list or not?"

Tazzy rolled her eyes. "Of course, I am. Let me get some paper." Tazzy rummaged through the satchel she called a purse and pulled out a small notebook. "Okay, what do you want on your bucket list?"

"Hold on," Georgia said. "I already have one started. Let me run upstairs and get it."

She took off up the stairs to her apartment for her list, feeling lighter than she had in years. She returned, list in hand and slapped in on the counter in front of Tazzy. "Here is what I already have."

Georgia called out all the new things she wanted to try. Tazzy added them with the occasional 'it's your funeral' look, but without comment.

Mostly.

She did pause when Georgia added base jumping. And when the cage diving with sharks in Australia came up, Tazzy said, "I don't know of anyone who's done that, and neither do you. We can add that later if you survive all the other crazy things on this list."

Georgia looked over the list to make sure Tazzy hadn't left anything off. Before she could read to the bottom, however, someone snatched the page from her hand.

Georgia spun around to find Hutch standing behind her, his deep blue eyes shooting sparks. "Little girl," he said, "we need to talk."

CHAPTER 11

Georgia took a moment to calm her racing heart. Hutch didn't like her bucket list. Well, that was too bad. If he made her list, it would include bowling with bumpers in the gutters and walking around town inside one of those giant plastic bubbles.

Actually, that might be fun. If it were an inflatable ball, she could strap herself in and bounce down some of the mountainsides nearby.

How long had he been standing behind her anyway? Was the tandem paragliding through the Grand Canyon what upset him? He was just a big worry wart. She would have an experienced instructor with her. Maybe he would let her steer.

"I'll... just go straighten those bookshelves now," Tazzy said and scampered to the bookshop. Coward.

She lifted her chin and met his glare head-on. Sheesh, he could be scary.

It didn't matter. He was not the boss of her, regardless of what he thought.

"That's where you're wrong, little girl. I am absolutely the boss of you."

Darn it! She'd said that out loud. Hutch stared at her with such a stern expression it made her gulp. It also made her hot.

Nope. Not going there.

Never ever. Not in a million years.

Didn't matter if her insides melted at the way his muscled arms crossed over his broad chest. Or his kissable lips tilted down in that deliciously disgruntled frown. Or those deep, mesmerizing eyes that gave her tingles in her most private places.

Wait. Where was she?

Oh, yes. He was not the boss of her.

A firm but gentle finger tipped her chin up so she was looking him in the eye. "Peaches, are you listening to me?"

"Um, no?"

"I didn't think so. Well, pay attention because you will not think ignorance is bliss if I catch you doing anything on this list," he said. "These things are all much too dangerous. This entire list puts your safety at risk. You remember what happens the next time you put yourself at risk, right?"

When she didn't answer right away, his frown deepened.

"You are so hot when you're angry," she blurted out. Her eyes widened in shock, and both hands flew up to cover her mouth.

Hutch's lips twitched. Darn it, that was hot, too.

"I'm glad you think so, Peaches. But that won't save your bottom if I catch you doing the things on this list. You got me?"

She couldn't stop staring at him. His eyes darkened to a deeper blue when he was upset.

"Georgia Anne, do you understand me?" he repeated.

"I understand you. That doesn't mean I agree."

"If I hear of you doing something from this list, little girl, I believe we will be able to come to a meeting of the minds quicker than you might think," he said.

"You two can talk that out later," Vivi said before focusing on Georgia. "I need to discuss something with you and Tazzy. Is she here?"

It wasn't like Vivi not to know who was working. She was always on top of the schedule. Georgia took in Vivi's worried expression and braced for bad news. Had she messed up so badly in the three weeks she'd worked at Books-N-Brews that Vivi was firing her?

That couldn't be it. Vivi wouldn't need Tazzy if she was firing Georgia. Besides, she had done her best and then some. She clocked in first every morning and worked well past closing. Hutch wouldn't be happy if he knew about that, but she owed Vivi more than she could ever repay for the job and the apartment.

Had Jarrod decided to get to her by putting pressure on Vivi? Her heart plunged. Nothing would surprise her when it came to Jerkface. How had she wound up with someone worse than Mara and Nevada? Jarrod would think nothing of using her friends to get to her. She wouldn't allow anyone else to pay for her mistakes.

Georgia put a hand on Vivi's shoulder. "What is it, Vivi? Have I done something wrong?"

Vivi's eyes widened, and her smile relaxed a little. She shook her head and placed a cool hand on Georgia's cheek. "No, sweet child. You have been nothing but a blessing these past few weeks. As providence usually works, you arrived just in time." She glanced over Georgia's shoulder and crooked a finger. "There you are, Tazzy. I need to let you and Georgia know what is going on."

Tazzy threw Georgia a questioning glance as she hurried over, but all Georgia could do was shrug.

Vivi's smile disappeared. "My sister in Asheville has been feeling poorly for a while now, and she got news last week that she has cancer."

Georgia gasped and threw her arms around Vivi. "I'm so sorry. Is she going to be alright?"

Vivi nodded. "The doctors think so. They caught it fairly early, but she is going through a particularly harsh regimen of treatments and needs someone to be there with her. Her children are all grown with their own families, so I told her I would come stay with her as long as she needs me."

Georgia's heart broke for Vivi. How like her to drop everything for someone she loved. That was what Vivi did. "Of course, you'll go to her. Don't worry about anything here."

That earned her a smile that reached Vivi's eyes.

"I'm not worried, sweet girl. I know the shop will be in good hands. Tazzy has worked here for years. She knows more about this place than I do. Now that you are here to manage the books, I can focus on my sister."

"Absolutely," Tazzy said.

Georgia's mind raced through all the new things she and Tazzy needed to learn. She could put in the book orders and deal with the vendors. Vivi could show them the accounts, and they'd figure that out.

They'd have to stay on top of the young people Vivi hired to help out at the shop. The schedule might be tricky, but they could figure that out, too. Was there time for Vivi to show them what to do? She tried to swallow her fears.

Vivi needed her strength. Georgia would find a way to keep her promises. She owed Vivi so much. Loved her so much. The new Georgia never let down those she loved.

But what if she couldn't do it? What if she ruined everything?

It was suddenly sweltering, and Georgia couldn't catch her breath. Sweat coated her skin, and her stomach rolled. Standing as straight as she could, she tried not to draw attention to herself. She didn't need to add to Vivi's burdens.

"Georgia, are you alright?"

She heard Hutch's words, but they seemed to be coming from far away. Spots danced before her, and she thought her knees might give out. Just as they buckled, a strong arm encircled her waist, lifting her to sit on the barstool behind her.

"I've got you, little girl," Hutch said.

He pressed his forehead against hers, speaking quietly while he caressed her back. The spots disappeared, and the world stopped spinning. Then Vivi was there with a bottle of water for her. Georgia flushed with humiliation.

She was a big baby. Now Vivi would spend all her time worrying. Tears stung her eyes. She was so stupid. So weak. She always let people down when they needed her the most.

"I'm sorry," she said. "I promise I'll do a good job. I don't know what came over me. I'm such an idiot."

Georgia stopped speaking when a growl rumbled from Hutch's chest. Did people growl? Of course not. That would be silly. "I won't let you down. I promise I won't."

Vivi gifted her with a smile. "That isn't possible, sweet child. You have nothing to worry about."

Georgia could think of a billion and one things to worry about, and she hadn't even put any real effort into it yet.

Then Vivi did the oddest thing. She placed Georgia's hand into Hutch's. Weird.

"I don't expect you to run the shop. I have a silent partner to oversee things when I'm called away. It won't be the first time he's stood in for me."

The tightness in Georgia's chest relaxed a bit at Vivi's words. A silent partner was perfect. Vivi could focus on her sister without worrying about what was happening in Darling. And she wouldn't single-handedly ruin the financial foundations of Books-N-Brews.

Who was the silent partner? So many people came into the shop regularly. It could be anyone. She had to ask. "Do I know them?"

Vivi's eyes lit with mischief. "He invested in the shop years ago and became my silent partner. You'll have time now to turn Hutch into a voracious reader."

Georgia froze, wide eyes glued to Vivi. Did she mean? No, that couldn't be right.

Hutch cleared his throat, and her gaze swung to him. He was laughing. Not on the outside, of course, but she could tell from his expression he thought the situation was hilarious.

"I guess now I am officially the boss of you," he said.

Yep, he thought it was funny.

She ignored the relief filling her heart. It was simply because it didn't all depend on her. The relief had nothing to do with Vivi's partner being Hutch. Nope. He was bossy and opinionated. And bossy.

The clock on the fireplace mantle chimed. Of course, Vivi noticed the new plant. "When did we get that?" she asked.

The last thing she wanted to discuss was Nevada delivering gifts from her ex. "Nevada dropped it off. It was, um, a gift to… welcome me back to town," she said.

She detested lying, but couldn't tell the truth. Tazzy coughed but didn't contradict her. She had sworn her friend to secrecy. The fewer people who knew about Jarrod and what she had gone through, the better.

Vivi's expression grew tight. "That doesn't sound like Nevada. I know she is your sister, but be careful around her, sweet girl. How you can be twins is a mystery to me."

Time for a change of subject.

Best to separate work and pleasure from the start. That was the only way to handle the situation. She probably wouldn't see him anymore than she did now. He was a, well, she wasn't sure exactly what he was. She needed to ask him more questions about Sabre Security.

He took her outstretched hand with a grin. "It will be a pleasure doing business with you."

Darn, that sparkle in his eyes did tingly things to private places that shouldn't tingle at work. "I know Vivi is relieved you are stepping in."

Hutch smiled at her emphasis on Vivi's name, the rat fink.

"Yes, I'm glad I can ease Vivi's mind," he said, also emphasizing her name.

Vivi patted his hand. "Well, I'm glad that's settled. Call me sexist, but knowing Hutch is keeping an eye on things while I'm gone is a relief."

Unfortunately, it made Georgia feel better, too. She had to put a lid on those feelings. Hutch didn't want a relationship, no matter how often he took her to dinner and checked in on her.

It was for the best. Hutch didn't need someone so damaged. No one needed a broken person who constantly swung between being too much and not enough. Georgia should focus on her adventuring no matter what her heart or her tingles had to say.

"Is that clock right?" Vivi asked. "Goodness, the time got away from me. I told my sister I would be there before dark." She gave Georgia a tight hug and whispered in her ear, "Lean on Hutch, sweet girl. He can handle anything."

Hutch looked her over, apparently satisfied with whatever he saw. "I'll stop by after closing. I have a few things to go over with you."

Tazzy coughed, though it sounded suspiciously like a laugh. Georgia glared at her friend, then asked, "What kind of things? Does Tazzy need to stay, too?"

"No, just you."

She didn't like that, but her lady bits sure did. "I thought you were a silent partner."

"Lots of things don't take words, little girl." He winked. "We'll grab supper and talk."

Oh, this was so not good. And she looked forward to it. Darn it!

CHAPTER 12

*H*utch climbed into his truck and smiled as he watched Georgia through the window of Books-N-Brews. She'd headed straight for the counter, taken out a notebook, and began making a new bucket list. Stubborn.

Well, he was stubborn, too.

He had always had a protective streak where Georgia was concerned. But now, it was so much more than that. When he had heard her talking to Tazzy about everything she wanted to put on that damn list, he'd almost marched her back to Vivi's office and explained a few things.

Things like how she'd better think again if she planned on doing any of those bucket list items. Some of them were just ridiculous. No one in their right mind wanted to face a tiger in the wild.

Georgia needed someone to keep an eye on her. Good thing Vivi had asked him to step in while she was gone. Honestly, he needed to take on another responsibility like he needed a hole in the head. His job with Sabre kept him plenty busy.

But he would never turn Vivi down when she needed his help.

He knew she was downplaying her sister's condition. She had enough to worry her. The least he could do was help with the shop.

He'd had to step in before since he'd become her partner. Mostly he just kept an eye on the place. This time it was helpful to both of them since Georgia was determined to carry on with her adventuring, as she called it.

He had to get back to work, but first, he pulled into the alley behind the shop. He'd been trying to talk Vivi into upgrading the security in her shop for years. At least Vivi's absence would allow him to take care of that for her. He had never pressed the issue, but now that Georgia was there, he was making the necessary improvements.

Vivi didn't talk about it much, but she was concerned about the unsavory people hanging outside the doors of the shelter, harassing those in need. Sabre kept an eye out in an effort to keep the people the shelter served safe. And with it on the block behind Books-N-Brews, he wasn't willing to put off the upgrades any longer. Especially with Georgia alone there at night.

He smiled at the memory of Georgia's face when she realized he was Vivi's silent partner. Vivi announcing she was leaving had Georgia on the verge of a panic attack. She had leaned into him at the news he was the silent partner and didn't think she even realized the relieved sigh that had escaped her.

When she'd looked at him, he'd also seen the flash of excitement in her eyes before she'd shut it down. Oh, yeah. She wanted him to be there. Whether she was willing to admit it or not was a different matter.

She had instinctively known she could trust and depend on him. That made his Daddy side swell with pride. Letting her down was not an option.

He would do anything in his power to keep her safe. This weekend, he had plans for making the building more secure. The first step, however, was going over some basic safety rules she would follow or she wouldn't be sitting comfortably any time soon.

The thought of her squirming over his knee, promising to be a good girl and begging him to stop, had his cock stiffening. He remembered every moment of that night eight years ago when he had blistered her ass.

Tazzy had already irritated him that night by not being at his going away party. She'd been upset he had enlisted. To her, he was another big brother, and she couldn't understand why he'd wanted to leave. He'd understood, but he'd wanted her at his party. It had taken over an hour to track her down for her dad since no one knew where she was. Anything could have happened. He'd lectured her all the way home.

He had his windows down with Blackberry Smoke's *Like I Am* playing as loud as he could get it. He almost hadn't noticed Georgia Donnelley struggling to get away from the three guys, obviously drunk, trying to force her into their car on an isolated dirt road. No one else in sight. He had passed by on his way home. Thank fuck.

His jaw clenched. He knew where that road led, and she had no business being near it.

He'd damn near had a heart attack when he'd gotten a better look at her. What in God's name was she wearing? Not enough, that was for damn sure.

Her hair was a mess, and someone had torn the sleeve of her shirt. It was apparent she had been crying. Once he'd dealt with the fuckers who'd been manhandling her, he'd gotten her into his truck and headed to Graceview. When she'd told him about sneaking out of her house and going to the weekly Friday night booze bash at Taylor's Point, he had almost lost his mind.

He'd pulled over and let her have it. Her actions had been foolish and more than a little dangerous, as evidenced by the condition of her hair and clothing. He'd held on to his temper until she had smarted off at him. Her sassy tone was all it took to push him over the edge. He'd yanked her out of her seat and dragged her to the back of his pickup. She'd yelped in shock when he'd pulled her over his lap and spanked her ass right over the skintight jeans she'd worn.

At first, she had howled like a banshee, protesting he couldn't spank her. He'd quickly disabused her of that notion. Then she'd tried pleading and promising all sorts of things if he'd stop, but he'd needed her to learn not to pull stupid stunts like she had that night. He was leaving for boot camp soon and then probably the middle east. He wouldn't be around to protect her. By the time he finished, she was a very sorry, very sobbing mess.

He had held her in his lap until her tears calmed. She'd clung to him, pressing closer instead of demanding he take her home. He'd known then that he wanted to pursue a relationship with her. She had needed him and was willing to let him take care of her, and that did something for him, even at twenty-two. Their connection had been intense.

The next day, Tazzy barged into his apartment, crying her eyes out because Georgia was gone.

He still couldn't believe it. After what they had shared, Georgia had moved to California with her new husband. She'd been engaged and hadn't told him. Had let him kiss her. His emotions had clouded his judgment. He had been furious.

In reality, she had every right to do whatever she wanted with her life. He had made no claims or promises. But he hadn't expected her disappearance. And the confusion and rejection wounded him. He'd nursed his wounds by heading out to fight for kin and country without looking back. He should have investigated more. She'd hurt his pride and he'd been a dick.

It gutted him to think of what she might have endured. She

hadn't given him any specifics, but no one got that haunted look in their eyes without cause.

They also didn't put distinctive ringtones on their phones. It was obvious the calls she had been receiving upset her.

There were only two kinds of people who warranted unique ringtones. People whose calls you didn't want to miss and those you didn't want to take. He had always been good at reading people. It was one of the things that made him good at his job.

It wasn't just that Georgia didn't want to talk to whoever triggered that ringtone. She had a visceral reaction to it. Her face lost color and her hands trembled as she silenced the calls. Those calls were freaking his girl out.

If they were coming from who he thought they were, he was going to find her ex and make sure he never bothered Georgia again.

Her mother had a hell of a lot to answer for, too. How could she look at her twin daughters and think one was perfect and the other was worthless? The fact she thought Nevada was perfect and Georgia was worthless was insane.

Georgia's ex-husband had not corrected her belief that she was lacking. His grip on the steering wheel tightened at the thought of him still terrorizing her.

Most people didn't want to spend time on the phone with their exes, especially right after a breakup. But it was more than that with Georgia.

Georgia wasn't just annoyed. Her whole body had stiffened, and she had put a hand on the nearest chair to steady herself. She had lied to him about the call.

They would be talking about that tonight, too. Lies would never be okay between them. Not blatant lies and not lies of omission. She needed to be completely honest with him, and he would do the same with her. Trust was too easy to lose and too hard to regain.

She needed protection from Jarrod Jemison. He knew it down to his bones.

What kind of person stole someone away from everyone they knew and loved in the middle of the night? And what kind of person refused to let said person call the people who were important to her? A narcissistic dick, that's what kind.

Going no contact hadn't been Georgia's idea. No, Jarrod had separated her from everyone in Darling. What had the past eight years been like for her? They hadn't been good, that much was obvious.

He needed Reid to look into Jarrod Jemison. Something was off. He could feel it in his bones. Maybe Georgia's bucket list wasn't the most dangerous thing in her life after all.

If there was a way to get into a scrape, she found it. She led with her heart, which was one of the things he loved about her. But she needed someone to help her think things through before she acted.

Things like buying that crazy truck. Sure, it was adorable and fit her personality, but it needed to be scrapped. He'd almost had a heart attack when he realized the condition the thing was in as she drove it across the country.

He couldn't believe she'd let him leave it at Lowell's Garage. She'd asked about it every day since. If she found out he'd told Winnie to take her time, she'd be furious. He needed to get her a safer ride.

She needed a protector. Who was he kidding? She needed a keeper. He would be the one to keep her safe and help her see the amazing woman she was. Her being with anyone else was unacceptable. And if she wanted to explore her Little side with him, even better.

He wanted a Little to call his own, and she called to the Daddy inside him. Georgia was a Little. He knew it. The question was, did she?

She needed time to figure things out without feeling any pressure from him. And she needed to find those answers before his heart got involved. As if his heart wasn't already involved. Self-delusional, much?

She responded to him. His kisses. His Daddy voice. She shivered every time he called her little girl. So, yeah. Hutch was doing this. He was going to find a way to make Georgia his.

He would go slow, for her sake and his. He needed to make sure she wanted the same things he did. And then he needed to give them to her.

CHAPTER 13

Of all the Darling restaurants Hutch had taken her to so far, *That's Italian* was her favorite. And it was going to be a problem.

This place was a-maz-ing! It was bright and loud and colorful, and smelled the *bestest* in the whole world. She almost slapped her hands over her mouth. She glanced across the table at Hutch to make sure she hadn't said anything out loud. He wasn't staring at her in horror, so she must not have.

Whew! That was close.

The best part was the plain white paper covering the tables and the basket of crayons sitting on each one. Georgia barely contained her squeal. She picked a red crayon and practiced drawing the outline of the apple Tazzy was teaching her to make. Crayons were way easier than coffee as an artistic medium.

This place was drawing her Little out in a big way. She loved everything about it, and by all the filled tables, she wasn't alone. There were couples everywhere. She would have to work hard not to let her Little out, which made her sad. If Hutch were only her

Daddy, she would be free to enjoy everything without worrying she'd embarrass herself.

Hutch picked up a pink crayon. "Here, Peaches. Why don't I add a fat, juicy worm?"

She gasped and covered her drawing with both hands. "No worms in the apples," she said, injecting all the haughtiness she could muster into her tone.

His eyes twinkled as he placed the crayon back in the basket. "I guess you're right," he said.

She nodded. "Silly Daddy," she said, returning to her picture.

Then she froze. Literally froze. Ice coated the inside of her chest. Her hands went numb, and her brain spasmed.

What had she just said? She could not have just called him Daddy. She wanted to slide under the table and hide.

He was going to think she was an idiot. A kinky idiot. Crayons had always been a gateway for her into Little headspace. Something about losing herself in coloring made all her cares disappear. She should have known better. She could just die!

He hadn't said anything. Maybe he didn't hear her. She peeked up at him, only to find him staring at her with a stunned expression.

So, yeah, he'd heard her.

Her stomach lurched, and a cold sweat broke out all over her body. She scooted to the edge of her seat, needing to get to the restroom. Fast. She was going to be sick.

Once that was over, she was going to climb out the bathroom window and disappear into the night, never to be heard from again. She would run away to outer east Mongolia to stand on the street corners and sing Disney songs for spare change.

Maybe she should buy a tambourine. She'd seen that before. She would be a full-fledged street performer in a foreign land.

If only her shaking legs would support her escape.

"Excuse me," she mumbled and stood, poised to run.

Hutch grabbed her hand. "Hold on, Peaches. Sit back down, and let's talk."

She was shaking her head before he finished speaking. "I need to go." Maybe she could fake the 'gotta pee' dance. But that wouldn't help him forget what she'd said. "Now," she added and took a step.

Hutch didn't let go of her hand. She tugged at his hold, but he wouldn't let go.

Tears stung the back of her eyes. "Please," she whispered.

Tenderness filled his eyes. He placed his other hand on top of hers. "Little girl," he said. "I am not upset or embarrassed by your calling me Daddy. I am thrilled you feel the same way I do. Please sit back down so we can talk."

She continued to struggle against his hold until his words penetrated. Wait, what? He was thrilled?

She scoured his face, seeking any sign he was lying or trying to make her feel better about what she had blurted out like a big-mouth idiot. The only thing on his face was concern and hope.

It was the hope that made her sit back down.

He placed his hand in hers and pressed her fingers around his. "Now, tell me what you were thinking."

What was she thinking? She was thinking about how expensive plane tickets to outer east Mongolia were. And who would take care of Petals while she was gone? And how she was going to make herself get on a plane to Mongolia when she didn't like to fly. Did they have boats to outer east Mongolia?

Stop. She needed to get a grip. What was she doing?

This wasn't who she was now. She was the new Georgia. An adventurer, and adventurers showed no fear. She could be brave for Hutch. He cared about her. Maybe not the way she cared about him, but he cared. She could talk to him.

"I felt stupid. That you like me, but not like that. That calling you Daddy was weird. That wanting a Daddy at all is weird." Her voice wobbled when she added, "That now you'll hate me."

When she looked down, she was surprised to see she was squeezing his hand so tight her fingers were white. "Oh my gosh! I'm so sorry," she said, releasing his hand. "I hurt you."

He took her hand and put it back around his. "You didn't hurt me. Thank you for telling me your thoughts. We'll have to work on those, won't we?"

She nodded and waited for him to continue, thankful he didn't want to leave. She didn't want to know what he was going to say, but had to know what he was going to say. Luckily, he didn't make her wait.

"Georgia, nothing would make me happier than being your Daddy. I was planning to discuss our relationship when we got back to Books-N-Brews tonight. Since you opened the door on the subject, let's talk about it now."

Was he kidding her right now? Just like that?

Hutch was a Daddy.

She had known that deep down. He was kind and patient but stern and protective. He was everything the Daddies in the book she read were and more.

Glancing around, she tried to judge if the other tables were close enough for anyone to overhear their conversation. She knew it was packed but hadn't noticed the table spacing. The décor and the crayon baskets had stolen her attention.

Now that she looked around, she noticed some things. A few tables had groups of teenagers, and others had tourists in town on vacation. But most of the tables had couples that looked suspiciously like Hutch and her.

Her eyes widened when she caught sight of a man and woman sitting on the other side of the restaurant. She was dressed similarly to Georgia and was busy coloring on the paper table covering. She beamed up at the man, pointing excitedly at her picture. He nodded and kissed the top of her head.

As she looked at the other couples more closely, several appeared to be Mommies or Daddies with their Littles. Her eyes shot to Hutch. "Are there a lot of Daddies and Mommies in Darling?" she asked.

He smiled. "Yes, Peaches. Darling is a special town that draws people who enjoy that dynamic."

Georgia fell back in her seat. "How did I miss that growing up here? No wonder Mara had a corncob up her butt. She would never approve."

And how had she not noticed that since she'd been back? She'd been here for weeks and weeks. Hope swelled inside her. "So, you aren't shocked or horrified at all?"

"No, little girl, not at all. I am thrilled."

Who knew butterflies could tap dance when they were happy? At least the ones in her stomach could. "I'll try hard not to be bad," she promised, trying to sound as serious as she felt.

Hutch took her cheeks in his hands, tilting her face to him. "Sometimes little girls can be naughty, but never bad. You're strong and brave. I'm proud of you. And if you get carried away with your bravery, that's what Daddies are for."

Wow. He thought she was strong and brave. She didn't think she was either of those things. She wanted to crawl into his lap and let him wrap his arms around her. In his arms, she felt safe and protected.

But she was a mighty adventurer. She was going to be brave for her Daddy. She was going to be brave for herself. And he would be there to encourage her each step of the way.

Mr. Bianchi, the owner, chose that moment to plop a silver pan with his famous two-pound calzone on their table. It was the largest one Georgia had ever seen.

"I hope you enjoy," the man said with a thick Italian accent.

Georgia blushed when she blurted out a loud, "Wow!"

Mr. Bianchi laughed and ruffled her hair. "You let your Daddy get yours for you. It's hot." Before she could respond, a bell dinged in the kitchen, and he disappeared behind a swinging door. Startled, she looked back at Hutch, but he just grinned and started cutting a slice off the calzone for her.

"I hope you are going to eat most of that," she said. "It smells amazing, but it's huge!"

"Well, we better get started then," he said with a laugh. He put a slice on her plate. Her first bite proved it tasted even better than it smelled.

When they finished their meal, Hutch ordered tiramisu for dessert with coffee and a glass of milk for her.

While they waited for dessert, Hutch handed her the crayons. As soon as she started coloring, he said, "Georgia, I want you to be my Little girl. I think I've wanted that for the past eight years. It felt like something started the night you left. I tried to bury what I felt because I was hurt, but the minute you showed up in that crazy pink truck, I knew those feelings were still there. What I need to know is how you feel. Do you want me to be your Daddy? You don't have to answer me now if you need time to think about it."

Georgia didn't have to think about it. She knew. Hutch was the only man she'd ever wanted. She would love nothing more than to have him as her Daddy. She jumped up and threw her arms around his neck. "Yes! Yes, I want that more than anything!"

He beamed down at her, then lowered his mouth to hers, kissing her as if they were not in the middle of a public restaurant. His kiss stole her breath. Stole her mind. Stole her memory of where they were. Gradually, clapping and whistling broke through her reverie, reminding her they had an audience.

She pulled back, burying her face in Hutch's chest. His chuckle filled her with warmth, and she smiled. But she still didn't want to lift her head and face all the people applauding their public display of affection.

"Alright, that's enough," Hutch called across the room, but she could hear the smile in his voice, too. He bent close to say, "Eat your tiramisu, Peaches. We still have some things to discuss back at Books-N-Brews."

She wasn't sure how to feel about that. What was left to say? She finally settled for, "Yes, Daddy."

CHAPTER 14

*H*utch took his time driving back to Books-N-Brews. He needed to think through what came next carefully. His conversation with Georgia had gone exactly as he would have planned it, but now things could get tricky.

He wanted to give her exactly what she needed from him. She told him she was ready, even eager, to be his Little girl, but was she? He wanted nothing more than to pack her up, move her to his cabin, and start their happily ever after.

But it was his job to put her needs ahead of his own. If he handled this wrong, it could ruin everything.

He didn't like long lists of rules. He liked broader rules. He knew Daddies who used a notebook to keep track of all their rules, but he liked heart rules.

Rules should help a Little develop the proper attitudes and mindset. If you made a rule for each infraction, there was always something you missed. Nothing would be more exhausting than chasing after a Little who tried to get attention through negative behavior.

He wanted a Little he could lavish attention on for the right reasons. A Little like Georgia.

After arriving back at the store, he sat beside her on the couch. God, she was beautiful. Excitement, joy, and apprehension filled her eyes. He'd installed shades on the store windows, so now he had her to himself.

He needed her lips again. They were warm and tender, and he wanted to taste them again now that they were alone. Running his fingers into the depth of the midnight blue waves of her silky hair, he tilted her head, pressing kisses along her jaw until he reached the sensitive spot behind her ear.

He pulled her closer until his chest met her body. His cock pulsed as he raised his other hand to the swell of her breast and ran his thumb across her tight nipple. Her soft gasp of pleasure did nothing to calm his pounding need.

Her breath came in shallow pants. Then her moan drew him back to her lips. They parted slightly, allowing his tongue to slip inside. He tasted their shared breaths and felt the pounding of their combined heartbeats.

He needed to stop. The first time he had her would not be on the couch in the middle of Books-N-Brews. He pulled back, gazing into her passion-filled eyes. He wanted nothing more than to toss her onto her back and shove his cock deep inside her.

With a herculean effort, he sat her up and put space between them.

"Peaches, do you know what you do to me?"

Staring at his lips, she answered in a breathy voice, "I know what I want to do to you. Why did you stop?"

That brought a smile to his lips. He liked that she wanted him as much as he wanted her. "This isn't a stop; this is a pause. We need to talk about a few things. Then, I plan to have my wicked way with you." He wriggled his brows at her and twisted an imaginary mustache.

Georgia stifled a giggle and shook her head. "Silly Daddy," she said again.

"You made me the happiest Daddy in Darling tonight, but I want to make sure we are on the same page about what that means."

Suspicion flashed through her eyes. "How many pages are there?"

"Not too many," he answered with a smile. "I need to know what you want in a Daddy. And I need you to know what I expect from my little girl." Georgia's mouth formed an *oh*. Cute. "Why don't you tell me what a Daddy looks like for you."

Her eyes widened then she scrunched her brow. "I don't know, exactly. I've only read about Daddies in books."

"That's a good start. What is it you like about those books?"

He appreciated that she gave it some thought before answering.

"Well, I like that the Daddies are kind. They don't say mean things when they're angry. I guess I like that they are safe."

It hit him hard that she mentioned emotional safety first, but he wasn't surprised. "I can't promise I'll never get upset, but I won't ever use my words to hurt you."

"I know that already. I trust you, Daddy."

"I'm glad. What else do you need from your Daddy?"

"In my books, Daddies are protective. And they take care of their Littles."

"Good, I like taking care of you. I know what happens to Littles who misbehave in your books. Do you like that?"

A beautiful red filled her cheeks, and she dropped her eyes. She nodded her head. She also squirmed in her seat. His Little girl liked punishments, at least when they happened to the Littles in her books. Would she feel the same when it was her bottom getting roasted?

"That's good, Peaches. I definitely know what to do with a little

99

girl who is having trouble following the rules." Her eyes shot up to his, dropping back to her lap when he winked at her.

"What kinds of punishments do the Littles in your books receive?"

She shrugged. "All kinds. They have to stand in the corner and write lines."

"Do they get spankings when they are naughty?"

She nodded again. That wasn't going to do. "Eyes to me, Little one. When we are having a serious discussion, I expect you to look at me. Understand?"

She met his eyes. "Yes, Daddy," she said.

"Is there anything else you want me to know? Anything else you need from Daddy?"

She nodded again. "I like it when the Daddies take care of their Littles, like drawing them a bubble bath or brushing their hair. Oh, and when they cut their sandwiches with cookie cutters, things like that." A mischievous glint sparked in her eyes. "My favorite part is when they get ice cream whenever they want and never have to eat yucky veggie tables."

He lifted one brow. "I'm afraid I might have to disappoint you about that. A Daddy's job is to give his Little girl what she needs to be healthy and happy. So, veggies will remain on the menu."

She looked so sad he had to laugh before pulling her to sit in his lap.

"Would you like to know what I expect from my Little girl?"

She practically bounced on his lap. "Yes, Daddy. I want to be who you want me to be."

He needed her to know he was not her ex. "You already are who I want you to be, Peaches. You don't need to become anyone different, even when you're naughty. That's what you do, not who you are. You are perfect for me right now."

Her shoulders slumped. "I don't always like me. I can be selfish and lazy and stupid—"

Oh no. He was not having that.

He placed a finger over her lips. "I'm going to stop you right there, little girl. None of that is true. Those are lies people who should know better told you. That's not who you are. You are not to say mean things about yourself. Not out loud and not to yourself. That will absolutely get you corner time or a trip over my knee."

"But, Daddy!" At his expression, she sighed and said, "Yes, Daddy."

He pulled her in for another hug. If he could have a few minutes alone with the Donnelley's and Jemison, he would make them pay for hurting his girl. They had a lot to answer for.

He set Georgia up to look at him but kept her on his lap. "Now, to avoid those punishments you read about, let's discuss rules. I only have four rules, and we'll both follow three of them."

"But, Daddy, I thought rules were just for Littles."

He shook his head. "Three for us both and one especially for you."

He had her full attention then. She waited for him to explain. Such a good girl.

"Rule one; we treat people and things with respect."

"That doesn't seem hard," Georgia said.

"It doesn't, does it? But if you respect someone, would you call them lazy or selfish?"

She narrowed her eyes. "No, Daddy."

"But you said all those things about yourself. Hmm. You have a face like a person." He prodded her face gently, then moved to her arms. "You have arms and legs like a person."

When Georgia giggled, he reached for her ribs, tickling her. "You have ribs like a person."

"Stop, Daddy," she shrieked, laughing and wiggling. "I gonna pee!"

That stopped him short. "Do you need to go to the bathroom?" he asked.

"No, but if you tickle, I might have a accident." Her voice took on a Little tone.

"Alright, no tickling for now. Rule two; we are always honest. Honesty builds trust. I will never lie to you and expect the same in return. Do you agree with that?"

"Yes, Daddy. I don't like cheats and liars."

That came with a scrunched forehead and a vigorous shake of her head.

"Good," he said. "Rule three, we choose safety first. That means you don't do things that put your health or safety in jeopardy."

She stared at him, then slipped her hand behind her back. He grabbed it and put it back in her lap.

"No crossed fingers on the rules. That counts as not being honest," he said. "We'll be talking about your bucket list again."

No way in hell was she doing the things on that list. He'd almost had a heart attack just reading it. He liked adventure, but he would be setting some firmer boundaries for her. And no list would include sharks or tigers.

"When am I getting Petals back? I need my truck."

Clever girl. Winnie was having the time of her life putting the pieces of her truck back together. Hopefully, by the time she finished, Hutch would have convinced Georgia to purchase something easier to handle.

"Winnie is still trying to make Petals road ready."

"It's taking forever," she said. "You're sure she's working on it?"

"She is. They have to work on more than just your truck. Don't you like riding around with Daddy?"

"Course I do. But I can't ride 'round with you forever."

"Why not?" As far as he was concerned, that was the best place for her.

"Maybe I should go by and talk to Winnie," she said.

"We'll try to run by there soon," he promised. He would take her to the garage, but he wasn't in any hurry. "We still need to go over rule four. This rule is just for you."

She didn't object, so he kept going. "Rule four is very important. Are you ready?" At her nod, he said, "Little girls always mind Daddy."

"I can do that. I good at minding," she said.

He appreciated her confidence, but they hadn't discussed her bucket list. He'd save that for when she was in a more adult headspace.

She smiled, and it lit up his world. He was going to bust his balls to be the Daddy she wanted. The Daddy she needed. The Daddy she would stay with forever.

He wanted nothing more than to take her upstairs and make love to her all night. But she needed time to think about what he had shared with her.

He couldn't change who he was any more than he wanted to change her. He wanted a sweet Little who was loving and obedient. He didn't expect perfection, not even close. But he knew himself. He had friends who loved brat-taming, and that was fine for them. It just wasn't what he wanted.

He wanted peace. He wanted a Little girl to take care of and keep happy in every way he could. He wanted his forever Little girl. And he wanted her to be Georgia.

CHAPTER 15

Someone was pounding on the door of Georgia's apartment. She jerked up in bed, almost smacking her head on the ceiling. She had the most incredible raised platform bed. It looked like a bunk bed, but instead of a bottom bed, she had a beanbag chair, a table, and a lamp. The perfect play nook.

She canopied purple chiffon curtains covered in glow-in-the-dark stars around the bed. The extra fairy lights kept it from getting too dark at night. She loved it.

Whoever was at the door banged again. She hadn't slept, thinking, ok, worrying, after Hutch left the night before.

She still couldn't believe he was her Daddy. Her life didn't come with happily ever afters. If it did, it would be Hutch. She shivered at the memory of his kisses the night before. They had curled her toes.

He said to make sure he was the Daddy she wanted. She wasn't sure how to want anyone else. She had loved him for years. Granted, he didn't know that and she couldn't tell him. Not until he had a chance to love her back.

She loved everything about him. Even all his rules. She'd stay with him as long as he'd let her. That wouldn't be forever. Eventually, he'd realize she hadn't been honest about who she was.

Hutch and Tazzy were the only ones who thought she was anything special. Well, Vivi always treated her like she was special, but she treated everyone that way, so that didn't count.

Georgia had enough emotional baggage from Jarrod the Jerkface to fill a Samsonite warehouse. Now he was calling her phone nonstop. She'd never have left if he'd paid so much attention to her in California. Perish the thought.

The pounding on the door started up again. Who pounded on doors at god-thirty in the morning on a Sunday?

Like she didn't know. Only Jedidiah Hutchinson would be banging on her door like that. She ran to the door and snatched it open. Over-eager much? She leaned against the door and grinned, giving him her best attempt at a sexy, "Hi, Daddy."

He grinned back. "Good morning, sweet girl," he said. "That was the perfect greeting. I love your jammies."

Oh. Good. Lord.

She was so eager to get to the door she hadn't thought about her clothes. She glanced down at her pajamas as if she didn't know what he saw.

She wore a light pink, hooded onesie with cat ears. A Disney kitten on the front said, 'Purrfect in Every Way.' She was going back to bed, hiding under the covers, and never coming out again.

At the thought of her bed, her heart stopped. What if Hutch saw her bed? I mean, yes, he knew she was a Little. But there was knowing, and then there was *knowing*. She had bought stuffie friends for Penny, and now had a dragon and a mermaid.

She had a thing for imaginary creatures.

They were all clearly visible on the bed in her studio apartment. Grown women didn't have so many stuffies. He was going to think she was crazy.

"You woke me up, Daddy," she said.

"Well, rise and shine, beautiful," he said, delivering a playful swat to her bottom.

"Ouch!" she yelped, even though it didn't hurt.

Then he was inside her apartment, looking around the entire space.

She'd decorated her apartment in soft pink and purple things she'd picked up garage sale hunting before work. She loved it, but what would he think? She stared up at him, not even breathing, as he took it all in.

He smiled and said, "Nice lava lamp."

He crossed to her bed and lifted Singe, her dragon, off the floor. Could the floor open up and swallow her?

She waited for him to ask her what a grown woman was doing with so many stuffies. Jarrod would have. Her ex had found Penny once and thrown her in the trashcan. He called her infantile and an embarrassment. Then he'd told all his friends, and they'd laughed at her.

Hutch brushed her dragon off and lifted him to soar over the bed, then put him back down next to Penny and Bubbles, her mermaid. Georgia stared at the carpet under her bed, waiting for his scorn and amusement.

"Hey," he said, placing fingers under her chin. "What's wrong, little girl? I should have asked before touching something so special, but I didn't think you meant it to be on the floor."

He wasn't freaked out. Distracted, she corrected, "Him."

"What?" he asked.

She was such an idiot! Blushing, she explained. "Singe is a him, not an it. And thank you."

"Of course." He nodded. Then to Singe, he said, "I apologize, Singe. Obviously, you are the king of the dragons." His gaze shifted back to her. "Would you introduce me to everyone else?"

Ok, what was going on? Not only was he not angry, he wanted to know all their names. Was he really like the

Daddies in her books? He wasn't just being nice. She could tell.

"You don't think I'm weird?" She tried to laugh, but it sounded forced. "I mean, grown women don't name their stuffed animals. That's just in the books, right?"

"Actually," he said, "I know several women who name their stuffies."

Was he trying to make her feel better? That wasn't necessary. She had armor plating instead of skin. Tough as nails, that was her.

Right.

"Did you just roll your eyes at me, Little girl?" Hutch asked, his voice growing stern and growly.

Her nipples grew tight. She prayed her pajamas were thick enough they didn't show.

"I wasn't rolling my eyes at you. Honest," she assured him. "I was rolling them at myself." And now she owed herself another eye roll.

"You were rolling your eyes at yourself. I haven't heard that one before. Why were you rolling your eyes at yourself?"

Of course, he hadn't, because he didn't usually talk to idiots.

"It doesn't matter. Why are you here so early?"

His face shifted from amused to stern. "I tried to call you several times to let you know I would be here early this morning. It went straight to voicemail, and you never returned my calls. Why didn't you answer your phone?"

Drat! She had gotten tired of Jarrod calling her nonstop yesterday, and had turned off her phone. She must have forgotten to turn it back on.

"Sorry, Daddy. I got... so busy with work I must have turned off my phone. I guess I forgot to turn it back on." Shoot, she broke rule three, and it hadn't even been a whole day. She was a horrible Little.

Her explanation didn't satisfy Hutch.

"I don't like not being able to contact you. If something happens to you when it's off, I won't be able to find you."

Find her. What? "How would my phone help you find me?"

"I added an app to your phone that tells me where you are."

He just said that like it wasn't creepy or stalkerish or anything. "You can't just put stuff on my phone."

Hutch crossed his arms over his chest. Uh-oh. "Do you remember last weekend?"

Darn it! She should have called Tazzy. But it was early, and Tazzy slept in on her day off. She wouldn't have called her anyway. She would always call Hutch when she was in trouble. She'd settled the minute he'd answered the phone.

Still, he was tracking her. What about privacy? "Sorry I bothered you," she said.

His scowl deepened. "Watch your tone, little girl. You call me if you need anything. But I can't help you if I can't find you. Now I know where you are, so I can help if you get lost again."

Darn it again! That made sense. Still, she wasn't ready to let it go. She said, "Fine. If I need privacy, I'll leave my phone here." It was the wrong thing to say. She blamed her lack of sleep.

Hutch's frown turned into a glare. "You try that, little girl, and see what it gets you."

Her hands reached for her bottom without her permission.

Hutch nodded. "I see we're on the same page. We talked about your safety last night. If you put yourself at risk, I will put you over my knee. Understand?"

She nodded. Wowzers. That escalated quickly.

"Words, little girl."

"Yes, Daddy, I understand." Her lady bits got squirmy. His scolding turned her into a puddle of goo.

"And Peaches, if you put yourself at risk intentionally, I'll use my belt. Are we clear?"

Why did people talk about butterflies in their stomachs? She had bees, killer bees. And they were buzzing. She stared at him, eyes wide, and nodded again before adding, "Crystal."

He nodded toward her phone. "Why don't you make sure it's on now? I wouldn't want you to miss another call."

She hurried to the phone, turned it on, and made sure the ringer was at the highest volume. She held it out in case he needed proof. "Sorry I snapped at you. Real Daddies are different from book Daddies."

His face softened, and he enveloped her in a bear hug. "Good girl," he said. Her insides buzzed again. "Sabre is working downstairs this morning upgrading the alarm system. Once that's done, we'll head up here to put a new lock on your door and extend the system into your apartment."

"I don't want an alarm system up here," she said.

There had been a coded alarm at her house in California. The code had changed weekly. She could never remember the current code, which caused the alarm to go off. Jarrod would get furious and spend hours telling her how stupid and useless she was.

Besides, she didn't want them in her apartment. This was her Little space. She would never be able to explain it to strangers.

Before Hutch could respond, her phone rang. She cringed when Jarrod's stupid ringtone echoed around her apartment. The name Jerkface lit up her screen. The time on her phone said 6:17 a.m. She wasn't surprised. He had been phoning her all day and night for weeks.

Hutch stepped closer. She tucked the phone behind her back.

"Who's calling at this hour, Georgia?" he asked, but by his tone, he already knew.

"Um, nobody." She wracked her brain for a reasonable explanation. "It says Jerkface whenever it's a wrong number."

Just shoot her! She was a terrible liar.

Hutch's scowl returned.

"Little girl, I'm going to remind you, just this once, of our rules. I get you've been living with vipers. But we don't lie. And in case I wasn't clear, you never lie to Daddy. Got me?"

"I got you, Daddy. I'm sorry, I panicked."

"Tell me if you don't want to say who's calling. Don't lie. Trust is too hard to get back once it's gone."

Her nose burned as she tried to blink back her tears. Her stomach ached. She had disappointed him.

But she had to protect him from Jarrod. Jarrod was like poison, and no one was immune. Hutch was the opposite of Jarrod. He didn't deserve the trouble she'd bring if Jarrod came after her. She would deal with Jarrod herself.

Hutch wrapped his arms around her again, cocooning her away from all her problems. When he released her, she wanted to grab him and pull him back.

"I'm going back downstairs. If you wanted to brew some coffee later, no one would object."

"I can do that," she said. It was the least she could do if they gave up their Sunday to help her Daddy.

"That's my girl." Hutch smiled and lifted his chin. "See you downstairs."

She watched the door in case he decided to come back. When that didn't happen, she snapped into motion. She had work to do before a bunch of strangers entered her apartment. Hutch might be a Daddy, but the men he'd brought with him weren't. She had a lot of de-Littling to do.

CHAPTER 16

*a*n hour later, Georgia looked down at her latest latte art. If she squinted her eyes, she could almost see the leaf. Steamed milk was hard.

"Here." She offered the mug to the man named Deke. Hutch had introduced her to all the guys working for Sabre Security. She liked them, but they made her feel tiny. The shortest man was half a foot taller than her.

Deke stared into the steaming cup. "That's funny," he said. "I've never seen poop emoji latte art before."

"That's not a poop emoji. It's a leaf."

He looked again. "Right. I knew what it was. I was just joking." He headed back to the others.

"See if I make your coffee pretty again," she called after him, then spun around and plowed into a solid chest.

Two big hands steadied her. "What's wrong, Peaches?" Hutch asked.

"Deke made fun of my latte art," she told him. "I'm not making him another one. I can make you one."

He glared at Deke. "That's alright, babygirl. I'm not thirsty right now. Have you had some water this morning?"

"Coffee isn't for thirsty. Coffee is for goodness."

He had this weird affinity for water and made her drink it all the time. If there was such a thing as water addiction, he had it.

"Are you sure?" She didn't want him to feel left out.

"I'm sure. Why don't you go back upstairs and play? I know you're working more hours than you are turning in. You don't want to get sick."

She gasped and covered his mouth with her hands. "Don't say that, Daddy. The universe is listening."

He kissed her palm, and she snatched her hands away, giggling. Turning her toward the stairs, he swatted her bottom.

"Daddy, someone will see," she said, running up the stairs.

"No running on the stairs," Hutch called after her. "You might fall."

She groaned. Could she get any more embarrassed? She probably imagined it, but she could swear all the men from Sabre gave off Daddy vibes.

Upstairs, she finally let her Little out to play. She would hear Hutch and the other men coming up the stairs in time to hide her things. Then she lost herself in coloring books and rainbow scratch art pads.

The next thing she knew, her Daddy walked through the door, followed by Deke, Reid, Jaxon, and Sawyer. Georgia squeaked and threw her blanket over the crayons, stuffies, and blocks spread over the floor. It didn't help because they had already seen everything.

Her whole body burned with humiliation, and she thought she might pass out. She scrambled around on her hands and knees, trying to gather everything without uncovering anything else. What would they think of her, a grown woman lying on a floor cluttered with stuffed animals, coloring while she watched cartoons? She even had pigtails in her sapphire hair. With bows!

Her efforts were useless. She jumped up, intending to run for the bathroom to hide, but Hutch put an arm around her waist and pulled her close.

"Guys, give me a few minutes," he said. The next thing she knew, they were alone. She buried her face in his chest and burst into tears.

He lifted her off the ground and she wrapped herself around him. As if she weighed nothing, he carried her to the worn couch and sat with her in his lap.

"Where's my suitcase? I have to move," she sobbed into his chest.

"Where are you moving to?" he asked.

"Outer east Mongolia!" she wailed. "Or maybe Siberia. No, not Siberia. Bubbles doesn't like cold water."

"Why would you do that?" he asked, his low voice rumbling in her ear. It sent warm fuzzies all over her, which she ignored. She could never show her face again. And now Hutch was going to be mad at her.

She studied him. He didn't look upset. He looked relaxed, caressing her back and rocking her back and forth. Why wasn't he yelling about how embarrassed he was?

What the heck? He wasn't angry at all. His eyes were gentle and kind. But he had to be upset. Maybe he was just good at hiding it.

"I'm sorry," she said. Her voice was still thin and wobbly from crying.

"Sorry for what, little one?"

"You know. Acting like a baby, wasting time coloring, and having toys out for everyone to see. I didn't mean to embarrass you."

She continued to search his face. Something flashed through

his eyes, but it was gone before she could read it. He wiped away her tears with his thumb.

"Little girl, no one gave it a second thought. You didn't do anything wrong. Enjoying yourself on your day off isn't wasting time. It's healthy. And why would I be embarrassed? I love watching you play. It's one of Daddy's favorite things to do."

He had to be joking. Of course, he was embarrassed. She certainly was.

"Look at me, Georgia Anne." He waited for her to comply. "I told you I knew other women who liked stuffies."

Her cheeks burned, but she nodded. Once again, even having lived here growing up, she had missed the glaringly obvious.

"That's because I know several women who are Littles. Most of the men who live in Darling are Daddies."

That would explain some of the men who frequented Books-N-Brews. Overall, the men of Darling were polite and kind. They also tended to be protective of their women and more than a bit bossy. And, she'd overheard threats of a spanking or two.

Darling was full of Daddies!

"You aren't just saying that, are you?" She had to ask. "You know other women like me?"

"I do. I can introduce you to some of them. We'll have a welcome back home party and invite everyone."

That brought her up short. Did she want to do that?

On the one hand, she would love to meet others who felt the same way she did. It would be wonderful to have friends who understood. She could talk and ask questions. Oh! She could have Littles over to spend the night. They could color and drink all the different flavors of hot chocolate.

On the other hand, they might hate her even more than some already did. Maybe they would think she was a fake or doing it wrong.

What if she was doing it wrong? What if she had a party and nobody came? And they laughed at her behind her back.

"Georgia," Hutch interrupted her thoughts. "Where did you go?"

She shook the thought of not fitting in out of her head and focused on Hutch. "You promise all the guys with you are Daddies? They didn't think I was weird?"

He frowned at that. "Of course, they didn't. They think you're almost as adorable as I do. I can tell we will have to work on building trust."

Those bees flew back into her stomach, but they didn't sting this time. They buzzed and tickled. Hutch thought she was adorable.

She had been wondering about something since last night. True to form, she blurted it out. "When did you know I was a Little?"

One side of his mouth quirked up. God, that was sexy! "My first inkling was Petals," he admitted. "I didn't say anything because I was shocked to see you. Then I didn't want to scare you off. How long have you known?"

He wanted to know her better, too. That was good, right? Her tingles got stronger. She'd promised to be honest, but it was uncomfortable. "Um, about eight years."

Her answer surprised him. "You knew eight years ago? You were only eighteen."

She knew her cheeks were red because she could feel the heat. "Not exactly, no. But that last night when you... I mean when I... um," she stumbled over her words.

Hutch smiled. "The night I spanked your bottom for putting yourself in such danger?" When she nodded, he added, "I remember."

A thought occurred to her, and she asked, "Did you know you were a Daddy then?"

"I wouldn't have called it that back then. I knew I needed to take care of the important people in my life, protect them, and correct them if necessary. I'd never spanked anyone before. But this is Darling. So, I figured out I was a Daddy after you left."

Her heart kicked up a notch. "Does that mean I was important to you?"

"Absolutely." He didn't hesitate to answer. "I told myself it was because of Tazzy. That night, I realized it was more than that. But before I could explore it with you, you married another man and left."

She needed to explain the truth about what had happened. Now wasn't the time. But soon.

She could answer his question. "I realized some things that night, too. I didn't like the spanking. It hurt. But when I thought back on it, I felt valued for the first time in my life. You cared enough to get me safe and keep me from making a mistake like that again."

Memories of that night had turned her on. She hadn't known why, but it had. Then she'd stumbled across a romance book about a Little who found her Daddy. She'd related to almost everything she read.

Hutch took her hand. "I've been searching for a Little to call my own for a long time. When you came back to Darling, I realized I hadn't found anyone because no one else was you."

They had lost so much time. The past eight years could have been so different. She could have been safe and happy. Loved. It was enough to make her heart break. How could Mara have done that to her?

"I know it's soon, Georgia, but I don't want to waste any more time. I want to spend the rest of my life with you. You don't have to commit to anything right now, but I want you to know this isn't casual for me. When you're ready, I want to talk about the future. Is that something you're willing to explore with me?"

God, did he even have to ask? "I want that, too."

He grinned at her. "You'll have to be patient with me. I haven't been in a relationship with anyone in a while."

"Me either. I mean, not a good one, and I've never had a Daddy."

"We'll work through it together, little one. It's like riding a bike. Once you learn, you never forget."

"I never learned to ride a bike."

Hutch stared at her, finally asking, "You've never ridden a bicycle?"

Great, now she felt like Orphan Annie. She shook her head. "No one ever taught me," she said.

"Well, today is your lucky day, Peaches. It just so happens I have the afternoon free. And I have a bicycle at my house just waiting for a special Little girl."

"Today?" she all but screeched. That was not happening. She needed time to build up her courage. Then she would have to add it to her bucket list to mark off. "I can't. I'll mess it up like I do everything else."

Hutch got that stern face again. "Look at me and tell me I always mess everything up, little girl."

Georgia gasped. She couldn't do that. "Daddy, no!"

He lifted her hand to his lips and pressed a gentle kiss there. "Of course not. If you did, you'd expect consequences, right?"

She looked down at her feet and nodded.

"And you should," he said. "I expect you to give yourself the same kindness and respect you give me. When you don't, it hurts you. I will never let anyone hurt you, little one. Not even you."

No one had ever protected her from anything, especially unkind words. She wanted to press into him and feel his arms around her again.

"Now, you keep playing while we install your alarm, then we will head to my place and learn to ride that bike. Sound good?"

Good? It sounded amazing.

She just hoped he was as excited about it at the end of the day.

CHAPTER 17

*H*utch glanced at Georgia as he opened his shed. Her hands gripped each other so tight her knuckles were white, and she bounced up and down on her toes. Cute. Her reaction went straight to his dick.

He walked the bike onto the grass and she froze. The only things open wider than her mouth were her eyes. Then she squealed, clapped her hands, and raced toward him. She reached for the handlebar but pulled back as if touching it would make it disappear. Instead, she hit him with a bear hug that almost sent them both to the ground.

"It's beautiful!" Her cheeks flushed with excitement. She was the prettiest little girl he had ever seen.

"I'm glad you like it," was all he got out before she turned back to her new bike.

"Can I touch it?" she asked softly.

"It's going to be hard to ride if you don't," he teased.

She stroked the handlebars and ran her hand down the streamers. His cock pulsed with the need to feel that hand stroking him.

She flicked the button on the bike's bell and giggled at the chime it made.

"It's the most wonderful thing I've ever seen! Where'd you find it?"

"Daddies have their ways," he said. He'd found it at a garage sale and taken it to Winnie. She loved 'Littling' things for her friends and was good at it. She'd outdone herself this time. She'd turned a rusted old bike into a mermaid bike, sea blue with sparkly pink handle grips and rims. She'd added a white basket on the front and long pink and white streamers on the handles. He knew Georgia would love it the minute he saw it.

Winnie had added everything he'd asked for; most importantly, training wheels, which would come in especially handy since she'd never ridden a bike. He'd had it back for a week, waiting for a day like today when he could give it to Georgia.

"Do you want to help me push her to the driveway?" He smiled as she practically leaped for the bicycle. As soon as they reached the drive, she tried to climb on the sparkly banana seat.

"Not so fast, little girl." He took her hand and led her into the cabin. "First, we have to get you geared up."

"What do you mean, geared up?"

"It means wearing a helmet and knee pads whenever you're on your bike. Riding a bike is fun. Cracking your head on the ground if you fall is not." No way was she riding a bike without safety gear.

"It already has training wheels on it! I don't need a helmet if it has training wheels."

"Training wheels are helpful, but you could still get hurt if you lose your balance. You will wear your helmet and knee pads every time you ride, or you'll lose the privilege of riding. Remember your safety rule?"

"A'course. We talked about it last night. Are you so old your mem'ry is that bad?" Her voice drifted into a Little's higher pitch.

She patted his hand and added, "Don't worry. I can member for both of us."

Sassy minx. It seemed they needed to go over a few things again before she learned to ride.

"I remember a lot of things," he said, taking her hand. "Come with me."

He walked to an oversized leather chair and sat down. Once she sat on his lap, he asked, "What is the rule about safety, little girl?"

She frowned at him. "I don't wanna talk about rules. I wanna ride my bike."

She was already in her Little headspace, which was just where he wanted her. He hid a smile, deepened his voice, and asked, "Who decides when you ride your bike, young lady?"

She scrunched up her face but answered, "You do."

"That's right. And I want to go over a few things first." He chose to ignore her dramatic sigh. It actually pleased him that she felt safe enough to let her emotions out. "If you get sassy with Daddy, this will take longer than I planned. What did we say last night about respect?"

"Treat people and things with respect," she recited with exaggerated patience. "Can we go now, Daddy?"

"The only place you're going is the corner if you don't pay attention. What we are talking about is important."

He gave her a stern look and stifled a groan when she squirmed on his lap.

"Is it respectful to call Daddy old and not listen to him?" She shook her head with her lip poked out. "No, it isn't. You want to try again?"

"Yes, Daddy."

"That's my good girl. Now, what is the safety rule?"

"We choose safety first."

"Good girl."

She nodded. "Ok, noooowww can I ride my bike?"

"Georgia Anne, you are still not listening. Pay attention or you'll wind up with a hot bottom."

She slumped against him and stared at her knees. "I'm sorry, Daddy. I wanna listen, but my ears keep thinking about the bell on my bike and how it sounded when I rang it. I didn't mean to be bad."

He tilted her chin up so she could see his eyes. "I might be getting old, but I still remember what we said last night about your being bad. You are not bad. You are a thoughtful, generous, and brave person. I've never known anyone as good as you. From now on, every time you call yourself bad, you will list five true things about yourself. Bad is not true. Understand?"

She nodded, but her eyes shone with doubt.

"Let's try it now. Tell me something good about Georgia Anne."

She caught her bottom lip between her teeth as she tried to come up with something to say.

With tears in her eyes, she shrugged. He hated she couldn't see herself as he did. They would be working on that.

"How about I start? I already told you that you are thoughtful, generous, and brave. You are also fun to be around. That's four things. You add the last one to make five."

After more deliberation, she looked up at him and said, "I like helping people. Does that count?"

There were thousands of things that made her special. He was going to make sure she knew and believed every one of them. He hugged her to him and kissed the top of her head. "It absolutely counts. You are a wonderful helper. I'm proud of you for thinking of it."

Her smile at his praise warmed and broke his heart. Yep, one hour alone with her family. Maybe two.

"Pretty please with sugar and a giant cherry on top, Daddy, now can I ride my bike?"

"You can," he said. "I just have to adjust your gear to fit."

She groaned. "Do we have to?"

"No," he answered her. "But it will make sitting on your bike much more comfortable."

"How will a helmet and knee pads make the seat more comfortable?"

"Oh, it won't make the bike's seat more comfortable, just yours." Color infused her cheeks when she caught his meaning. Adorable.

He grabbed her helmet and put it on her. She wasn't impressed. "It's gonna squish my hair."

"Better than the road squishing your brain."

"Good point," she called in a sing-song voice. "I've never seen a unicorn helmet before. It's the most beautifulest helmet ever I seen! I love it!"

"I'm glad, Peaches. Now hold still long enough for me to fit the straps."

Two swats to her bottom later, she ran back outside. Her twirling in the driveway, watching the rainbow reflections dance off her helmet, was the cutest thing he'd ever seen. He had looked long and hard for the perfect one, and it was worth every second.

He guided her onto the bike and slid her feet into the foot guards. She pedaled slowly at first then picked up speed. He'd held onto the seat for a while until she demanded, "Let go, Daddy. I do it myself."

After that, he leaned against the side of his truck and watched his girl go. His girl? Damn, that sounded good. She was his girl, and he would take care of her.

An hour later, Georgia pulled up in front of him. "I wanna take the training wheels off, Daddy."

"Are you sure, Peaches? You're still learning. Maybe we should leave them on for a day or two until you're steady."

"I am steady," she insisted, and he saw the determined glint in her eyes.

Still, he had to think about what was best for her. "I think waiting until tomorrow would be better."

She wilted in front of his eyes. "You're right, Daddy. I probably couldn't do it anyway."

Damn. He hadn't meant to discourage her. She was doing a great job, and he was holding her back.

"No, you're right, Peaches. You are ready. Just hold on a second and let me get my tools."

After removing the training wheels, he held her bike again until she learned to balance without them. Soon she was riding around the cul-de-sac in front of his house.

His heart swelled at the joy on her face as she cried out, "I'm doing it. See me? I'm doing it."

Yes, she was. His girl could do anything she put her mind to. He'd tell her to add determination to her list of positive things about herself.

"Daddy, these knee pads are too tight on my legs. They're slowing me down." She pulled beside him. They were a bit snug. She stuck out her closest leg and demanded, "Off!"

Uh, no.

"Excuse me?" Someone was headed for a timeout.

She backtracked quickly. "I mean, can you please take them off, Daddy?"

That was more like it. He pulled the knee pads off and removed the short straps.

She couldn't ride without kneepads, but he could make them more comfortable. He needed to go inside for the longer straps. His was the only house on the road, so no one else ever drove down it. She'd be fine on the driveway. He'd grab the straps and come right back. "You wait right here. Do not ride until Daddy gets back. It won't take long."

"Hurry, Daddy," she called after him.

Just as he located the straps, a scream followed by wailing pierced the air. He raced back outside to find Georgia sitting on the pavement at the end of the drive beside her toppled bike. She hugged her knee to her chest.

Hutch took off at a dead run. The only thing pounding faster than his feet was his heart. He knelt beside her and brushed her hair from her eyes.

"Let me see, Peaches," he said, lifting her knee gently.

"Don't touch it! You'll make it hurt more," Georgia yelled and tried to pull free.

"Georgia Anne, be still and let me check your scrape." His stern Daddy voice stilled her instantly.

Why the fuck had he let her wear shorts? Everyone knew you wore long pants to ride a bike. He shouldn't have left her unattended. He'd fucked up, and now she was bleeding.

"It hurts, Daddy," Georgia cried, tears streaming down her face.

"I know, little one. I'm sorry you had a wreck. You're lucky it wasn't worse. You could have broken your leg."

Then she held up her hands and showed him the scrapes crisscrossing her palms. "Oh, baby, that looks painful. That's why Daddy said not to ride until he got back."

"I know!" Georgia sobbed harder. "I'm s-sorry. You were t-taking forever, and I didn't think it would h-hurt to ride up and down the driveway. I was doing good. And then the wheel w-wobbled, I fell, and my bike was on top of me."

He lifted her in his arms. "It's alright, Peaches. Daddy's here."

CHAPTER 18

*H*utch sat Georgia on the bathroom counter. Her knee throbbed, and her hands stung. "I'll get you all fixed up, little girl, and then we are going to talk."

From the look on his face, she didn't think talking was what he had in mind. Even with her scrapes, that's all she could think about.

He pulled a first aid kit out of the towel closet, but she stared at what he held under his arm.

The most precious narwhal stuffy she had ever seen peeked out from the crook of his elbow. She was beautiful, complete with an ice cream cone for a horn. Pink ice cream with sprinkles dripped down her white body, and she had the biggest, bluest eyes Georgia had ever seen.

Except for her Daddy's eyes.

They were even bluer.

"I thought Nellie might love a hug while we take care of your owies." He held Nellie up for her to see.

"Thank you," she said, fighting the urge to snatch her new friend from her Daddy's hands. "She is perfect!"

"Well, she's needed a friend for a long time. I know she loves hugs as much as you." He smiled as he took out the antiseptic. "This won't sting. You hold on to Nellie and keep her from being scared, okay?"

Georgia nodded. Why had he brought Nellie to her? She was so soft, like hugging a cloud. But Georgia didn't deserve a new friend. "You don't have to be nice to me. I know I'm too much trouble."

He stopped tending her scratches. "You will never be too much trouble, Georgia. You made a bad choice. We'll discuss that shortly. But after that, we're going to the kitchen for supper. And if you eat your vegetables, you can pick out the movie we watch later."

Long before she was ready, he shut the first aid kit and announced, "All done. Now, let's go to the playroom and have that chat."

The playroom? He had a playroom? He carried her down the hall as she tried to imagine a playroom designed by Hutch. When he opened the door, she froze. Nothing could have prepared her for what she saw.

The walls were pale teal blue with three large windows adorned with white chiffon curtains. Rugs of different sizes and colors decorated the cream-colored wooden floor. A velvety purple armchair sat before one window, with a padded rocking chair before the other. Shelves lined the left wall with toys – Lego blocks, dolls, and stuffed animals. There were even craft supplies and coloring books. Everything she could wish for and then some.

But what captured her attention was the castle-shaped bed taking up almost one wall. Two massive box-shaped shelves stood like towers at each end, almost reaching the ceiling. A set of curving steps bracketed the bed, leading to a top bunk. Pillows, stuffies, and twinkle lights flooded the entire space. It. Was. Gorgeous.

She wanted to race everywhere in the playroom at once. Then she caught a glimpse of Hutch, eying her with worry. Did he think she wouldn't love it? It was incredible. She would tell him, but she had no words.

"Well, do you like it?" he finally asked. "If you don't, we'll redo it however you like. I want you to be comfortable."

She threw her arms around his neck. He'd fixed this magical playroom for her.

It was spectacular. It was too much.

It was Hutch.

For the first time in her life, she had somewhere to call home.

At least, she hoped she did. Her heart tripped with fear. She couldn't mess up again, or he would find someone else. Someone better.

"I love it," she said. "It is the most beautiful thing I've ever seen."

She felt his muscles relax, and he set her on her feet.

"I'm glad you like it," he said. "I hate the first thing we have to do in here is discuss your misbehavior." He led her toward the large armchair.

Hutch sat down and pulled her to stand between his thighs. Her bottom tingled while nerves and regret tickled her tummy. Why hadn't she just done what he said?

"When Daddy went inside, what did he tell you to do?"

Her bottom clenched. It wasn't like she had chosen to disobey him. Not exactly. She had waited and waited for him to get back. She could feel the knowledge of how to ride her new bike draining from her brain.

She just needed to ride her bike up and down the driveway one time to make sure she didn't forget how. But it had been so fun she made just one more trip up and down. And then another.

She knew she was pushing her luck. Thoughts of getting caught made her twist the handlebars too fast when she turned. And that made her fall.

So, it was his fault. She opened her mouth to explain that to him, but one look at his expression had her changing her mind.

He quirked just one eyebrow up. "I don't think you're about to give me the answer I'm looking for," he said. "What did I say, naughty girl?"

She didn't want to say, but she had no choice. "To stay where I was and not ride my bike."

"That's right. And what did you do?"

Tears already stung her eyes. "I rode my bike."

"Yes, you did." His voice grew more stern. "Were you listening earlier when we talked about safety?"

Guilt dropped heavy bricks on her chest, making it hard to answer. "Yes, Daddy." Her voice was barely more than a whisper.

"So you deliberately chose to disobey."

"Yes, Daddy." A tear slid down her face and dripped off her chin.

"I'm not going to spank you for that."

Her head shot up. He wasn't going to spank her? Why did that disappoint her? She should have been relieved, and she was, sort of. But she also felt let down. She was crazy.

Then he continued. "Not only for that."

Wait, what? "What do you mean?"

"What did I tell you about obeying Daddy?"

Her voice still trembled. "Always mind Daddy."

"And did you do that?"

She laced and unlaced her fingers and whispered, "No, Daddy."

"No, you did not. Were you being naughty?"

She wanted to say no, but she'd known she wasn't minding him. She'd wrecked trying to get back in place before he caught her.

Her lips trembled as she admitted, "Yes, Daddy."

Hutch sat her on his knee. "There are consequences for breaking the rules, little girl. I'm going to spank you, but I want you to stand in the corner and think about what you could have done instead first."

He pointed to a corner with a sign that read, 'Thinking Corner,' and she reluctantly did as he asked.

"I'm setting the naughty girl timer for five minutes, which is the length of time I was in the house getting the knee pad straps. When the timer rings, come back to me."

She sniffled, humiliated to be in such a childish position. At least he didn't make her lower her shorts like the girls in her books.

She should have minded her Daddy. If she had, she wouldn't have gotten hurt. Her butt wouldn't be getting smacked. And her Daddy wouldn't be disappointed in her. She had ruined their good day, just like she always ruined everything. She did her best to blink back her tears.

Time crawled by, and she decided she'd been right. Five minutes was forever. When the timer finally rang, she shuffled back to Hutch. He waited for her, still sitting in what would forever be the spanking chair. At least to her.

He guided her back between his legs. "Tell Daddy what you thought about."

Her nose stung, and she sniffed back a tear. "'Bout how I should have minded you. An how, if I had, I wouldn't have got hurt."

"Thank you, Peaches. Now, let's get this over with so we can have more fun."

He guided her over his knee. Once her bottom pointed to the sky, he placed his hand at the top of her shorts.

"Daddy will always spank you on your bare bottom," he said before pulling her shorts and panties down to her knees. She gasped as the cool air touched her backside.

He rubbed his hand over her bottom and explained, "I don't give warmups for punishment spankings. This spanking is to help you think twice before disobeying Daddy."

With that, his hand left her bottom, and she held her breath. It came crashing down on her right cheek. Her breath escaped with a huff as his hand then branded her left cheek. Those stung!

He landed two more hard smacks. It felt like the killer bees had left her stomach and were now stinging her rear. She tried to cover her behind with her hand, fingers spread wide.

When he grabbed her hand and settled it in the small of her back without missing a beat, she yelled, "Wait!"

Smack. Smack. Smack.

"No, ma'am," he said. "This stops when you have learned to mind your Daddy, little girl."

Was his hand made from hot iron? Her bottom was on fire. She burst into tears.

She kicked her legs, hoping to lessen the effect of the smacks while begging him to stop. She promised never ever to disobey again. And she meant it. No bike ride was worth this.

"Will you mind me from now on?" he demanded.

What did he want from her? She'd already promised never to do it again. "Yes, I promise!"

Finally, after exhausting herself, she went limp. As soon as she did, his smacks slowed.

"Alright. Five more swats, one for each minute you should have waited."

Keeping track of each smack as it fell, she tried to hold still. Then, finally, he was finished.

She lay across his lap, focusing on his warm hand as it rubbed her back. "I'm proud of you. You took your spanking like such a good girl. Now sit in my lap and let me hold you."

She pushed off his knee and climbed onto his lap. With her face buried in his neck, she continued to cry. Not because her butt was throbbing, though it was. No, she was crying because she'd ruined their perfect day.

There was no way he would want her now. Her mother had

known she wasn't worth the effort. Now Hutch knew it, too. He'd hold her for a while, then take her home.

That made her cry harder.

"Hey, now," Hutch said. "What's all this? It's all over now."

"Y-you don't have to s-say that. I kn-know I ruined everything." She'd finally had a Daddy of her very own, and she'd ruined it.

He leaned back and searched her face. "What did you ruin, Peaches? What is going on in your head?"

"You know," she said, but he remained silent. He was going to make her say it. "I proved you can't trust me. You don't want someone like me as your Little girl."

"All you proved today is you're a Little girl who needs her Daddy. Little girls sometimes have a problem being patient. That's why they have Daddies. You don't have to be perfect, Peaches. I'm sure not. You want to know a Daddy secret?"

Daddies had secrets? This she had to hear. When she nodded, he leaned forward, looking right and left as if making sure no one was listening.

"Don't tell anyone, but Daddies make mistakes, too."

Georgia studied him. Was he serious? "You don't want to find someone else?"

"No, Peaches. Never."

She collapsed onto his chest, hugging him as tight as she could. "I'm sorry I didn't mind you, Daddy."

Hutch hugged her back. "All's forgiven, little girl. That's what spankings do. They wipe the slate clean."

He held her for a long time, whispering sweet things. Her eyelids grew heavy. How could she be this relaxed? This at peace? All the guilt and fear was gone.

She had read a lot of books about Daddies and their Littles, but none of them were as good as the real thing. She smiled and let sleep claim her.

CHAPTER 19

*H*utch took another swig of his beer and tossed the potatoes in the oven. A glance at the video monitor assured him Georgia was still asleep. He wasn't surprised. She had been pushing herself since she got to town.

Georgia had no idea of her worth. That was about to change. He was going to show her just how valuable she was. The castle bed fit her. She was his sleeping beauty. His princess.

His armor might be tarnished, but her knight had arrived. He would slay every dragon that tried to scorch her. While he couldn't promise every day would be a fairy tale, he'd work his ass off to give her happily ever after.

Georgia stirred in bed, so he downed the rest of his beer and headed to the playroom.

She had kicked back the covers and was picking at the bandage on her knee. "Leave that alone, Peaches. The bandage keeps the germs out and the medicine in." He kissed her forehead and sat on the edge of the bed.

She stared at him with a dreamy look on her face. Adorable.

She reached for her knee again, but he stopped her. "Do you need another reminder to mind Daddy?"

She yanked her hand back as if it had been burned. "No, Daddy. But it itches."

"Let me show you what will help." He took her hand and rubbed her fingers softly over the bandage. "Better?"

After a contented sigh, she stretched her arms over her head. She froze when she arched her back and pressed her bottom into the mattress. "My bottom hurts."

Hutch grinned back at her. "That's what happens when little girls fall asleep after their spankings."

"That was mean, Daddy," she pouted, but her eyes told a different story.

"That was earned, little girl," he said, ruffling her hair. "Now, I thought we could get a snack and watch cartoons until we're ready for dinner."

Her mouth dropped open. "You'll watch cartoons with me, Daddy? Don't you have something more important to do?"

"What's more important than spending time with you?" he asked as he helped her out of bed.

"Just about anything, I guess."

Oh, no. Absolutely not.

It was time to start showing his little girl what a relationship should be. He sat on the bed and pulled her onto his knee, smiling when she shifted her bottom off his thigh.

"Spending time with you isn't keeping me from something important. It is the most important part of my day."

She searched his eyes. "I've never been most important before," she whispered.

His heart ached at her words, and he hugged her close. "Well, you are now," he said.

After settling her on the sofa, Hutch went to the kitchen to grab juice and snacks.

He'd found the perfect cup for a Liddle, a blend of Little and Middle, which was what he thought she was. He took out a spill-proof water bottle covered with cute little unicorns.

They spent the rest of the afternoon watching Powerpuff Girls. They moved to the kitchen, and Georgia colored while he grilled the steaks.

He didn't miss how her nose wrinkled when he pulled out the asparagus and salad fixings.

"I don't like green stuff," she said. "It's gross."

"You don't like green apples?" he asked.

"Well, apples are okay, I guess," she said, focusing on her coloring. The tip of her tongue rubbed the corner of her lips when she concentrated. It was endearing.

His dick liked it, too. Too bad his dick wasn't allowed to participate today. Today was about getting used to their dynamic outside the bedroom. There'd be plenty of time for sexy games if all went according to plan.

He kept the conversation light. "How about green grapes?"

"Green grapes are yummy."

"So, it's just green vegetables that are the problem."

"Pretty much veggies in general. They're slimy and icky."

"Well then, you are in for a treat, little lady. I'm a superb veggie chef. No slime allowed. All I ask is that you try everything on your plate. How will you know you like something if you never try it?"

She shook her head without looking up. "That's Daddy logic. Real logic says if it looks like a veggie, smells like a veggie, and acts like a veggie, run!"

Hutch gave her a stern look. "Little girls who don't try their vegetables don't get dessert."

"That's not fair!"

"Five out of five doctors agree. I don't make the rules, I just enforce them."

He took special care with the asparagus, roasting it in garlic and olive oil until it was tender but not overdone. He must have done a good job because her plate was clean by the time their meal was over.

After dinner, she picked a book for him to read. She fell asleep again, leaning next to him. He watched the news and sports highlights and was about to carry her back to bed when her phone rang with the ringtone he'd come to despise.

Georgia was startled awake and stared at the phone like it was a snake. His jaw tightened as she reached for it. These calls had been going on long enough. Ignoring them wasn't working. This guy wasn't getting the message.

She tried to silence the phone, but Hutch grabbed it. "What are you doing? Give me my phone," she demanded, but Hutch saw panic, not anger.

This asshole would not terrorize his woman for one more second. Ignoring her protests, he answered the call on speaker.

"Georgia, beautiful, it's about time. I knew if I kept calling you'd answer eventually. I always have been able to outlast you. Listen, gorgeous. I'm sorry for our little misunderstanding."

Georgia stiffened beside him. "Little misunderstanding? Jarrod, you cheated on me with seventeen women. That I know about. I can't—"

"Georgia, sweetheart, they didn't mean anything. You're the only one that matters. I love you, babe. You know that. You have my heart. I'm just weak, darling. Come back home, and I promise I'll make it up to you."

Hutch gritted his teeth. What a jackass. He started to speak, but Georgia shook her head. He didn't like it, but he complied. The asshole didn't even give her a chance to speak.

"Nevada said you got the flowers I sent. I ordered them just for you. And the necklace and matching bracelet? Those came from Barons. I know how much you love that store. I picked them out myself. You can wear them to the firm's annual benefit ball. We'll send Phyllis with you this year to ensure you buy an appropriate dress. I don't need a repeat of that rag you picked out last year. I almost never lived it down."

Hutch didn't take his eyes off Georgia, so he saw her fold in on herself. When she raised her hands to cover her face, they shook.

Jarrod's voice took on a darker tone. "You know, I don't appreciate the silent treatment, Georgia. It's childish, though I don't know what else I expected. You're coming home. Don't bother driving. I'll have a ticket for you at the Knoxville airport tomorrow afternoon. It's time to stop the temper tantrums and come home where you belong."

Hutch had heard all he could take. Before Georgia could respond, he took charge of the conversation. This guy wasn't getting the satisfaction of ever hearing her voice again.

"You listen to me, you stalker son of a bitch. I don't know how you made your money in court when you're too stupid to read people. But I'll lay it out for you. Georgia is no longer your concern. Lose her number. Forget her name. You seem to get your sick as fuck rocks off terrorizing women, but if you bother her again, you'll be answering to me. Tell me you get me."

Georgia looked as if she might be sick. She grabbed a sofa cushion and hugged it to her chest.

Jarrod was silent for so long Hutch reached to disconnect the call. But then he said, "You have me at a disadvantage. Who are you, and what the hell are you doing with my wife?"

Satisfaction settled in Hutch's chest at the change in Jemison's tone. This wasn't the wooing, apologetic husband, or the condescending asshat. Now he had the real man, cold, controlling, furious. Ignoring Georgia's frantic gestures, he answered. "Jedidiah Hutchinson. I'm the man your *ex*-wife now calls her man. I don't put up with pencil neck dickwads like you giving her grief. You were too stupid to hold on to her. Learn from your mistakes. But do it chasing someone else. This woman is off limits. If you cannot comprehend my words, I'll be happy to fly to California and explain it to you. Painfully and thoroughly. Now, I still haven't heard you say you get me. Do you get me?"

Another silence, then, "Georgia, you little whore. When I get you home—"

Hutch disconnected the call. Georgia's face had lost all color.

Eyes blank, she asked, "What did you just do?"

"I let your ex-husband know he lost, little girl. Do not answer the phone if he calls. If he does, you let me know immediately. Do you understand?"

Georgia jumped up and began pacing around the room. "Okay... alright... okay... this is good."

He hated seeing her so upset, but he had to protect her. Jarrod Jemison was not going to back off. He was a sociopath fixated on his little girl.

Georgia turned to him, and her expression made him brace. "How could you do that? He wasn't supposed to know about you."

The words punched him in the gut. He was no high-powered lawyer, but what the hell? "Sorry, Georgia. Didn't know I was your dirty secret. You ashamed of me?"

Her shocked eyes met his. "Of course not. You don't understand. Jarrod is more powerful than you can imagine. His connections are untouchable. You shouldn't have to deal with him because of me."

Something was going on here. Something he didn't get. "Don't worry about me. I can take care of myself and you. That's what Daddies do."

She grabbed her phone. "Not this time, Hutch."

So now he was back to being Hutch, not Daddy.

She stuffed her phone in her purse. "I need to go."

He took her hand. "Hold on, Georgia. I get that was whacked."

"I want to leave. Now," she said. "If you don't take me, I'll call an uber."

Goddamit. "The fuck you'll call an Uber. They aren't safe. If you insist on leaving, I'll take you."

She walked out the front door without looking back. Shit.

He grabbed his fucking keys and followed her out the fucking door to his fucking truck. She thought he didn't understand the danger. But he knew Jarrod Jemison's type. Sabre dealt with them every damn day. Not that he'd ever shared with her who Sabre was or what they did. Fuck.

When they made it to Books-N-Brews, she was out of the truck and racing to the door before he got it in park. He stopped her before she unlocked the door. "Don't you ever do that again! You don't touch your seatbelt. I will help you out of the truck."

He sucked in a deep breath. She'd scared the fuck out of him jumping from the truck like that. When he could speak without yelling, he asked, "Do you remember the alarm's deactivation code?"

She rolled her eyes and snapped, "I'm not stupid. Of course, I remember."

He swatted her backside. Hard. "Check the attitude, little girl, or I will check it for you."

She glared at him and rubbed her bottom. "I don't need you to walk me inside."

"I'm doing it just the same." He retook her hand and led her up the stairs, trying to devise a way to penetrate the wall she was building between them.

He didn't see a lot of choices. He wasn't going to force her to do what he wanted. She'd had enough of that in her life.

It was late. She was tweaked. He would leave, but she was damn sure going to know this conversation wasn't done. "Activate the alarm when I leave. I have a meeting at Sabre in the morning, but I'll be here as soon as I can. We will talk this out then."

"You don't need to do that," she told him. Jesus. How had this night gone so wrong, so fast?

"Yes, I do. Regardless of what you're telling yourself in that head of yours, we'll talk tomorrow and fix this."

"I won't be here."

"Oh yeah?" There was only so much attitude he was willing to take. And he was done. "Last chance to check your attitude. Where will you be tomorrow?"

"Tazzy and I are going out to the lake. We'll be there all afternoon." She notched up her chin as if daring him to contradict her.

"Okay. Keep your phone with you. I want to know where you are in case you run into trouble."

"Fine," she said.

Okay, suffice it to say he was over the snippiness.

"Little girl, you need to listen to me. I know you're upset, but I will not tolerate your disrespect. How do you answer Daddy when he tells you to do something?" His patience hung by a thread.

He thought she wouldn't answer him, but she finally gave him a grudging, "Yes, Daddy."

He pulled her closer for a quick kiss goodbye until she tried to remain stiff and unaffected. She might as well have thrown down a red flag.

He deepened the kiss and forced her back to the door, leaning into her with his entire body. He ground his hips into her, making sure she felt how hard he was.

She tried not to respond, but slowly she melted against him. He kissed her long and hard. When he pulled back, she stood there for a minute, lips open and swollen, eyes closed.

He tapped her nose and her eyes flew open. "We're not finished. You be safe tomorrow. Or else."

CHAPTER 20

Georgia tossed and turned all night. With a groan, she punched her pink satin pillow with the giant eyelash print as hard as she could.

Guilt flooded her instantly. She hugged the pillow, smoothing the spot she had just pummeled. "Sorry, Lashes. It's not your fault I can't sleep. I shouldn't take my mood out on you."

And now she was talking to her pillow.

She should be punching Hutch, not an innocent pillow. Yeah, right in the nose.

Well, not in the nose. That would hurt him. She didn't want to hurt him. Maybe in the arm. That would work. His arms were all muscle. She couldn't hurt his arm.

But it would still show him how mad she was. How dare he take her phone? Who did he think he was?

He thinks he's your Daddy, that's who.

Georgia scowled. Sometimes she wished the voice in her head would shut up.

No matter what he thought, Hutch didn't have the right to act like he had last night. Even if he was her Daddy.

Only now, he couldn't be her Daddy. Not anymore.

Her eyes burned but she blinked back tears. She had to be strong to protect her Daddy from himself. From Jarrod. He wanted to make her problems go away, but he had no idea who he was dealing with.

And there was something he didn't know. Something that would make him hate her. She shouldn't have let things get this far with Hutch. It wasn't fair to him.

She couldn't stop the tears now. She was a horrible person, and now she had put her Daddy in danger.

Because her Daddy... no, Hutch, not her Daddy... Hutch was in danger now, and it was all her fault.

She should have turned off her phone so Jarrod couldn't call. Then Hutch wouldn't have challenged Jarrod. Now he was on Jarrod's radar.

It was five o'clock in the morning. The sun wasn't even up yet. She paced around her apartment, arms wrapped around her middle. She knew what she had to do, but the thought made her tummy ache.

She had always known she wasn't good enough for Hutch. He was handsome and intelligent and brave. He looked out for people and kept them safe.

He thought he could do that for her, but he couldn't. Jarrod was a classic psychopath and the poster child for narcissistic personality disorder.

He honestly felt no remorse. Ever. Not for anything.

He did whatever he wanted, and no one could stop him. His wealth and reputation protected him. He was a shark in the courtroom, helping the worst people in the world get out of paying for their crimes. He did horrible things to people and slept like a baby at night. She'd seen him do it.

Now Hutch was on his radar because of her. Nothing could happen to her Daddy.

No. Not her Daddy anymore.

The only way to deal with Jarrod was to ignore him. He thrived on attention. He had to have a steady supply of beautiful women telling him how amazing he was. And he had an endless supply of beautiful women.

She had planned to disappear from Jarrod's life. Oh, he would know where she was, but with Jarrod, it was out of sight, out of mind. Eventually, anyway. He would give up and turn to someone else if she could just lay low and not react.

Her plan wasn't working yet, but it would. It had to. Jarrod's calls would become less and less frequent. It was only a matter of time before he'd find someone new to torment.

Then he'd need to give her what she wanted. The trick was not to let him know she wanted it. It had to be his idea because his ideas were the only good ideas.

But last night, Hutch flushed all her plans down the toilet. But it was so much worse than that.

Now Jarrod knew about Hutch. Hutch was now in danger. Jarrod had been picturing her suffering alone in small-town America, a fate worse than death.

But now he knew she wasn't suffering. Now he knew she wasn't alone. A sob clawed its way up her throat, choking her. She couldn't breathe.

What would Jarrod do to Hutch? It could be anything.

Hutch would fight him, thinking he could win. He was everything she wanted, the Daddy of her dreams. And now she had to let him go. Again.

She had to make him want to let her go, too. Then Jarrod would see Hutch didn't matter. Her heart shattered, but she would do anything to protect her Daddy.

At least she'd downloaded the pictures of the women he cheated with onto a spare flash drive she'd found in his desk drawer. Women he'd slept with starting a week after they got married. What a jerkface!

Jarrod didn't know she'd copied them, but she would show him if he went after her Daddy. The possibility of being outsmarted wouldn't occur to Jarrod. Especially by her.

The threat of those pictures becoming public might be enough to send him slithering back under his rock. He was vain, and he guarded his reputation. He needed to think people respected him. Jarrod had never understood the difference between respect and fear.

She dressed and went down to the shop. She would distract herself with work until lunch. Then she and Tazzy were going to tackle one of the things on her bucket list.

She hadn't lied to Hutch. At least, that's what she told herself. She just hadn't told him everything. He would probably still say she'd told a teeny white lie.

She and Tazzy were going to the lake. Well, close to the lake. Okay, not really the lake. They were going to the sinkholes, not hiking or sunbathing as he thought. But the sinkholes were close to the lake.

And Hutch wasn't her Daddy anymore. So, it wasn't his concern. And that sucked, but that was her life. She couldn't think about a life without Hutch. Not right now.

She could, however, think about her bucket list. Now she could start her grand adventure.

She could do whatever she wanted. No one could stop her.

Or care if she got hurt.

But her adventures were all she had now. She needed something a little, not dangerous, but definitely something to push her out of her routine, boring life.

Something to help her forget the clusterfudge her life had become.

After lunch, Georgia jumped when the door jingled, but it was only Tazzy.

"You ready?" Tazzy asked. "I can't wait to get to the lake. My roommate is driving me crazy. She started writing a pen pal. Sounds great, right? Well, it's not. Her pen pal is in prison. Not jail. Prison."

Georgia tried to follow her friend's conversation, but between her lack of sleep and breaking up with Hutch, her brain wasn't working.

"Wait, the roommate that moved in with you two weeks ago?"

"That's the one," Tazzy said, tossing her bag onto the counter. "Are you ready to go?"

"I thought she was a corporate executive at one of the local hotels or something."

"She is. She's also a little quirky. Like writing someone in prison for murder quirky."

"Holy moly! That makes my bucket list sound tame."

Tazzy tilted her head. "I wouldn't say that. You, my bestie, are also quirky."

Georgia did something she thought she would never do again. She laughed. "I can live with that," she said.

Tazzy smiled. "So, again, ready to go? I want to take some pictures up at the lake."

Georgia crossed her arms over her chest. "I don't see any bathing suit straps under that top. Are you changing when we get there?"

Tazzy wrinkled her nose. "I'm thinking no." She rushed to add, "But I have my camera with me to capture the momentous occasion. Hopefully, the first of many."

"Tazzy, you were supposed to be my partner in crime!" Georgia tried not to whine.

The truth was, she needed Tazzy to do it, too. That way, she wouldn't be doing it alone. She might chicken out by herself. She needed someone to share the consequences if they got caught.

But no one would find out. And even if Daddy did, he was not — that is, no one was— the boss of her. She didn't have a Daddy anymore.

Hutch no longer factored into her decisions because he was no longer part of her life. That was how it had to be, even if it killed her.

She forced a smile on her face, hoping it didn't look as fake as it felt. "That's ok. I'm glad you thought of a way to remember these adventures. Just promise if I start to chicken out, you'll give me a push."

"Are you sure you want to do this?" Tazzy asked.

"Do what?" Deke asked.

Darn!

Georgia had completely forgotten Deke was there. Before she could tell him it was none of his business, Tazzy announced, "Georgia's going cliff diving. It's on her bucket list."

Deke's gaze swung to Georgia. "Hutch knows about that?"

Darn!

She shot Tazzy a glare and faced Deke. Notching up her chin, she informed him, "I don't have to tell him. He's not the boss of me anymore." She had to force the vile-tasting words out.

Deke snorted. "Since when?"

"Since last night when we broke up."

Darn it! She hadn't meant to say anything. Especially to one of Hutch's friends. She pressed her lips together as Deke stared down at her.

He held her eyes for a long time, searching. Finally, he shrugged. "If you say so," he said. "But I got to tell you, little girl, it's a bad play."

"I can do whatever I want." Great, she might as well stomp her foot and stick out her tongue.

"Didn't say you couldn't, just said you shouldn't." He continued to look her over, then nodded. "Okay then. Your choice. Thanks for the joe." He gave both Tazzy and her a chin lift and left.

Tazzy grimaced. "Sorry about that. I wasn't thinking. You may have broken it off, but you know Deke is right. Hutch is going to be furious when he finds out."

"So what if he is?" Georgia asked with a confidence she absolutely did not feel. She had to concentrate on not covering her bottom with her hands. Hutch no longer had a say in her life.

Besides, he couldn't punish her if he wasn't her Daddy. True, that hadn't stopped him eight years ago. But she wasn't a teenager anymore. She was a grown woman. Yeah, that would convince him.

Right. You were a grown woman yesterday afternoon, too.

She needed to hold auditions for a new voice in her head.

"Let me run upstairs and put on my swimsuit," she said.

Upstairs, she pulled on the scraps of material she had worn only once. She'd never been comfortable in the skimpy swimsuit, but today was about living her life large for the first time ever.

She thought it would feel better than this. It should feel good, right? She couldn't feel anything but the empty hole in her chest where her heart used to be.

She straightened her shoulders and gave herself a pep talk. If she wanted to jump off a fifty-foot cliff into freezing water, she would. She grabbed her purse before she could change her mind and headed to the door, pausing when she noticed her phone in the side pocket. She pulled it out with two fingers and held it away from her as if it might bite.

Hutch would be furious if she left her phone behind, but if she kept it, he could track her. Did she dare?

She didn't answer to him anymore. So, it didn't matter if he knew. But there was no sense asking for trouble, right?

Memphis could call Tazzy if anything happened at the store. Setting her phone on her kitchen table, she headed out.

CHAPTER 21

*H*utch pulled up in front of Deep Dive. Reid had texted he had information about Georgia last night. Hutch wanted that information. He didn't know the specifics of her life for the past eight years, but he knew enough.

He didn't believe in coincidences. Jarrod had conveniently visited the Donnelleys for the first time a year before her eighteenth birthday, then swept her off her feet? That she'd married and left with him, all without saying one word to her closest friends?

No, something was off, and her family was neck-deep in whatever it was.

He checked his phone as he entered the building. Yep, Georgia was right where she should be at Books-N-Brews. She and Tazzy must have changed their plans. That was fine with him.

She'd been so upset when he'd left her last night. He'd intended to talk to her first thing this morning. He would never have left the shop where he had been parked all night if he hadn't gotten an emergency call from Sabre. As it was, he'd had to go, which pissed him off. When his meeting finished, he was headed straight back to Books-N-Brews.

He hadn't liked her going to the lake and possibly swimming without him. He wanted to be there in case she got into trouble in the water or hiking trails. If she was still at the shop, then she was safe.

He entered the warehouse size room that made up the second floor. The only person with an enclosed office was Reid.

Most people would be hard-pressed to decide if they had entered an office or a gym. The guys working there needed to stay in peak condition.

In the far-right corner, a full-size boxing ring allowed them to practice their fighting skills and work out their frustrations. Speed and heavy punching bags, reflex bars, and gloves lined the walls, and a bell painted to look like a target adorned the closest support beam. There were also areas for weightlifting and treadmills for conditioning.

In the center of the room, tables stood far enough apart to work on separate cases without disturbing the other teams. They could also be pulled together if they had an all-in case.

State-of-the-art windows lined the entire second floor. They were bullet-proof and could be blacked out at the push of a button.

Reid stepped out of his office and shook Hutch's hand.

"I was glad to see your text, man," Hutch said. "What did you find?"

Reid frowned and led him to a group of leather chairs across the room. "Oh, I found plenty, but you won't like any of it."

He sat down, so Hutch did the same. Reid got right down to it.

"Your girl has had a rough time of it. She moved to Los Altos eight years ago and has been a prisoner in the lap of luxury."

Hutch blanked his expression. He'd asked for this information. Now he needed to hold his shit tight while he got it.

"She never left her mansion without her husband by her side.

She might as well have been living in Stepford, man. He had total control of every aspect of her life. The man wanted a beautiful doll to distract his clients while he robbed them blind and got them out of whatever shit they had gotten into."

Hutch was going to kill him. Slowly, with extreme prejudice and a smile on his face. "Did he hurt her physically?"

"Likely. We couldn't find any evidence of that. The occasional long sleeve shirt in July, sunglasses on cloudy days, things like that. But no medical reports were ever filed. He had a Dr. Rheinstein who made house calls. Not daily, but often enough."

Hutch shoved off his chair and strode to the window. He needed a minute to get a handle on his rage. The need to pull out his phone and book a plane ticket to California was strong. Instead, he drew in a deep breath and walked back to Reid. "What about her life aside from Jemison."

Reid looked through his notes. "He enrolled her at Stanford University. She got her B.A. in English and her Master's in Comparative Literature. Graduated summa cum laude both times. After that, she was in all the appropriate clubs and societies. By then, I guess she'd learned to play her part. She smiled on cue and never said a negative word against her husband that we could find." Reid tossed down the file.

Acid burned Hutch's stomach. His precious girl had lived through hell for eight long years. He had served his time in the military and seen things too horrific to describe, but nothing had made him feel the way he did right then.

He lowered his head to his hands. "I shouldn't have taken her back to that viper's nest she called home. She would never have gone through that shit if I hadn't."

"You couldn't have known what would happen," Reid said. Hutch was right, but it didn't ease his guilt one bit.

He hadn't even known where she was. But now that he knew

what her ex had done? Well, he was damn sure going to do something about it now.

"I want a deep dive search on Jarrod Jemison. Offshore accounts, legal dealings, client lists, and how he got them off. I want it all. And I want to know the connection between Jemison and the Donnelleys. How in the hell did a high-powered lawyer from Los Altos, California, wind up in the home of someone in Darling, Tennessee?"

"I'll get Sawyer on it."

Deke chose that moment to join them. He grinned when he spotted Hutch. "The best at what, making the ladies run?"

Reid threw the ball he had been tossing at Deke. "Not the time. We're going over our current info on Jemison."

Deke lost his smile. "What's going on?"

Hutch's rage resounded in his answer. "We are nailing his ass to the wall. I know men like Jemison. He thinks he's powerful. I want him to disappear so no one will ever find him. But we take him down publicly first. Ruin him. It will hurt more if we humiliate him by exposing his dirty secrets. I want him to be a laughingstock. A pariah. He needs to suffer for a long, long time before he meets the devil who made him."

Deke nodded. "I get you. I saw your girl earlier, by the way. She and Tazzy were on their way out the door."

Damn it.

He took out his phone. It still showed her at Books-N-Brews. Her bottom was toast. She hadn't taken her phone. "Yeah, she said they were going to the lake."

"Oh, so you know."

"Yes, Deke. I know. Tazzy is with her. I'm sure they'll be fine. She's going to be in trouble when she gets home, though. She didn't take her phone with her." He had just talked to her about that. He obviously hadn't made himself clear, but he would.

Deke smirked. "I'm not surprised."

Hutch was not in the mood. "What's that mean?"

Deke shrugged. "It means if I ever find my Little, I won't let her go cliff diving. I'm surprised you let Georgia go."

Wait. What?

"What are you talking about? Georgia's not going cliff diving. She is going to the lake to hike the trails with Tazzy and maybe get some sun."

He didn't appreciate Deke's snort.

"She's not going to the lake. She's going to the sinkholes. Something about a bucket list?"

Hutch's head was finally going to explode. "Why didn't you call me?"

"I told her you wouldn't like it. She said, and I quote, 'Hutch isn't the boss of me anymore,' and ran upstairs. Tazzy said you had a fight and were no longer together."

"Damn it!" Hutch gritted his teeth to hold back the rest of his words and stalked to the door.

There was no way Georgia was doing something so dangerous. He would handle her instinct to run from him once she was safe. After that, her ass would pay.

He peeled out of the parking lot and headed to the sinkholes. Had she already jumped from one of those cliffs? Paramedics rescued people who thought jumping from that height would give them God only knew what all the time.

Yesterday had been perfect until that damn phone call. She had taken to riding her bike like a champ. When she realized he had let go of the bike and cried, "I'm doing it!" his heart melted.

Then, when he'd heard her scream, well, he didn't even know he could run that fast. It had taken all he could do not to take her to the hospital when he saw her on the ground cradling her knee.

And when she'd fallen asleep in his lap, he could have held her the rest of the night. She'd known she was safe with him. Even in her sleep, her face glowed with peace and happiness. He planned to keep her world right and safe for the rest of her life.

All that peace and happiness had vanished with the ring of her phone. Her face had blanked. Her Little had disappeared. Was it any wonder he had lost it?

All he could think about was the pain and terror her ex-husband caused. He wanted, no, he needed to protect her from that dirtbag.

But she had rejected him. She hadn't wanted his protection, and that stung. She hadn't even wanted her ex to know that he existed. What was that about? Was she ashamed of him?

He'd never be able to give her everything she had with Jemison. She'd lived in a mansion and gone on world-class vacations. He couldn't lavish her with jewels.

With him, she would be the treasure. He would make sure she knew it.

If she didn't kill herself jumping off a fucking cliff. He drove faster.

Sure, he had messed up last night. But hearing Jemison's voice for the first time, knowing he was trying to bully and manipulate her, made him lose it.

She had shrunk into a shell at that asshole's voice. It was all the Daddy in him could do not to pull her into his lap, wrap his arms around her, and promise her to make it all go away. The beast inside him had wanted to rip Jarrod Jemison apart piece by piece.

But she hadn't wanted him to hold her. She hadn't even wanted him to talk to her. So even though the Daddy in him balked, he had taken her home to give her time to calm down. He should have listened to his gut. He had mishandled the whole damn thing, and now his Little girl thought she had to fight her battles alone. Someone should kick his ass.

He tried calling her again. Then he tried calling Tazzy. Both calls went straight to voice mail.

Again.

His little girl, and she *was* still his little girl, was racking up the punishments. When he finished holding her and making sure she was unharmed, she would be one very sorry little girl.

It took an eternity to reach the sinkholes. He drove by the first one because he could see no one was there. He jumped from his truck at the second area and raced to the closest sinkhole. There were only three, so that narrowed the search. When he didn't find her at the second one, he ran straight through the small copse of trees to the third sinkhole. The highest.

As he cleared the tree line blocking his view, his heart nearly stopped.

Georgia stood at the edge of the cliff, peering over the side to the water fifty feet below. His heart tried to bust through his chest. He tore into an all-out sprint, yelling out her name.

She spun toward his voice. Her eyes widened when she saw him. As she tried to step away from the edge, she stumbled. Her arms flailed as she screamed and disappeared over the side of the cliff.

CHAPTER 22

*G*eorgia stared down at the dark sparkling water far below her and swallowed hard. Fifty feet looked a lot longer from up here. Like, a lot.

Maybe this bucket list thing was overrated.

She had already jumped off the ten, and the twenty-foot cliff, and almost chickened out at twenty feet. It would not bother her to go ahead and check the cliff diving box off her list. And a big part of her wanted to.

But if she didn't do this, she would be disappointed in herself. That's what bucket lists were for, right? To do exciting things that push you out of your comfort zone.

She glanced down at the water below. It was dark. That meant it was deep, right? So, no rocks or logs or anything to worry about.

Of course, there was the fact that it was cold. Frigid. It was fed by a mountain spring, so, yeah. She hated cold water.

Her stomach hurt. This was a bad idea.

Come to think of it, there were no specifics about exactly how high the cliff she jumped from had to be. Twenty feet was like jumping off a two-story building. Fifty feet would be more like four stories tall. That seemed excessive.

Yeah, there was bucket list excitement, and then there was death wish excitement.

She gazed down one more time and came to a decision. She wasn't jumping off a cliff that high. And she was going to be okay with that.

At least Hutch wasn't there to see. He would have a coronary. Not that he mattered anymore. She was moving on. The hole in her heart would heal. This had to be done for his sake.

The hollow ache in her stomach slid into her chest. She felt lost without him already, and it hadn't even been a day.

Feeling like a wimp and a failure, she stepped back from the edge.

The breeze kissed her damp skin, and she shivered. If Hutch were here, he would demand she put on a jacket.

Someone called her name. She could have sworn it was Hutch, but it couldn't be. Probably. If he looked for her, her phone would send him to Books-N-Brews, not the sinkholes.

There it was again, only closer this time. She was losing it. Unless Deke had ratted her out.

The third time she heard his voice, she turned to see who could sound so much like him.

No one, that's who.

It didn't sound like him. It *was* him. Racing across the clearing toward her.

He was here, and he was pissed. Very, very pissed. Instinctively, she took a step back. Only when she did, there was nothing there.

Her other foot slipped on the scattered rocks, and she plunged downward. Somewhere in the back of her mind, she remembered a video she had seen that said to curl up in a ball. She pulled her knees to her chest, but nothing could stop the scream that ripped from her throat as she fell.

She'd been right. Fifty feet was a long, long way down. She fell forever. Then the surface of the water smacked into her, stealing her breath.

Ice-cold water shocked her skin, and she instinctively tried to suck air back into her lungs. Only she was underwater, so there was no air to be had.

Adrenaline flooded her insides. She dropped down and down and down. Her lungs burned. Why had she screamed out all her air?

Was she never going to stop sinking?

Ha! She was sinking into a sinkhole. She made a mental note to slap herself if she somehow made it back to the surface.

Releasing her knees, she tried to kick her way to the surface, but she didn't have enough air. Her panic increased. She was going to drown in a sinkhole.

Without warning, a strong hand grabbed her arm and tugged her toward the surface. She didn't have to open her eyes to guess who it was.

Hutch had jumped in to rescue her. Hopefully. It would be a lot of effort to save her just to kill her later.

When they broke the water's surface, Hutch flipped her to her back and wrapped his arm around her. He shifted her so she was floating on top of him as he swam for the edge of the sinkhole.

Tazzy was waiting by the ladder to help her out. She looked as pale as Georgia felt.

"Oh, my gosh, Georgia. Are you alright? When I saw you fall, I thought I would have a heart attack!"

Hutch broke in before she could answer. "Take your car and go home. We'll talk tomorrow about your part in this little stunt."

Tazzy opened her mouth to say something but apparently thought better of it. She nodded and raced away, leaving Georgia to her fate.

Flipping fantastic.

Hutch may have saved her, but the likelihood of her imminent demise had not changed. Merely the location. Now they would find her dead body beside the sinkhole instead of at the bottom of it. She didn't count that as much better.

As Tazzy drove away, Hutch's hand fell on her shoulder. He spun her around, and she got her first close-up look at his face.

Yep. He was furious. She should say something, but shock and fear had frozen her brain.

He looked her over from head to toe. She must have passed inspection because he said, "Right," before dragging her to a boulder hidden from view by the base of the cliff.

"Um, Hutch?" she asked as if she didn't know. "What are you doing?"

He stopped and pivoted to face her. "When you are in trouble, little girl, you call me Daddy. And believe me when I tell you, you have never been in so much trouble."

Without waiting for a response, he dragged her the rest of the way to the giant rock. Without so much as a pause, he sat down, and over his knee she went.

"Wait, Hutch!"

Smack!

"Ouch! Daddy, I meant Daddy," she said. "Wait, Daddy. We need to talk."

"We are communicating just fine, little girl. My hand will say it all. Consider it Daddy's form of sign language."

And with that, he began to spank her in earnest.

The books were not lying when they said getting spanked on wet skin hurt more. Holy moly! She would have told him to stop, but the hard, rapid swats stole her ability to form words.

After several blistering swats, she cried out, "Wait, Daddy. Owie! Stop. Stop! That hurts!"

"That's the idea. You'll find I'm fluent in Daddy sign language."

He stopped, but only long enough to yank down the bottoms of her bathing suit.

"Daddy, someone will see!"

Her legs started kicking of their own accord as he punished her poor bottom. Her butt was already on fire.

"What were you thinking?" His hand didn't slow down at all. "Do you have any idea how dangerous that was? What if you had hit the water wrong? You could have broken your damn neck!"

He punctuated each word of the last sentence with a smack to her bottom.

Once, she had stepped on a hill of fire ants. She would never forget the sting of those bites.

This was worse. Each smack drove the sting higher and deeper. How was that even possible?

"I wasn't going to jump," she wailed. "I was trying to move back, but I slipped when I saw you running toward me." She wished she was back in the icy water of the sinkhole.

"You shouldn't have been there in the first place. You could have been killed," he said, still smacking.

"Are you going to do something that dangerous ever again?"

She shook her head as hard as she could. Cold droplets of water flew everywhere. "No, Daddy. I promise."

Hutch stopped spanking her for a moment.

"Damn right you do. Now, let's talk about not minding Daddy." With that, he began smacking her bottom again. The fire instantly reignited. She wailed in protest.

He paused, resting his palm on her roasted butt. "Did I not tell you, specifically, not to try to do anything on that bucket list?"

She did not want to answer that question truthfully, but she was in no position to fib. "Yes, Daddy."

"Yes, I did. Do you think I'm just trying to keep you from having fun?"

His hand fell over and over while he waited for her answer.

"No, Daddy." She was never going to be able to sit again.

"No. Am I trying to stop you from exploring who you are? No. I am trying to protect you from things like what just happened. Do you understand?"

"Yes, Daddy," she repeated. It had been a dangerous thing to do, but she would have agreed to anything he wanted to make him stop. Hopefully, it worked.

He rested his hand on her backside. "You are my world, Peaches. Nothing is going to happen to you. And if I have to spank your bottom every day from now on to make that clear, I will."

That was all she could take. Georgia burst into tears. "I'm sorry, Daddy. I won't do it again. I promise."

He gave her ten more hard swats, then lifted her to sit on the rock beside him. The hard, rough surface bit into her tender flesh.

She tried to find a more comfortable position, but there wasn't one. She reached to pull up her bottoms, but he stopped her.

"Eyes on me, naughty girl," he said.

She didn't want to face him. She was not a pretty crier. Her face must be swollen and splotchy.

When her eyes met his, fury no longer burned, but she could tell he wasn't done. She braced for whatever he was going to say.

"Why did you leave your phone at Books-N-Brews?" he asked.

She dropped her gaze so he wouldn't see the guilt in her eyes.

"Answer me, Georgia. Did you leave your phone by accident?"

She should tell him yes, and he'd believe her. She could avoid all the trouble telling him the truth would cause. But she couldn't.

She wasn't a liar. She knew leaving her phone at her apartment was wrong. She wouldn't be able to live with a lie.

"No, Daddy," she admitted. The hurt that flashed across his face stabbed her heart. "I'm sorry." Her voice wobbled. She wanted to explain but couldn't find the words.

"Disobedience is not acceptable, little girl, but deliberate defiance is something else entirely. Why did you deliberately leave your phone at Books-N-Brews? Were you bratting to get Daddy's attention?"

She couldn't meet his eyes. She was trying to protect him, but this was so hard. She had expected him to be angry, not hurt. With her gaze fixed on her knees, she shook her head.

"I'm glad to hear that. Bratting is not something I tolerate. Were you angry at me for answering your phone last night? Is that why you didn't want me to be able to call you?"

No. Well, maybe a little, but she'd needed the adventure to distract her from the heartbreak.

Once again, she shook her head.

He took a deep breath. "You told Deke we broke up. That you were free to do whatever you wanted. Is that why you left your phone? Did you think it through and decide you don't want me as your Daddy?"

She had to stop him. His words were destroying her. Of course, she wanted him to be her Daddy. No one else could make her feel like he did. She died inside at the thought of being without him.

She had disobeyed to force his hand, to make him be the one to walk away. That way leaving wouldn't be her fault.

Leaving was for the best. Not for her. She would lose the sun from her sky and the breath from her lungs. Her entire world would turn black.

She deserved that. He didn't.

Fresh tears tracked down her cheeks. This time it would be different. She would not be weak. This time she would do the right thing. She would make the sacrifice for his sake.

"Georgia, I asked you a question. I want an answer. Did you change your mind? Do you still want to be my Little girl?"

Yes.

She took a deep breath and steeled her nerves. "That's what I've been trying to tell you, Hutch. I don't want a Daddy, and I don't want you." Her voice cracked as she attempted to get the words out.

She had to be done. Make it believable because she would never be able to do it again. "I miss California. I have gotten accustomed to a life I could never have here. I... I think it would be best to return to where I belong. So, if you could please take me home so I can collect my things, I'll go back to the apartment. Then we can both move on with our lives."

CHAPTER 23

*H*utch walked Georgia up to her apartment and left as soon as he heard the door lock engage. Silence had blanketed the ride, except for Georgia's sniffles as she tried not to cry.

She had talked about California, but she called his cabin home. When she said she didn't want a Daddy, it hit him like a sucker punch to the gut. His insides grew cold, and he thought he was going to puke. Then he realized she had lied. To him and to herself.

If she had stopped at comparing her life in California to Tennessee, she might have fooled him. She was right. He would never be able to give her all the things Jemison could.

He might have bought everything she'd said, but then he'd met with Reid. Now he knew better.

There was no way his Little girl would ever value the things Jemison could give her over her love for him and the people of Darling. How she had gotten the words out of her mouth, he didn't know. And when they got all this straightened out, he was going to wash that beautiful mouth out with soap for those lies.

She wanted him out of the picture, and now he was beginning to get why. She didn't hate him. If that were true, she wouldn't be trying to protect him from Jemison.

His phone rang. "What's up?" he asked Reid.

Reid got right to it. "Sawyer uncovered some things you need to see. You got the time to run back by here?"

Hutch had nothing but time. "Be there in ten," he said.

Pulling up to Deep Dive, he headed straight to Reid's office. The look on Reid's face didn't bode well.

"Did you get to Georgia?" he asked.

Hutch nodded. "That's why you called me back down here? To ask me about my girl?"

Reid frowned. "No. Have a seat."

It was Hutch's turn to frown, but he sank into the chair closest to Reid's desk. "Okay, I'm sitting. What have you got?"

"Sawyer was able to hack into a few places he couldn't get into earlier, and found some things you need to know." Reid opened the file on his desk. "Dr. Varick Rheinstein, turns out, is a good doctor, but he's not a good man. People call on the good doctor for medical attention under the table. For a substantial fee, he keeps quiet about the dirty little vices of the rich and famous. He sets bones and hides bruises without talking. He does, however, keep excellent private records. He treated Georgia forty times in eight years."

Hutch sat up straight in his chair. "He beat her? Tell me you're shitting me."

"Wish I was. Did Georgia tell you she had a dog in California?"

"No. Why?"

"According to sources, she had a dog that she adored. Dog got out one morning, and Jemison *accidentally* ran over it."

Hutch closed his eyes. He'd thought he was ready to hear this, but he'd been wrong. He could feel the veins in his head pulsing. But Reid wasn't done.

"Jarrod bragged he'd 'taken care of that damn mutt' because it distracted his wife."

Hutch came to his feet. "That fucker killed her dog?"

"Yep," Reid said. "Calm down, man, because that's not all."

Calm was not happening. All Hutch could see was his hands wrapped around Jarrod Jemison's throat, squeezing the life out of him. He forced himself to sit back down.

Reid gave him the last of it. "You can read Sawyer's report on what he found. It's what he didn't find that worries me."

"For fucks sake, just spit it out."

"Sawyer's report has a lot. Pre-nup, marriage certificate, property records. But no divorce decree."

Hutch must have missed something. That couldn't be right. "What are you saying?"

"I'm saying Georgia is still Mrs. Jarrod Jemison."

HUTCH PARKED BEHIND BOOKS-N-BREWS. HE'D RIDDEN AROUND A long time after leaving Deep Dive. Everything Reid had told him cycled through his head, so it was late by the time he let himself in Books-N-Brews and reset the alarm.

He took the stairs two at a time and banged on Georgia's apartment door. Minutes passed, but she didn't answer. He tried again. No response.

Then he heard shuffling on the other side of the door, and a muffled voice said, "Go away."

Not likely.

"Peaches, we need to talk," he said. "Open the door."

A pause, then, "We don't have anything left to say. Please just go away."

"Open up for Daddy. Right now, little girl. I won't tell you again."

He heard a thump and then quiet sobbing from the other side of the door. "Georgia, move away from the door. I'm coming in."

Pulling out the key Vivi had left him, he opened the door and scanned the small space. One dim lamp burned, and he spotted Georgia huddled on the floor next to the couch.

His heart crumbled. She leaned into the chair, sobbing as if her world had ended. He strode across the room and sank beside her, pulling her onto his lap.

She had her stuffed unicorn, Penny, pressed to her chest. Her lips and eyes were swollen, and her nose was red.

His poor girl. He hugged her tighter. "Stop crying, sweet girl. Daddy's going to make it better, I promise."

That only made her cry harder, slicing his heart into pieces.

"Y-y-you c-came back," she said, clinging to him as if he might disappear. "I th-thought you were g-gone for good. I'm s-s-sorry, Daddy."

"I'm not that easy to get rid of, little girl."

Tears streamed down her face as she looked up at him. "How come you c-came back? I'm the worst person on the planet!"

"Don't talk like that about my girl," he said gently. "Now, five good things. She's kind and brave, loyal and tender. And mine."

He gazed down at her tear-stained face. She was the most beautiful woman he had ever known.

Once he'd calmed down enough to think, he had pieced together what had happened. At least, he thought he had. Now he just needed to explain it to Georgia.

"I'm sorry I left the way I did, Peaches. Daddy listened to what you said instead of hearing what you didn't say. Once I remembered which was more important, I spent a few hours with Reid coming up with a plan."

She sniffled against his chest. "I thought I'd chased you away. I was so awful to you. I'm so sorry. I didn't know what to do. I said I wanted you gone, but it wasn't true."

"Hush, little girl. I know. I know what is best for both of us. There is no one in the world for me but you."

She immediately started shaking her head. Her breath still hitched as she spoke. "Nuh-uh, Daddy. I got so scared when you answered my phone. And then you told him your name and that we're together. I didn't want him to know about you. Now, because of me, he'll hurt you."

He's welcome to try.

"No one is going to hurt me, Peaches. Especially not some slick lawyer who abuses women half his size and hides behind his father's money to get away with it."

Georgia froze at his words. She stared up at him, eyes wide. "You know he hurts women?"

He placed his palm on her cheek. "I know he hurt you, Georgia. But there are a few things you don't know about me."

"Like what?"

He didn't like the guarded tone that entered her voice. He wanted to shield her from his work with Sabre, but she'd made herself sick with worry. She needed to understand he could take care of himself and her.

"My time in the military wasn't spent behind a desk, little girl. They recruited me into the SEALs. I have more than enough training to handle your ex-husband. Sabre is a personal security company. We don't usually install alarm systems like we did at Books-N-Brews. Our clients hire us for protection and to solve problems no one else will touch."

"Oh," she said. "I see."

He smiled. She didn't see anything. How could he explain what he did without scaring her?

"We are the people who bring down the Jemisons in the world. And the clients who hire him."

She went pale. "That sounds dangerous."

He wasn't going to lie. Not when he was demanding total

honesty from her. "It can be. But all of us have specialized military backgrounds. We know what we are doing, and we are very good at it."

She didn't say anything, so he gave her time. Then she rocked his world. She looked straight at him and asked, "Can I hire Sabre to help me?"

Thank God.

He pulled her closer and held her tight. "We've already started, little girl. Jarrod Jemison is now a bad memory I'll work the rest of my life to help you forget."

"I can pay you," she said.

He gave her a gentle shake. "Don't add to the punishment you've already got coming. I haven't forgotten everything that happened this afternoon. We weren't done."

She buried her face in his chest and groaned.

"We'll deal with that later. Right now, I want you to tell me everything." He tilted her chin up so she could see how serious he was. "And, Georgia, I mean everything."

She nodded. "Can you ask me questions so I don't leave out anything important?"

His girl. "Absolutely. Do you need to go to the bathroom or get a drink?"

Pink rosied her cheeks. She dropped her eyes and nodded. She was so adorable.

"Okay, you go potty, and I will get you a water bottle."

She wrinkled her nose and countered with, "Diet Coke?"

He gave her his best Daddy look. "Water," he said, standing them up and guiding her to the bathroom. "Now, scoot!" He couldn't resist giving her a swat to the rear that sent her squealing on her way.

He grabbed two bottles of water and settled on the sofa. He had to handle this right, especially after the way he'd messed up by leaving her alone earlier.

She snuggled onto the sofa beside him, and he handed her the water. "Drink," he ordered. She saluted and eyed the water as if it might bite her.

"Are you ready?" he asked.

She shrugged. "As ready as I'll ever be."

"Okay, let's start at the beginning. How did your mother meet Jarrod Jemison?"

Her brow wrinkled as she thought. "I'm not sure. I know they were in some online group together, but I have no idea what it was. One day she just started talking about him. It grew from there. I didn't think anything about it. She talked to lots of people online."

"But you don't know what group it was?"

"No. My mother wasn't fond of questions."

That screamed of understatement, but he needed to move on.

"Tell me what happened after I dropped you off that night."

She stiffened but nodded. "I tried to sneak back in the house, but my family and Jarrod were waiting in the den. I had never seen him in person, so it was a shock."

Hutch bet it was. He forced himself to remain quiet and let her talk.

"They were sickly sweet, and my mother acted like she knew where I'd been. Nevada was the only one not there, which was weird because I thought she liked Jarrod. But I was suddenly the center of attention. The next thing I knew, they were talking about engagements and weddings. No one would listen to me."

Her words grew more rapid, and her breath quickened. Hutch put a hand on her thigh. "It's alright, little girl. None of this was your fault. Take your time. If you need a break, tell me."

She nodded and took a sip of her water.

"I told them I didn't want to get married, but they said they knew what was best for me and I should be grateful someone like Jarrod was interested in someone like me."

175

Hutch ground his teeth to hold back the words he wanted to let fly.

"The next thing I knew, a minister was there and pronounced us husband and wife." She gripped his arm. "You see? This is all my fault. I went along with them. Why didn't I refuse? I could have refused. But instead, I married a man I didn't even know. Who does that?"

Someone groomed to crave her mother's approval. She'd had no say in anything her entire life. Jesus, no wonder it was so important to her that she got to choose the things on that insane bucket list of hers and do them.

He would have to find a way to be okay with at least some things on that list. She needed that from him. Now that he saw that, he would find a way.

It was evident she needed a break. So did he.

"That's enough for now, brave girl. Let's go downstairs and find a book to read. How does that sound?"

She attempted a smile and asked, "Can I pick any book I want?"

"Of course, little one."

Downstairs, Georgia headed straight for the kid's section. She pulled out the book *Ella Enchanted* and handed it to him. They cuddled on the couch in front of the fireplace to read.

She jumped in with each new character and demanded, "Do the voices, Daddy!" He read three more chapters before she suggested they make milkshakes.

"As long as you brush your teeth when we get back upstairs," he said.

She got right to work. He scanned the shop, his eye catching on a large, wrapped box, complete with a bow and card.

He held it up and asked, "What's this?" before thinking.

Georgia glanced up and froze. "Who is it for?"

The card read *'time to pay the piper'* in a sprawling script.

It didn't say, but he knew. Damnit! He should have kicked it under a chair and gotten it on his way out. "It doesn't matter," he said.

She shook her head. "You have to tell me."

Fuck. "It says,"

Time to pay the piper.

He dropped the box and ran to Georgia when the glass she held shattered on the floor.

"Don't move, little girl. You'll cut yourself. Are you alright?" He lifted her and sat her on one of the bar stools. Tremors shook her tiny frame.

Georgia reached for the package he'd tossed on the counter before he could stop her. "It's from Jarrod." She told him something he already knew. "It's what he always said before one of his correction sessions."

"The ones that required a visit from Dr. Rheinstein?"

She jumped at the doctor's name but nodded. Yeah, he'd be visiting the good doctor when he finished with Jemison. He was going to need an industrial slaughterhouse when he got his hands on these guys. One they could hose down to dispose of bodily fluids.

"You stay right there while I get this cleaned up."

What had he been thinking? He knew she was getting gifts and flowers. He saw her pulling the ribbon from the corner of his eye.

"Don't open that," he said. "Just put it down. I will take care of it."

She placed the box back on the counter and stared at nothing, blank-faced, while he finished cleaning up the broken glass.

He picked her up and settled her on his hip.

She yelped and wrapped her legs around him as he headed up the stairs. "Put me down. I'm too heavy for you to carry."

His only answer was a swat to her bottom.

When they reached her apartment, he said, "Pack a bag. You're staying at my place until further notice."

She froze. "I can't stay with you. It will put you in more danger."

"Now is not the time for debate. Now is the time to mind your Daddy. Pack a bag now, or I will pack one for you."

"But—"

"Now, Peaches."

"You don't understand."

"No, Georgia, you don't understand. There is no way I am leaving the woman I love at the mercy of a psychopath. It's not going to happen. Now, pack."

She froze. What now? Then it hit him what he'd said.

Well, shit.

CHAPTER 24

"You love me?" Georgia stared up at Hutch, both hopeful and fearful at his declaration.

"I do," he answered immediately. "I always will."

She needed to stop him. He would hate that she had allowed him to declare his feelings when he learned her secret. "You can't. There are still things you don't know. When you find out, you'll change your mind."

"Won't happen, little girl. You're it for me. Now go pack."

She searched his face, not sure what she was looking for. The only thing she found was love and acceptance, at least for now. A tentative smile braved its way across her lips.

After she packed, they rode to Hutch's cabin. She didn't remember much of the drive. Her mind was too busy working through everything he'd said.

He loved her. At least, that's what he believed. He wouldn't believe that when he knew everything she was hiding. When he found out, he would see she wasn't worth loving.

She would add being loved by Hutch to her bucket list. It was the one item she never wanted to check off her list because then it would be over.

But she wasn't going to think about that now. She would live in the moment and enjoy her dream life. A Daddy who loved her. One who read books to her and kept her safe. Who made rules to help her and cared enough to hold her accountable when she broke them.

She would cherish each moment. Those memories would have to carry her through the rest of her life.

When they reached Hutch's cabin, he set her things in the play-room. She adored her space. He let her play there while he took care of a few Daddy things.

She found him in the kitchen once she had unpacked. He had started dinner and was staring out the window at the lake-sized pond behind his cabin. Country music played through the cabin's sound system, and she couldn't help but move to the song's rhythm. Her dance caught his attention and he smiled. Putting his beer down, he crossed to the middle of the room and held out his hand.

She ran to him, leaping up when she got close enough. He caught her easily and held her close. Her heart danced along with the beat of the song. He put her down, holding her hands as he twisted her back and forth until she was laughing too hard to breathe.

It turned out Jedidiah Hutchinson could dance. Like really dance.

She had never danced before. Initially, she was shy, but Hutch was so good she soon relaxed. He spun her, dipped her, and held her close. She loved it!

"Cabin, play a slow song," Hutch said.

He smiled down at her as soft music drifted through the room. One of his hands slid down to the small of her back. His heat radi-ated through her, shooting tingles to all the right places. She pressed her cheek to his chest and listened to the steady rhythm of his heart.

That was Hutch. Strong, steady, masculine, sexy hot. Daddy.

Yep. She definitely had tingles in places that felt good. Glancing up, she found him staring down at her, his cobalt blue eyes blazing. She was suddenly aware of how much their dance was affecting him. His cock was hard.

Then he lowered his mouth to hers. When their lips touched, fire shot straight through her. No one had ever kissed her like this. All tender and passionate at once.

He teased her lips with his tongue, and she opened for him. He explored her mouth with wet, hot, demanding insistence. Then he pulled her even closer, and she clung to him.

Never had she been so excited by a kiss. Jarrod couldn't even excite her when they made love. Not that he tried.

She ran her hands through Hutch's hair, reveling in the softness. Tightening her grasp, she tugged, and he groaned into her mouth. She wanted more.

So. Much. More.

But then Hutch pulled away and brushed her hair back with a reluctant grin. "Peaches, as much as I love this, we need to talk. And talking will be the last thing on my mind if we keep going."

There was a pounding in her pussy that echoed her heartbeat, and she wanted to pull him back down to continue their kiss.

But he was right. She couldn't go any further without telling him her secret. After that, he might change his mind.

God, she hoped he didn't change his mind.

At her nod, he led her to a large armchair in the living room, pulling her onto his lap. She rested her head on his shoulder, desperately fearing what she might lose.

She had known walking away from him would be almost impossible, but now that she knew he loved her, leaving just might kill her.

Hutch spoke before she could say anything. "I want to go first. Before we start down this road, I want you to know I will understand if you don't feel the same thing for me that I feel for you, little girl. Our feelings are something we can't control. I'll still help you deal with Jarrod. You and Tazzy will still be friends. I want a life with you, but I would never make that a condition of my help."

She already knew he would never do something like that. He was a good person. Too good. That's what scared her.

She placed a hand on his cheek. "I already know that, Daddy." She should call him Hutch until they settled things, but that's not who he was to her. He was her Daddy, pure and simple. And she would call him that as long as she could.

He nodded. "I hope what I say will convince you to stay here. But if you need to leave, I will take you to Tazzy's house or anywhere else safe. Just not back to Books-N-Brews. Not until I can get some protection lined up."

He was wrong. He wouldn't want her to stay once she shared her last secret. He seemed to be waiting for her response, so she said, "Alright."

"Good," he said. Relief flooded his eyes. "I knew something was going on when you gave your ex-husband's number that ringtone but used it to avoid his constant phone calls. *Goodbye Earl* was a good choice. You were hiding something, and I let you. But I worried it was something you might need help with. So, I asked the guys at Sabre to investigate him."

Her heart almost stopped. What had Sabre uncovered in their investigation? Her breathing sped up as she went through the possible consequences.

"You shouldn't have done that. You should have asked me."

"Would you have told me?"

"Maybe not, but you should have tried."

Her heart needed to stop beating so fast. Hutch couldn't know her secret. If he did, he wouldn't be talking to her anymore, much less dancing with her in his kitchen.

She would have pushed off his lap, but he held her there. "What did you find out?" she asked.

"Jarrod Jemison is in some serious shit. We know he's dealing with some powerful people overseas in the Middle and Far East. He's willing to get creative with the law to keep his clients out of jail, and they pay him well for his talents."

"I know." Really, what else could she say?

His eyes, already cold, grew glacial. "We also know about all your visits from Dr. Rheinstein."

This time, he couldn't keep her in his lap. She leaped up, needing to move. Needing to hide. Shame swept through her. She was going to be sick.

He knew what a pathetic victim she'd allowed herself to become. She was one of those women who filled the self-righteous with indignation when they had no idea what she had endured.

Her eyes flew to his, waiting for the condemnation she saw in most people, but it wasn't there. He wasn't condemning. He was furious.

But not at her. For her.

He held out a hand to her. "Please, Peaches. I need you to be close to me right now."

She went to him without a thought. He pulled her back onto his lap and held her without speaking. She waited as the tension eased in his shoulders. At least a little.

"Just one more thing, Georgia, and then you can say whatever you need to. But you need to know that nothing can stop me from loving you. Nothing."

She believed he meant it. She just didn't know if it was true.

He pulled in a deep breath. "I know you filed for divorce and had those papers served as soon as you left. I also know he has not signed them yet."

She stared at him in horror. He knew she was still officially married.

He knew.

She couldn't breathe. She opened her mouth, but her lungs refused to work. Spots floated in her vision.

"Breathe with me, little girl. Slow deep breaths in and out. That's good, Peaches, now again."

Her heart rate slowly went back to normal, and her head cleared.

He knew.

Wait. He knew, and he'd still come back to her. He'd still brought her to his cabin to keep her safe. Still told her he loved her.

He loved her even though she'd lied. Even though she was broken. Even though her psychotic husband was bent on causing trouble. He loved her despite all that.

Warmth ate away the cold and spread throughout her body.

She stared at him, trying to find the words to express her feelings. How grateful she was that he accepted her, flaws and all. How she couldn't imagine her life without him. How, if someone had asked her to describe her perfect Daddy, it would have been him. How did you put all that into words?

"You are everything to me, Daddy. I want to be with you forever," she said.

The next thing she knew, she was in his arms. Her feet weren't even touching the floor. He held her so tight she had a hard time breathing.

"Thank fuck," he whispered in her ear.

Then, dinner forgotten, he carried her to his room.

Hutch kicked the door to his bedroom open and felt her shiver in his arms.

CHAPTER 25

*G*eorgia shivered as Hutch strode down the hall. They passed the playroom, thank God. She loved her playroom, but she was nowhere near Little head space. She was totally in grownup Georgia space. Her clit pounded, and her nipples pulsed with every step he took.

He set her down at the edge of the bed. Thankfully, her knees didn't buckle right out from under her. He stared into her soul with those intense blue eyes. "So beautiful," he said. "You are the most beautiful woman I've ever known."

Oh, God. His breath brushed her cheek as he nuzzled her ear. Shivers raced up and down her spine, settling in her core. She didn't dare move for fear he would stop. She needed his lips on hers. She'd never needed anything this badly. Not ever.

Slowly, he ran the tip of his tongue along her jaw, nipping her chin and immediately soothing the sting. At her gasp, he lifted his head to meet her eyes. He must have seen her longing because he smiled in pure masculine pleasure before lowering his mouth to hers.

Nothing could have prepared her for his kiss. The already

burning desire within her exploded. Needing to feel his skin against hers, she pulled at his shirt. It was a barrier, and she wanted it gone. He pulled back and looked down at her, his eyes deepening to almost midnight.

"What do you want, little girl?" he demanded huskily.

He wanted her to talk? She couldn't form words now. Tugging at the offending material, she managed, "Please, Daddy."

"Please, what? Do you want to feel your skin next to mine?"

Want was such a weak word. She needed to feel him more than she needed air. Yearning coiled in her like a tightly wound spring.

"Please," she repeated.

"Little girls first," he said, slipping his fingers under the bottom of her shirt. They trailed up her ribs, leaving scorch marks scoring their path. Fire shot straight to her clit.

He tormented her breasts with slow strokes, skimming right over her nipples. She had a mini orgasm on the spot. Longing and need coursed through her veins, and he hadn't even gotten her shirt off.

"Your skin is so soft, little girl." He pressed his hips into her. "Do you feel how hard you make me?"

She pressed back, reveling in the feel of his hard shaft. He wanted her as much as she wanted him. Another thrill shot through her.

When he finally pulled her shirt over her head, she returned the favor, pushing up his shirt so she could feel the heat of his skin on her own.

He undid the clasp of her bra. Then there was nothing between them. His lips recaptured hers as he pinched her nipple, swallowing her cries of pleasure.

She had never understood those spicy scenes in her books where the girl was drunk with arousal, but she did now. Her mind swam in a sea of bliss, unable to do anything except float from sensation to sensation.

"Let's get the rest of these clothes off you. They're in the way," he said. It didn't take him long to have her naked. He slid her pants down, kneeling, pressing his face into her soaked panties, and drawing a deep breath.

She knew he could smell how excited she was by what he was doing. What would he think? She didn't have to wait long for an answer. "You are wet for me already, aren't you? You smell incredible. It makes me want to taste you even more. Let's get you on the bed, dirty girl."

He chuckled at her whimper.

Hutch lowered her to the bed and lay next to her. "Are you comfortable, little one?" When she nodded, he asked, "Have you ever used a safeword before?"

Why was he talking? She could barely hear him over the need coursing through her. She shook her head. "I've read about them, but I've never had one." Was that her voice that was so breathy and filled with want?

"Safewords are important. If I do anything you don't like, you say red, and I'll stop immediately. I won't be disappointed or mad. I'll only be disappointed if you need to use your safeword and don't. I only want to bring you pleasure."

He had that down to an art. If it got any better, she might pass out.

He waited for her to respond, so she nodded.

"Words, Georgia Anne. Do you understand?"

"Yes, Daddy. If I need to stop, I'll say red."

She appreciated his caution, but she wasn't about to stop now.

"I want to look at you," he said, running his thumb over her lips.

Instinctively, she covered her buddha belly with her hand. His body had been chiseled to perfection.

He pulled her hand away. "I want to see all of you."

No, he didn't. "My belly is jiggly. I'm starting sit-ups tomorrow," she promised.

His brow furrowed. "If you want to exercise, that's fine. But you are beautiful just like you are," he said.

She snorted. Easy for him to say. He was carved like the statue of a god.

"And if you get rid of this adorable tummy, I'll spank your ass."

Her eyes shot to his. There was no way he liked her belly.

"Peaches, you are soft, just like a little girl should be. You don't have to change to please me. Got it?"

She nodded. What had she ever done to deserve a man like Hutch?

"Good. Now let me explore this gorgeous body."

She sucked in a breath as he trailed one finger from her collarbone, across her nipple, and down to her waist. If her nipple got any more pointed, it would cut glass.

"Your nipple is so tight and pink."

He lowered his mouth to her breast and pressed his lips against her nipple. Then he licked the tip of the sensitive bud.

She arched into his mouth. God, she was going to come just from his mouth on her nipples. He hummed while sucking her deeper, causing another shiver. Her pussy pulsed, and a moan escaped her.

"I love how responsive you are," he said.

He shifted to her other breast and, at the same time, ran his hand lower. He glided softly over her abdomen and stopped just above her clit.

She gasped and rocked her head from side to side. She was not going to be able to last long. He hadn't even touched her pussy and she was already on the verge of coming. The heat from his palm warmed her skin, and she lifted her hips.

"Be still, naughty girl," he said. "Let Daddy explore."

He slid his hand past her clit without touching it.

"No," she wailed. She needed his finger on her clit. The barest touch would send her flying. Instead, his finger traced her slit, gathering her arousal. He brought the glistening finger to his mouth and sucked it clean.

"So sweet. You taste delicious." He lowered his mouth to hers. "Taste yourself," he said, and his mouth was back on hers.

She had never tasted herself before. She tried to avoid his lips, but he refused to allow it. Opening her lips to him, she tasted her tangy sweetness on his tongue, and her pussy grew even wetter.

His fingers returned to her pussy, this time pushing inside. They were large and calloused, and felt incredible. He drew them in and out slowly, putting enough pressure on something inside her it drove her need even higher.

"Daddy," she gasped. So many sensations flooded her. She'd never experienced anything like it before. Never.

His voice was pure gravel as he spoke. "What do you need, little girl?"

"Daddy," she gasped again. "I need you, Daddy."

"And what do you want Daddy to do?"

Her desire blew past her embarrassment. "I want you to make me come."

His smile turned predatory. "That's my good girl," he said. "Daddy will take care of you."

He pumped his fingers in and out faster and curled them toward that spot he'd found inside her. She hoped it was okay to move now because she didn't think she could stop herself. The feelings he gave her couldn't get any better. She was sure of it. Until he ground the heel of his hand against her clit.

She screamed his name as a wave of pleasure swelled up inside her. It grew into a tidal wave of pleasure that crashed over her again and again.

· · ·

HUTCH

Georgia's skin flushed a pretty pink after her orgasm. She was the single most beautiful woman he had ever seen, and she was his now. He was never letting her go.

He stroked her silken hair and nuzzled soft kisses into the curve where her shoulder met her neck. When her heartbeat steadied, he lifted his head and smiled.

"That was amazing, Peaches. I damn near came just watching you."

His cock still throbbed with the need to sink deep inside her. But he needed to be sure she was ready for everything that step would mean for them both.

The dazed passion-drunk expression faded from her eyes, and she frowned when she noticed he still wore his jeans. "Why did you stop? I mean, what about you?"

"We'll get to me. First, I need you to know where I'm taking us," he told her. Even if that meant he had a hot date with a cold shower. "I told you before this isn't casual for me. You said you wanted to be with me forever. If I put my cock inside you, that's it. I won't be able to walk away. If we do this, it's the start of forever."

It was a risk, but he had to be honest. He wanted her to be his for more than a few nights or months. He wanted forever.

"I'm not trying to pressure you into a decision. But I have to know if it's what you want to, Peaches."

She stared at him like he hung the moon and stars. Maybe what he was asking wasn't fair, but he knew himself. If they took this forward tonight, he wouldn't be able to let her walk away. She'd take his heart and soul with him if she did. He'd never survive.

If she didn't see herself with him, he needed to know. But fuck was it taking a long time for her to answer.

Then she reached up to rest her palm on his cheek. He couldn't stop himself from nuzzling against her tender touch.

"Jedidiah Hutchinson," she said, "I've wanted to be with you since the seventh grade. I thought fate stole my future, but you got it back for me. I want to be with you forever."

Fuck. His heart almost exploded.

"You're sure?" he said. He wanted to toss her to her back and plant himself inside her. But he needed to make sure it was what she wanted. "There won't be any changing your mind, so be sure."

Her smile was what joy was made of. And she gave him what he had waited eight years to hear. "I'm sure."

The need to have her surged through his cock.

He retook her mouth and ravaged it. The need in him pushed to take all of her, fast and hard. And when she relaxed into him, he grabbed her hand and pressed it to his cock as it strained against his jeans. His chest swelled just a little at the tiny gasp she made.

He groaned with pleasure and need. Damn, he was going to come before he could get his cock free if she kept that up. He stood, shedding the remainder of his clothes.

Her eyes widened at her first sight of his cock. "Daddy, I don't think that will fit," she said.

"It will fit," he assured her. And the sooner, the better. "Take my cock in your hand. That's it," he said. He had never thought of himself as a masochist, but her tiny hand wrapped around his hard cock was the sweetest torture he'd ever endured.

He held her hand still when she tried to stroke him. He wanted inside her, needed it. But first, he needed to taste her.

He pushed between her legs and spread them further apart. Her pussy was so fucking wet. The fragrance of her arousal was perfect. He ran his tongue up her slit from the opening of her core to her clit, relishing her taste.

Her scream of pleasure was all the encouragement he needed. "Lie back, little girl. Let Daddy feast."

And feast he did. He circled her clit with his tongue while she tried to stay still. She failed, and he did not care. She bucked into him, and when her moans reached a fevered pitch, he plunged his fingers back in and sent her crashing into her release.

He lapped at her gently as she came down, sucking in every drop of her cream. The need to bury himself balls deep inside her drove him upward, kissing his way up her body until he reached her mouth.

"Are you ready to take my cock, naughty girl?"

"Yes, Daddy. I want you inside me."

That was all he needed. Pulling out a condom from his night-stand, he rolled it on and positioned himself at the mouth of her pussy. Her heat almost undid him.

He slowly worked his way inside her, careful not to cause her pain. God, she was tight, and her wet heat spiraled his need higher. Once he was fully seated, he held himself there.

"Are you alright, little one?" he asked, his voice strained.

"Yes, Daddy," she said. She rocked against him. Greedy girl. A surge of satisfaction crashed through him at her, "Please, I need you to move."

She did not have to ask twice. He pulled almost all the way out of her, then slowly pushed back in. She wrapped her legs around his ass and pulled him in harder.

That was all it took. His control snapped, and he drove into her. It was incredible. She was incredible. His balls drew up, and a fire of need and pleasure built at the base of his spine.

Her pussy spasmed around his cock, thank God, and when she broke, he let go and allowed the fire of his release to consume him.

He almost collapsed on her once he finished but caught himself on his elbows. He rolled to his back, bringing her to lie on top of him. She lay still with her cheek resting on his chest.

"Are you alright, little one?"

She nodded and hummed a contented "mmm-hmmm."

"I love you," he told her again. "That was amazing. Let me get a rag to clean you up."

Her head shot up. "I can do it, Daddy," she said and tried to crawl off the bed.

He stopped her before she could even move. "I know you can, Peaches. But I want to do this for you."

He walked to the bathroom and wet a cloth with warm water. He cleaned her gently and returned to the bath, cleaning himself.

That had been the most incredible orgasm of his life. And he had a lifetime ahead of him to enjoy.

But it had been a long, stressful day, and fatigue almost overwhelmed him. He lay back in the bed and pulled her to his side, cheek now resting on his shoulder. Her eyes were closed, but she had a smile on her face. His little girl. His.

He closed his eyes, but she placed her hand over his heart as sleep started to take him under. "Daddy, there's something I forgot to tell you."

He couldn't even open his eyes. "What is it, little one? What do you need?"

He fought the pull of sleep that tried to drag him under.

"It's important, Daddy," she insisted, though her voice was sleepy as well. "I have to tell you now."

He forced his eyes open and saw that hers were closed. With a smile, he asked, "Alright, sweet girl. What do you need to tell me?"

Without opening her eyes, she mumbled, "I loves you, too, Daddy." And then she was asleep. Peace warmed his heart as he let sleep pull him under.

CHAPTER 26

*H*utch stalked into Sabre and threw a large package on the conference table. He strode to the boxing area and punched a hanging bag, wishing it was Jarrod Jemison instead.

"What's up?" Deke asked from the table.

Hutch threw another punch and grunted out, "Georgia got another package."

Deke came alert. "Did she see who it was? I'll get Sawyer on the camera feed."

"I saw who it was. This time it was a tourist staying at the Crippled Creek. I've already talked to her. Jemison is getting the gifts to random people and tricking them into dropping them off without being caught."

Deke flipped the album closed. "How's he getting the gifts to the people?"

"Fucker's smart," Hutch answered, continuing to punch the bag. "Package comes to a resort, addressed to a random room with instructions. No prints, no trail. Basically, we've got nothing."

Hutch landed two double jabs.

Reid sat down and watched Hutch work out his anger. "You break it, you buy it, man," he said.

Hutch just glared at him and swung again.

"What's in this one," Deke asked as he picked up the box. "It's heavy."

Hutch gave the bag a final series of rapid-fire punches before returning to the table. "I didn't open it yet."

"They're coming more frequently. That's not a good sign. How's Georgia handling it?" Reid asked.

"She doesn't know," Hutch said. He ran his hand over his face. "Tazzy and Memphis grab them when they show up. So far, they've stashed them in Tazzy's car before Georgia notices. She is dealing with enough. She doesn't need this stalker shit."

Reid nodded. "I'd do the same thing. Protecting our Littles is priority one."

Our? Did Reid have a Little? He hadn't thought so, but he hadn't been around as much. Seemed a talk with his friend was overdue.

"Might as well open it and see what we're dealing with," Sawyer said, taking a seat.

Deke pulled on gloves, then snapped the tape and opened the package. He held up a ceramic jar.

Deke read the tag dangling from the lid and muttered, "This prick is spiraling." More of the team gathered around, and he held up the vase. Deke eyed Hutch and warned, "Brace, man. The tag's addressed to you."

No one spoke as Deke turned the blue glass urn he held. Stenciled peaches covered the sides.

Sawyer broke the silence. "Somebody tell me that is not a cremation urn."

Fuck. It was. Fuck. Fuck. Fuck!

"That's exactly what it is," Deke said, still looking at Hutch. "It's obviously a warning. The question is, is it for Georgia or you?"

Damned if Hutch knew. All he knew was this asshole was going to die. He'd be filling that fucking jar with Jemison's ashes and burying it somewhere up the mountain.

Sawyer spoke. "Well, he's telling Hutch he knows Georgia's nickname. Could be a warning for him. Could also be he's saying either Georgia goes back to him or she dies. Either way, Deke's right. A cremation urn is an escalation."

Hutch's temper broke. "Fuck!" He slammed his fist on the table. "I do not give the first shit what this fucker wants. I don't care what it costs. I want this fucker erased."

"I get you, brother," Reid said. "We'll get him. He'll slip up, and we'll nail his balls to the wall."

"This is my woman, my little girl," Hutch said, looking each man at the table in the eye. They knew what Georgia meant to him. They were all in. "I have to get back to Georgia."

Hutch headed back into town. Something was coming. He could feel it in his gut. He'd known it for days and had done everything he could to keep her safe.

He'd moved her into his cabin, where the security was better. No one could hack his system. Not that he couldn't handle it if someone did. He'd put her on total lockdown if he could.

Books-N-Brews was a much more challenging environment to control. He'd beefed up security there as well. They had a guy in the shop whenever Georgia was there. The shop and the alley were wired with video and sound surveillance.

It wasn't enough.

Somehow, Jemison knew when Georgia was at Books-N-Brews. She never got phone calls at home anymore, only at work. Jarrod's gifts showed up when she was at the shop, even if she hadn't been scheduled to be there.

They'd cleaned the shop of all the bugs and cameras once. Hutch tried to keep his eye out for more, but the shop was always full of customers. Tonight, he'd search again after they closed.

There had to be another camera there somewhere. Hopefully, today would be too busy for her ex to cause trouble.

It was Halloween, and Darling went all out to celebrate. The local businesses, including Books-N-Brews, gave the kids candy and put up kiosks and booths on the street during the dance.

During the day, there was a festival with old-fashioned games and activities. Trick or treating would start at 5:00 that evening, followed by a street dance until midnight, and ending with a massive fireworks show.

Kids and adults alike wore costumes all day. The town held a costume parade and contest. It was the perfect day for a town filled with Littles.

Georgia and Tazzy had picked out Powerpuff Girls costumes weeks ago. Somehow, Georgia had convinced him to dress up as the Professor.

Who was he kidding? He knew exactly how she'd done it. She'd been so damn adorable when she'd tried on that short dress, tights, and Mary Jane shoes that all the blood had vacated his brain and taken up residence in his cock.

He walked into Books-N-Brews and smiled. His baby had gone all out. A skeleton sat at the table in the window, with another flying on a broom overhead. Fake spider webs stretched across all the corners, and black garland sporting tiny orange jack-o-lantern lights adorned the fireplace. A giant cauldron on the hearth waited to be filled with candy for the trick-or-treaters to come.

He'd planned on shadowing her all night, but then Doc called. Fentanyl-laced candy a kid had found had sent him to the emergency room. That meant Hutch had to meet with his sources so Sabre could get the fuckers distributing the drugs before they killed someone.

But that left Georgia unprotected. When Hutch told Reid he would have to stay with his girl, Reid said he'd send Deke in as her bodyguard until Hutch could get back. But first, he had something to discuss with his little girl.

His girl was busy talking with customers, but her face lit up as soon as she saw him. She was already in costume, and he had to adjust his zipper. She was fucking adorable in that little pink dress. His cock appreciated the sight as much as he did.

She pretended to pout as she walked toward him. When she got close enough for no one to overhear, she said, "Daddy, you don't have on your costume."

"I'll put it on when I get back, little girl. Daddy has to work right now. I just stopped by to make sure everything's good."

"It's fantastic, Daddy. Don't you love what we did with the shop? I want to keep it up all year!" She spun around as she talked, pointing out her favorite parts.

He grabbed her waist before she made herself too dizzy to stand. "It looks cool, sweetie. You did a great job." She beamed at his praise. "But I don't think you can keep these decorations up all year."

"Why not?" she demanded. She was cute when she pouted.

"Well, if you leave up the Halloween decorations, where will you put all the ones you have for Christmas? If you don't put those up, you might confuse Santa. He is pretty old."

Georgia gasped and looked around as if an elf might be sitting on a shelf nearby. "Daddy, you shouldn't call Santa old. He might not bring you anything but coal and switches."

"Is that so?" He took her hand and led her back to the office. "If Santa brings me switches, it will be because I have a little girl who forgets her rules."

"I don't forget rules, Daddy!"

He put her mermaid water bottle on the large wooden desk. "You don't? Then who left your water bottle in my truck this morning?"

The cutest shade of red flooded her cheeks. "Um, it was probably Penny, Daddy. She can be forgetful sometimes."

"Well, I'm glad you told me. I'll just have to spank Penny then."

Georgia gasped. "Daddy, no! You can't spank Penny. That's mean."

"Well, I don't want her to think I'm mean. Rules are rules, though, and someone broke an important one. Do you want to rethink who left the water bottle behind in her hurry to open the shop?"

Georgia dropped her gaze to her shiny Mary Jane shoes. "I did, Daddy. I just wanted to make sure someone turned on all the lights and candles."

"I know, but your water keeps you healthy. Now bend over the desk, and we'll take care of this and get it out of the way."

"But, Daddy, someone might hear." She glanced at the door.

"Punishment works best given immediately. If someone hears, they'll know there's a little girl here whose Daddy loves her enough to make her behave. Now, over the end of the desk. I want you to look at your water bottle to remind you of the consequences of not drinking your water like a good girl."

If her lip poked out any further, she would trip over it. She threw him one last sad look then did as he instructed.

When she was bent over, he raised her skirt and lowered her tights and panties. Rubbing her bottom, he said, "The count is five, little one," and brought his hand down hard on the center of her right cheek.

She came up on her toes as a perfect handprint bloomed on her ass. He painted her left cheek with a matching one.

"Owie! Daddy, not so hard! That hurts!"

"It's supposed to hurt, little girl. That's what helps you remember."

He lowered his aim and gave her two matching handprints on her sit spots.

She stamped her foot and wailed, "I'm sorry, Daddy. I won't forget my water bottle again."

"I know, naughty girl. Last one." He brought his hand down in the center of her cheeks. Damn. He did love a pretty pink ass. After righting her clothes, he gathered her into his arms.

She sniffled. "I love you, Daddy. I promise to drink my water today."

"Good girl. I love you, too."

He led her back up front, smiling at the redness of her cheeks. Now they matched her lower ones.

Deke sat in a chair by the fireplace, reading the *Daily Nugget* with a scowl. For a man who valued his privacy, he spent a lot of time reading all the latest gossip around town.

Hutch kissed Georgia and let her scurry behind the counter to ring up the customers who had dropped by for coffee on the way to work and then crossed to Deke.

"I'll be back as soon as I can. Call me if there's anything I need to know."

Deke lifted his chin. "Will do."

Hutch and the rest of the Sabre team hunted until well into the afternoon. He made it back just in time for the costume parade. He'd thrown on his costume, ignoring Deke, Sawyer, and Reid when they gave him a hard time.

When his little girl danced beside him, hands held, arms swinging, at the parade, he did not give that first fuck about those jealous bastards or the ribbing he'd taken.

They were setting up the stage for the street dance when his phone rang. His caller ID showed Reid calling again.

"You got me," he said, scanning the crowd.

Reid lost no time. "We found something."

"Where are you?" Hutch answered, instantly alert.

"The old farmer's market. We found a couple of boxes of eye

drops in one of the old stalls under a tarp. The Taylor boys' dog sniffed it out. I'm pretty sure it's the synthetic liquid fentanyl."

Shit.

Hutch started moving toward his truck as he spoke. "I'm on my way."

Fuck.

He hung up and called Deke. "Deke, I'm headed to the old farmer's market." He filled Deke in on the detail. "This might take a while. Can you keep eyes on Georgia again until I get back?"

"No worries, man. Do what you gotta do. I'll keep your girl safe."

"Thanks, I owe you," Hutch said and disconnected the call.

Georgia skipped to his side. "I'm so excited," she said. "Don't forget you promised me the first dance."

Fuck, he hated disappointing his girl. "Sorry, Peaches. I have to take care of something. We'll dance as soon as I get back."

"Oh, okay, Daddy," she said. The disappointment in her voice was a slap to the heart.

"As soon as I can, Peaches. I promise. Deke's going to stay with you. You mind him and stay where he can see you. Understand?"

"I will," she promised.

"I mean it, Georgia Anne. If he tells me you didn't, I will blister your behind. Got me?"

"I got you, Daddy. Jeez." She rolled her eyes, earning her a swat to her bottom.

"Be good," he warned one last time.

"I will, Daddy," she said. "Be careful."

"Always," he said and headed for his truck.

That feeling was back, stronger than ever. Deke would take a bullet for his girl. Hutch knew it. Still, no one cared about Georgia as much as he did.

Bad feeling or not, children in danger trumped one asshat ex, so he headed to the farmer's market.

Fuck.

CHAPTER 27

The street dance was almost perfect, thanks to the crisp air and the fantastic music. The crowds of dancing people made for lots of thirsty customers. The only thing missing was her Daddy.

But now they were almost out of cups.

"I'll run back to the store and grab some more," Georgia shouted to Tazzy over the loud music.

Tazzy frowned. "Deke said to stay here until he got back. Why don't you send Memphis?"

Georgia shook her head. "Memphis can help you with the coffee. I can't," she called. She practiced her latte art, but her coffee art wasn't improving. "It's not far."

Deke had taken a lost child to the police booth at the other end of the crowded street. There was no telling how long it would take him to get back.

No harm running to the shop and back. Hutch would be mad, but he and Deke were being overprotective. And anyway, they'd never find out. Probably. Hopefully.

She hurried to Books-N-Brews to find the shop was dark.

She'd told Memphis to leave the lights on so people could see the sign directing them to their kiosk at the dance. The dark shop made her nervous.

She'd just call and make sure he'd left them off before she went inside. She searched her pocket for her phone, but it wasn't there. Darn it. She must have put it down when she was looking for her keys.

Hutch would be mad about that, too. But only if he found out. She crossed her fingers and prayed he wouldn't call or text until she had her phone.

She unlocked the door but had to force herself to walk inside. Everyone would think she was a baby if they knew she was scared of the dark.

All she had to do was grab some cups. Then she could run back to the kiosk. For exercise, not because she was afraid.

She flipped on the lights and headed straight for the supply closet. As she unlocked the door, she heard a thump in the office. She froze and tried to control her breathing. It was probably nothing. Gathering her courage, she stepped toward the office. She'd take a quick peek to ensure no one was there.

There was nothing to be afraid of. Memphis had locked the shop door and set the alarm system. If someone had unlocked the door, it would have sent a notification to her phone. The phone she'd left at the kiosk. Darn it!

She turned back to grab her keys from the closet door. She could use them as a weapon if she had to. But as she pulled her keys from the knob, someone shoved her from behind.

Her head smacked into the door, and the intruder shoved her inside the closet before she could react.

Her knees hit the floor, and she slumped forward into a shelf full of supplies. Cups, plates, and sugar packets rained down on her. The door slammed behind her, enveloping her in the blackest darkness she had ever known.

Her heart raced so fast she thought she might have a heart attack. She had to get up and get to the door, but a snick echoed through the tiny room before she could move. A minute later, a metal door banged shut as whoever shoved her escaped into the back alley.

She inched through the darkness to find the door locked. Being trapped in the dark shot terror coursing through her. She could cry for help, but no one would hear her. She was locked in the dark alone, with no way to contact anyone. Surely Tazzy would realize she wasn't back soon and send Deke to find her.

Had she relocked the front door? She couldn't remember.

Hutch was going to be so mad. Sliding to the floor, she hugged her knees to her chest and sobbed.

HUTCH

"What do you mean she's not where you left her?" Hutch roared into his phone. "Why the fuck did you leave her?"

"I had to take a lost kid to the cop's tent. I was gone for ten minutes, tops," Deke said. "I told her to stay put, but when I got back, Tazzy said she went to the shop for more cups. I'm headed there now."

"I'm on my way." Hutch was already speeding, but he still sped up.

Georgia was missing. Anything could have happened to her. Jarrod could have happened to her. "I'll call her and let her know you're coming."

"She left her phone at the kiosk," Deke said. "I fucked up. I should have told Memphis to take the kid. I thought she'd stay put. You need to spank that girl more."

Oh, he would be rectifying that as soon as he found her. "I'm almost there. Let me know when you have her. And keep her there."

What had she been thinking? She hadn't just ignored Deke. She'd disobeyed her Daddy. She would be one sorry little girl when he got his hands on her.

He drove in the back way to avoid the blocked roads and pulled up beside Books-N-Brews. Deke was nowhere to be seen, so Hutch tried the door. Shit. He headed back to the truck for his keys.

Where the hell were they?

Before he reached his truck, Deke raced across the street.

"Are you just getting here?" Hutch demanded.

"Fuck, no. The door was locked. I had to go back and get Tazzy's key."

Deke unlocked the door, and they entered the shop, ready for anything. The lights were on, so they should be able to see her, but the shop was empty.

"Georgia," he called out. "Peaches, are you here?"

He checked the kitchen and found it empty, too. Fuck! He tried to stay calm.

"Hutch," Deke called.

Hutch ran back up front to find the room empty. "Here!" Deke called from the hallway leading to the office. He stared into the supply closet and said, "I heard her inside, and the keys were on the floor. Get over here, man."

Hutch was already there. It took his eyes a moment to adjust to the dark room. When they did, he saw his little girl huddled in a tight ball against the far wall. She was crying but unharmed.

He ran to her, dropping to his knees and pulling her into his arms. She shook so hard he could practically hear her bones rattling. Her breathing was ragged. He rocked her in his lap and spoke softly. "It's okay, little girl. Daddy's got you."

"Turn on the light," he told Deke. "She's afraid of the dark."

She burrowed into him as light flooded the room. He ran a

hand through her hair as he held her close. "It's okay, little one. You're safe. No one is going to hurt you."

He kept his voice calm and low, which was a miracle because he wanted to shout. Whoever had done this to his little girl was dead.

He stood, lifting her with him. She wrapped her arms around his neck and buried her face in his shoulder. He carried her across the hall to the office but jerked to a halt at what he saw.

Someone had trashed the place. Chairs lay about the room, and the desk was on its side. Everything lay scattered and broken.

What the fuck?

He turned to block her view and carried her down the hall. Not ready to put her down, he sat in front of the fireplace and kept her in his lap.

What the fuck had happened? Had she interrupted a burglary? Whoever it was must have run out once they locked her in the closet, but what were they after? Why the office rather than the cash register?

Rubbing her back, he asked, "Did they hurt you?" He scanned her for bruises. All he found was a knot on her forehead. "What happened to your head?"

She looked up at him, her eyes dazed. "I was reaching for the keys in the closet door, but they jumped out and slammed my head into it."

He shut down the rage coursing through him. He had to think of her, and she didn't need to see him out of control. "Deke, call Doc and get him here to check her for a concussion."

"No doctor," she said. "I... I'm okay, Daddy. It was dark, and I was scared. I'm sorry I didn't mind you." She put a hand to the bump on her head. "Ow!"

"That was scary, little girl. It scared me, too. We'll talk about you not minding later. Right now, I want you to tell me how many fingers I'm holding up."

Hutch put up three fingers. She blinked at his hand several

times as if she were having difficulty focusing her eyes. She lifted her hand to her head again and said, "Owie."

"I know, sweet girl, I know. It's going to be okay. Doc Preston will be here soon. He'll make you feel better." His voice was thick with emotion. He hated seeing her in so much pain.

"I sleepy, Daddy," she mumbled. "I go sleep now."

"No, don't do that, sweetie. I need you to stay awake until Doc gets here." Wasn't he supposed to keep her awake if she had a concussion?

She threw her arms around his neck. "I sorry, Daddy. I sorry."

He held her close. His poor little girl. He should have been there, and then no one would have been able to hurt her. He'd let her down. He wished he could wipe away her pain as quickly as he wiped away her tears.

"Did you see who attacked you? What they looked like? Did they say anything?"

"No, Daddy. They pushed me. Mean, that was very mean."

She still sounded sleepy, but he thought she was becoming more coherent.

Damn it. Where was Doc? Maybe he should take her to the emergency room.

Deke flagged his attention. "Doc's on another emergency call. He said make sure she's steady on her feet and can answer basic questions. If she starts throwing up or passes out, bring her in."

Fuck waiting. "Tell Doc we're on the way."

Georgia put a trembling hand to his chest. "It's only a bump." She must have seen the resolve on his face. "I'll do what Dr. Preston said. I promise."

Damn right, she'd do what Doc said. And later, she'd learn what happened to naughty little girls who disobeyed their Daddies.

He almost lost his mind when he thought about everything that could have happened to her. She'd been alone, defenseless. Anything could have happened.

Tazzy and Memphis burst through the shop door and headed straight for Georgia.

"Oh, my gosh! Georgia, are you okay?" Tazzy asked.

"Tazzy," he said, quietly but firmly, "Georgia bumped her head. Loud noises hurt her, so you need to keep it down."

"Oh, sorry!" Tazzy said, whispering. "Georgia, are you okay?"

Georgia sniffled in his arms. "I'm fine. I'm sorry I didn't come back to the kiosk."

"It was fine," Tazzy answered. "Memphis went to Calico House's kiosk, and they let us have some cups."

"I should've thought of that," Georgia said. "I'm so stupid."

"You're in enough trouble right now, naughty girl. Don't call yourself stupid."

"Sorry, Daddy," she whispered.

Tazzy put a hand on Georgia's arm. "I didn't think of it either. We were crazy busy."

"I offered to buy the cups," Memphis added. "They said the advertising for their restaurant was enough."

Georgia slid off Hutch's lap and walked to the counter. She seemed steadier on her feet, but he would keep an eye on her. "We'll give them some free coffee coupons to show our appreciation."

Hutch took a minute to think. He needed to prove Jemison was behind Georgia's attack because he knew that fucker was involved. Maybe one of the cameras caught something.

Thinking of Georgia alone in that pitch-black room made him want to rip the guy in half. Jemison had to know she was terrified of the dark. It would be just like the asshole.

Hutch had bought a star projector night light to go in the playroom. It made her so happy he had bought one for their bedroom.

Deke walked up to him, his face tight with concern. "Sawyer reviewed the camera footage. It was a guy, but he knew where the cameras are. He kept his face hidden, even in the alley. Tire tracks show he parked just out of range of the camera back there."

Fucking hell.

Tazzy crossed to the cauldron that held the leftover candy. "We need to empty this."

"Let me help," Georgia said, joining Tazzy. "Memphis, will you get some bags? I don't want to go back into the storage room."

As the girls began sorting the candy, Tazzy frowned, lifting a crumpled piece of paper. "Some people! Who would throw trash in with the kid's candy?"

When she unfolded the paper, her eyes shot to Georgia. "I don't think this is trash." She held the note to Georgia, but Hutch snatched it away.

He read the note. It was definitely a threat meant for Georgia.

I can get to you any time I wish. If you want your friends to live, you know what to do.

Fucking hell.

Someone had to stop this motherfucker, and it would be him. Jemison thought he was invincible, but he was not. Hutch needed to figure out how Jemison did this, and then he would make him pay.

CHAPTER 28

Georgia stared out the window of Hutch's truck. Tree shadows reached out over the road as they sped past. Usually, she loved the canopy of branches. But not tonight. Now the branches were arms, waiting to snatch her away from everyone and everything she loved.

She jumped when Hutch's cell phone rang, and he snatched it from the seat between them. The caller ID showed it was Sabre. She tensed, bracing for whatever they had found on the surveillance video.

"This is Hutch. What did you find?"

Yep. Her Daddy was in a no-nonsense mood. Not that she blamed him. She had messed up big time.

He listened, gripping the phone tighter with each passing minute. "Can you tell for certain it was her?"

When Hutch disconnected the call, she asked, "What did they say?"

She could tell he didn't want to answer her. With a sigh, he said, "It looks like Nevada was the one who put the note in the cauldron. I'm sorry, Peaches, but it looks like your sister is up to her neck in this."

That Nevada was still helping Jarrod shouldn't have hurt, but it did. Did her sister not know she was putting good people in harm's way? Maybe not, or perhaps her sister could not consider anyone but herself.

She scrunched her forehead and winced. The pain medicine she had taken earlier that evening had worn off. She wanted to cry again, but that would only worsen her headache.

To top it all off, riding in the truck was making her sick. Those trees flying past the window had her stomach rolling.

She should have refused when Hutch told her it was time to return to the cabin. She should never have moved out there. If anything happened to her Daddy because of her, she would never survive.

She glanced at Hutch from the corner of her eye. He scowled at the road ahead, his body tight. She didn't blame him for being mad. She should have stayed at the kiosk with the others. All this trouble was her fault. If she suggested turning around, he would probably be glad. No one needed someone like her in their life.

He reached over to her and squeezed her hand. "Don't know what you're thinking, little girl, but whatever it is, get it out of your head."

"I'm sorry I caused so much trouble, Daddy," she said for the umpteenth time. It wasn't possible to say it enough.

"The only thing you did tonight was break a rule," he said.

But he didn't look at her. He glanced in the rearview mirror and then stared straight at the road. "That's what little girls do. That's why they have Daddies. We have a way of taking care of that, don't we, naughty girl?"

She nodded. "Yes, Daddy."

He gave her hand another squeeze before glancing at the

rearview mirror again. His brows dipped, and he put both hands on the wheel.

"When we get home, I'm giving you a bath, and then we will cuddle up and watch a movie."

"I thought I was getting a spanking," she said.

Relief and disappointment warred inside her. Didn't he care enough to correct her? Her heart dropped, and tears stung her eyes.

"Oh, you are, Peaches, you are. Just not tonight. Tonight, I'm taking care of you. We're relaxing and forgetting about our bad day. We'll take care of your punishment once you're feeling better."

Hutch glanced in the mirror again. He scowled at whatever he saw. "Georgia Anne, make sure your seatbelt's tight."

Her stomach dipped. Now what? "What's going on?" she asked.

She checked herself, but the five-point harness seatbelt he had installed when she started riding with him held her securely in her seat.

Another glance at whatever was behind them. "Probably nothing. Someone's coming up behind us faster than I like. They'll probably back off as soon as they recognize my truck." Hutch tensed, then yelled, "Shit, hold on!"

A jarring thud from behind them snapped her head forward. She screamed, and her heart thundered in her chest. She gripped the armrest so tightly she thought her fingers might snap.

Their truck swerved into the other lane, almost running off the road. Hutch pulled back just in time but stayed in the middle. He hit the gas. "Hold tight, little girl. I'm going to outrun them," he said, never taking his eyes off the road. "Sutton's Crossroads is after the next sharp curve. I'll pull ahead, and we can lose them there."

Georgia sent a prayer up to whoever was listening.

When Hutch sped up, the vehicle behind them matched his

speed. It pulled even with them on Georgia's side and slammed into them. Georgia's head smashed into the window.

"Fuck," Hutch cursed, then slammed on his brakes. The truck fishtailed, but he managed to keep control.

The black car sped away. She stared after it until the taillights disappeared around the bend of the curve.

Hutch reached for her, popping the lock across her chest and pulling her into his lap. He ran his hands over her arms and legs, checking her for injuries. "Are you alright?" he asked, already feeling the new knot on the side of her head. "That damned motherfucker! I'm going to kill him. Slowly."

Hutch hugged her tight against his chest. She could hear the rapid thump of his heart. The pressure of his chest against her aching head helped ease the pain a little.

"I'm fine," she tried to assure him but ruined it when she winced. Ouch! Her head was throbbing.

"Don't lie to me," he growled.

"Fine, maybe my head hurts a little." Hopefully, he didn't see her cross her fingers. Her head was killing her.

"That's it. I'm taking you to the hospital to make sure you don't have a concussion."

"No! I hate hospitals. I don't even like doctors. I'm fine, I promise."

"I'm not risking your health, little girl. I'll be with you. Doc can meet us there." He put her back in her seat and fastened the seatbelt.

"You can't just order a doctor to treat me," she said. Holy headaches, she wished the world would stop spinning. Her stomach lurched. "I's gonna be sick. Daddy!" she wailed.

Hutch pulled over. She unlatched her harness and flung open the door just in time. Hutch stood beside her, holding her hair back and telling her she'd be okay.

She hated throwing up. Hated it.

When she had nothing left to throw up, he lifted her back into her seat and strapped her in. First scanning the area around them, he rounded the truck and pulled back onto the road. "I'm sorry, Peaches. Just close your eyes. Daddy will have us there in just a few minutes."

Closing her eyes did help. She managed to make it to the hospital without throwing up again.

HUTCH

"Georgia's cat scan is normal," Doc said. "She doesn't have a concussion. She should be fine after a few days of rest."

"Thanks, Doc," he said. The goose egg that had popped up on Georgia's head had nearly scared him to death. "Anything I need to do?"

"Wake her every two hours tonight to check her symptoms. I don't expect anything to worsen, but better to be safe. For the next several days, keep her quiet. And no television, phone, or reading. Nothing to strain her eyes and no hanky-panky. If anything changes, call me."

Hutch took a deep breath and forced himself to relax. As someone who had patched him up many times at Sabre, Hutch trusted his friend as a doctor. He also trusted him as a fellow Daddy. "Thanks again," he said.

Doc gave him a chin lift and studied Georgia's chart with the nurse standing behind him.

Hutch needed to get back to his girl. He knew the way her mind worked. She'd figure out a way to make it all her fault.

She was the best thing to ever happen to him. She was the center of his world, and she was going to stay there.

That sick motherfucker of an ex had almost taken her from him today. Twice. That guy needed to be six feet under.

He had contacted Reid about the car that tried to run them off the road. The vehicle hadn't had a license plate, and the windows had been blacked out.

Georgia didn't recognize the car, either, but that didn't mean anything. People like Jemison could buy cars as effortlessly as they bought coffee. At least they had a car to look for. If it was in Darling, they'd find it.

There had been no relevant fingerprints in the shop or on the note. But this guy was getting bolder. Hutch didn't care why. He just knew Jarrod would fuck up soon, and he would be there to take him down.

He stepped into Georgia's hospital room and watched her sleep. His poor little girl had had a hard day. He was failing miserably at protecting her, but that was going to change.

Hutch hit the second person on his speed dial. Reid picked up on the first ring.

"Everything good? How's Georgia?" he asked.

"It's good. Doc says no concussion but to watch her for a few days. Listen, I need someone on Georgia when I'm not with her."

"You tell us when you need someone to cover her, and we're on it."

That was what Sabre did. They had each other's backs. Always had, always would.

Reid kept talking. "We protect other people every day. We're damn sure going to protect our own. She's yours. That makes her ours. She'd have our protection whether you asked or not."

"Thanks, man. I owe you."

"You never owe a brother. I'll let you know if I find out anything about the car. Later."

Georgia shifted to face him. "Right. I need to see about Georgia. Later," Hutch said, ending the call and focusing on Georgia. "Hey there, little girl. You ready to go home?"

Her eyes darted away at his words. "Um, yes," she said. "You could have been hurt tonight or even killed." Tears streamed down her beautiful face. "I should leave, but I don't think I can. I'd miss you so much. I-"

He put a finger to her lips. His girl's heart was as big as the sky, and it belonged to him.

"First of all, I wouldn't let you leave. And that's an extra ten smacks for even considering it. I love you. Losing you would kill me."

"But—" She tried to interrupt, but he held his finger over her lips.

"I'll keep you safe. That's what Daddies do. But not only me. Everyone at Sabre would lay down their lives to protect you. We'll catch Jemison."

"I don't even know why Jarrod wants me. He didn't like me at all when I was with him."

"You're harder to get over than you think, Peaches. But I'm not sure this is about you. Maybe it's about his losing control. Maybe it's something else. I don't know, and I don't care. What matters is stopping him."

"You're sure I'm not too much trouble?" She wouldn't meet his eyes.

"Look at me, little girl. I love looking after you. I love spoiling you and spanking you." He cupped her cheeks. "I love you, Peaches."

"I love you, too, Daddy," she said.

Hutch wrapped his arms around her. "Now, can we go home?"

She beamed at him and nodded. "Yes, Daddy. Let's go home."

CHAPTER 29

Georgia sat at the kitchen island, concentrating on the unicorn scratch art book Hutch had given her. She loved the rainbow colors she could uncover.

Thank goodness she was finally up and about. He'd insisted she spend the past three days resting in bed. Boring!

"You okay, little girl? You tell me if you feel dizzy. Understood?"

"I'm fine, Daddy! I haven't felt dizzy or even had a headache for two days."

Hutch set a plate of sausages and pancakes shaped like dinosaurs in front of her. "You're fine, huh?"

Uh-oh. He had that sneaky tone he sometimes used that usually didn't mean good things for her.

"Um… yes, Daddy." She had a bad feeling about the look in his eye. Suddenly, her plate consumed all her attention. She ate as slowly as possible, but eventually, her plate was empty. "Boy, those pancakes were tasty! Can I have some more? You are the bestest Daddy in the whole world. I love you thiiiiiis much!" She stretched her arms as wide apart as she could.

"I love you, too, little girl, but I think you've had enough pancakes for today. Since you are feeling all better, it's time for us to have that discussion about your behavior at the street dance. I love you enough to make sure you understand how important it is to follow Daddy's rules. Especially those concerning your safety."

Her tummy sank at his words, but she was also relieved. How could she feel both those things at one time? Guilt was an icky feeling. It made her tummy hurt way worse than any old bump on the head.

She knew Daddy's code words. Discussion was another word for spanking. *Discussing* things wouldn't be fun, but it would help her heart.

"Ready?" he asked. At her nod, he took her hand and led her to the playroom.

"I'm sorry I scared everybody, Daddy. Especially you. I won't do anything like that ever again."

"I'm glad to hear that, little girl. Your safety is the most important thing in the world. Not taking it seriously will always get you a sore bottom."

He was right. And as much as she dreaded getting a spanking, she knew Hutch loved her.

Once in the playroom, he said, "Take off your pants and panties. Then I want your nose in your thinking corner. Bottom out, legs spread. I want you to think about what you did to earn this punishment and what you could have done differently."

When she was in the corner, she heard him open the cabinet door where he kept the implements. Darn! She'd known he would use more than his hand for this spanking, but hearing him rifle through the different things in that cabinet made the bees in her tummy buzz faster.

She wished she could think as well in the middle of things as she could in her thinking corner. She should have let Memphis get the cups. Then she wouldn't be about to get her bottom smacked. She sniffled as a tear ran down her cheek.

She waited patiently, but he didn't call her. The skin on her bottom tingled, and the bees in her tummy buzzed harder. After a forever long time, he said, "Come here, little girl."

She dragged her feet until she made it to him.

"You were very naughty, little girl. So, this is going to be a hard spanking. You need to understand I am serious about your safety. What did you think about in the corner?"

"That I should have stayed at the kiosk. I could have sent Memphis or waited and asked Deke to go with me. I shouldn't have disobeyed you and caused so much trouble." Getting those last words out was hard because her throat was tight with unshed tears.

"Thank you, little girl. We'll take care of this, and then all will be forgiven. Daddy will never mention it again, and those yucky guilt feelings will be gone. Now, over you go."

He guided her over one hard thigh. She stared at the pale planks and squeaked when he shifted her further over his knee, dropping her nose almost to the wooden floor. She could see each nail and gap between the boards. At least her hands were free, so she could brace herself instead of dangling over her Daddy's leg.

He placed his other leg behind her knees, holding her in place. That wasn't a good sign. How fast could killer bees buzz inside one tummy?

"Give me your hands, little one. Your bad choices were too dangerous, so I'm using your hairbrush. It's going to hurt, and I don't want to injure your fingers if you reach back."

So much for bracing herself. She grimaced but gave him her hands. Now she was doubly exposed and vulnerable, knowing she could do nothing to protect her bottom.

He wrapped his arm around her waist, gripping her hip. No

chance to escape the hard swats soon landing on her bare backside. She swallowed hard, feeling vulnerable and exposed.

She knew he would let her up if she said red and devise another punishment. But she also knew, deep down, that she needed this to get rid of the awful, heavy guilt. She deserved every swat for putting herself in such danger.

"Now, young lady, why are you over Daddy's knee, about to get your bottom spanked?"

She hated this part. Why did she have to say it out loud? He already knew the answers. Why couldn't he just punish her and get it over with?

"I put myself in danger, Daddy." She sniffled, aggravated that her nose was running already. Tears stung her eyes, and he hadn't even given her the first smack! She was in such trouble.

"And how exactly did you do that?" He rubbed the smooth back of the hairbrush in small circles over her bottom, causing goosebumps to dot her butt and thighs.

"I went to Books-N-Brews by myself."

"That's right. And what did Daddy tell you to do?" He continued to coax her misdeeds out of her. He knew she just wanted to take her spanking and get it over.

"To stay at the kiosk or stay with Deke."

"And why did Daddy tell you to do that?"

He was going to drag it all out of her. Her eyes burned even hotter. She sniffled again. "Because you wanted me to be safe," she said, her voice wobbly with emotion. Lectures made spankings so much worse.

"That's right." He lifted the brush from her backside, and she held her breath. "I'm not giving you a set number of smacks. This spanking will last until you've learned your lesson. I don't want to have to do this again."

"Yes, Daddy," she said.

Why hadn't she obeyed him? The skin on her bottom crawled with dread.

Her mind flashed back and forth between wishing he would change his mind and wanting him to hurry up. The waiting was worse than the spanking.

Then he began her spanking, and she realized she was wrong. Waiting was better. Waiting was fantastic. How had she always managed to forget how much spankings hurt?

The splat of the brush against her bottom rang through the air, and at first, she thought maybe it wouldn't be that bad. Then fire blossomed across the center of her right cheek, and the breath left her lungs in one silent huff of pain.

He had spanked her before, but not like this. This brush was gigantic. It hadn't looked as big as it felt when he had brushed her hair with it. Why did they even make brushes that big? It almost covered her one whole cheek when he smacked her bottom.

She sucked in a lungful of air, but before she could do anything else, he brought the hairbrush down again in the same spot. This time her breath escaped with a loud squeal. She strained against the hold he had on her wrists. "Ow! Daddy, stop! That hurts!"

"Then I'm doing it right. It's supposed to hurt. That way, you'll think twice before disobeying Daddy again."

He spanked her right cheek twice before switching sides. Her left cheek received the same treatment. He kept a steady pace, not too fast, not too slow. Of course, she had never had this bad a spanking before, so who was she to judge?

Why had she left the kiosk? Oh yes, she'd thought he wouldn't find out. But Daddies always find out.

Smack. Smack.

She'd thought she was so clever and brave. She was just being naughty. She hoped he didn't take it easy on her.

She didn't have to worry. The brush smacked over and over.

She tried to hold in her tears. Her feet scissored in the air, at least as high as she could get them with his leg behind her knee.

Smack. Smack. Smack.

"Ow! Oh! Daddy, Ow! I'm sorry. I'm really sorry!"

"I'm glad to hear that, naughty girl. This brush must be doing its job."

He kept right on paddling her rear. She would never be able to sit again because she wouldn't have a bottom to sit on. The sting grew into burning flames dancing all over her backside.

Daddy was right. It really, really hurt.

If he would just move around more, that might help.

"Wait, Daddy. Wait! Not there. Not the same spot!"

"Am I not doing it right? Here, let's see what I can do."

She would have wriggled away, but he held her firmly in place.

He began to smack lower.

She began to howl.

Twice to the right. Twice to the left. She couldn't hold back any longer and burst into tears.

"Now we're getting somewhere," he told her. "Will you stay with your bodyguard from now on?"

"Y-yes, Daddy. I promise," she sobbed.

"Do you promise to mind Daddy?"

"Yes, Daddy, I'm sorry!" she wailed. "I will mind you from now on! I pinky promise! Is anything stronger than a pinky promise? I'll do that, too! I'm soooorryyy!"

"Alright, little girl. Just a few more to ensure you remember every time you sit down."

Then he spanked lower where her bottom met her thighs. He gave her five smacks on each side. Thankfully, this time he went back and forth. She collapsed over his lap and sobbed.

The brush clattered to the floor, and he lifted her to sit on his thigh.

The denim of his jeans scratched against her battered skin. She winced, crying even louder—aching, gut-wrenching sobs. Her face was red and swollen, and her breath came in hitches.

Her Daddy didn't say anything. He just held her tight and rubbed her back.

As she cried, the tears washed away all the yucky feelings inside. The only thing left was peace and the security of knowing her Daddy loved her too much to let her jeopardize her life.

After a while, the feeling inside her changed. She squirmed on Daddy's lap to still the feeling growing between her thighs. How could her bottom hurt like the devil, and her pussy pulse with desire? That wasn't normal. She squirmed again, but the feeling only grew faster.

"What are you doing, little girl?" Hutch asked. "Did my girl get excited by her spanking?"

Thank goodness her face was already red. She bit her lip and nodded. "Does that mean something's wrong with me?"

"No, Peaches. If you squirm a little more, you'll find Daddy is turned on, too."

She looked down and saw his cock was hard and pressing against his zipper. That couldn't be comfortable.

"We could do something to help us both," she said, already planning what she would do.

He shook his head. "That's not the way it works. Little girls don't get to come after punishments."

She thought he'd say that. It always worked that way in her books. "But, Daddy, what about you?"

He rewarded her with a kiss on her forehead. "We'll worry about that later. Right now, I feel like cuddling with my little girl. How about some popcorn and a movie?"

It wasn't as good as playing big girl things, but spending time with her Daddy was always good.

"Can we watch the Powerpuff Girls Movie?"

"We'll watch whatever you want, sweet girl."

She threw her arms around his neck and gave him a tight hug. "I love you, Daddy."

"I love you, too, Peaches. Now let's go pop that popcorn."

CHAPTER 30

"Two fucking weeks, Deke." Hutch told Deke something he already knew. He loosened his grip so he wouldn't crack his phone. He'd traced down useless leads all day, and his patience was gone. "Two weeks since that fucker broke into the shop and hurt Georgia." Two weeks searching in every nook and cranny of this county and finding nothing.

"I know, man," Deke said. "He's here somewhere. But Jemison's office still swears he's in California, just conveniently unavailable to talk."

Jemison wasn't available because he wasn't there. He knew it. Hell, everyone knew it. They just needed to find him.

The Graceview Retreat Center was his best bet, but Nevada wouldn't let him search the property. She was running the center while her mother was away. But she swore she hadn't spoken to Jemison since delivering the flowers for him when Georgia moved back. Which they knew was a fucking lie since they had her on camera putting that damn note in the cauldron.

She was lying now, but he couldn't prove it. Well, he was done waiting for permission. He would search for himself that evening.

"I want that asshole, Deke."

"On it," Deke said and ended the call.

Hutch sighed. He was taking out his frustration on the wrong guys. His brothers at Sabre were doing everything they could.

It was his job to keep her safe. No one would hurt her again. Not Jemison. Not anyone. Ever.

He had no idea why Nevada was helping Jemison. She must hate Georgia a hell of a lot.

When he arrived at Books-N-Brews, he stopped to enjoy the view. Georgia was at the counter with Tazzy, looking at a brochure. His little girl was bouncing excitedly.

Tazzy was less enthusiastic but nodded whenever Georgia looked at her. What was his naughty girl up to now?

A few nights ago, he'd come into the shop after closing and almost had a heart attack. Georgia stood on a bar stool, teetering on top of the counter. She was attempting to change out a light over the bar.

He barely reached her before the stool tipped and crashed to the floor. He hadn't wasted words on needless explanations. Flipping her over a bar stool, he spanked her bottom long and hard, not caring who might see.

Then he'd broken his rule and fucked her, still bent over the barstool. They'd both come fast and hard. His girl might not like spankings, but they excited her.

The bell jingled as he entered the shop. Georgia looked up, her eyes rounding when she saw him. She raced down the hall leading to the office. Perfect. This conversation probably called for privacy anyway.

He gave a chin lift to Sawyer, letting him know he could leave. Daddy was on duty now.

Georgia peeked out the office door, ducking back inside when she saw him. As soon as he entered the office, she hid whatever she had in her hand behind her back.

She gazed at him with wide, oh-so-innocent eyes. "Hi, Daddy. What are you doing here?"

Oh, the never-ending joys of being a Daddy. Her creative ways of getting away with things kept him on his toes. He couldn't hold back a grin.

"Just here to give you a ride home, little girl. What are you hiding behind your back?"

"Behind my back? Nothing," she said, holding out first her right hand and then her left. "See, nothing at all." She trapped her bottom lip between her teeth.

Nothing from his girl could mean anything. He strolled back to the door and clicked the lock in place.

She let out an *eek* and ran, but not before he managed to grab the brochure she had been hiding. One glance at the paper and his head almost exploded.

He held it up as she stared with wide eyes. "This doesn't look like nothing, Peaches. This looks like a brochure for off-trail snowboarding. At night. In Vermont."

Georgia opened her mouth to speak but then closed it again.

"I thought we agreed you wouldn't work on your bucket list anymore, little girl."

Her face flushed bright red. "Just because I have the brochure doesn't mean I'm going to do it, Daddy." She scuffed her toe on the floor.

"Uh-huh, and if I look at the work schedule for," —He glanced at the date circled on the brochure— "the last weekend in November, I won't see that you and Tazzy have those days off?"

Her brows scrunched, and he could practically hear the wheels in her head turning to try and come up with a reasonable explanation.

She was so fucking cute.

She was also about to get her butt toasted.

"Have you ever been on a snowboard before, naughty girl?" He crossed toward her, and she scurried behind Vivi's desk.

"No, but they have lessons. How hard can it be?"

When he reached the desk, he stepped to the right and she countered by stepping the other way. He was fast losing his amusement. They were not playing chase around the desk.

"Snowboarding is dangerous. You could crash into a tree."

He took another step. She countered again until they faced each other at opposite ends of the desk. The desk wasn't as big as she thought.

He kept his tone mild. "It isn't something you do off-trail or at night." He leaned across the desk, grabbing her wrist and holding her until he made it around to her. He made no effort to hide his displeasure. "It is absolutely not something you do without your Daddy."

A tentative smile crossed her face. "Does that mean I can do it if you go with us?"

"Nice try," he said with a smirk. "No, that is not what it means."

Her face fell.

"We can discuss it. I happen to love snowboarding. But first, we're going to discuss your planning to do something like this without telling Daddy."

"But, Daddy, other people snowboard all the time."

"Maybe, but I am not their Daddy. I'm yours. Now, what do you think I'm going to say?"

She sighed and mumbled, "That I'm not supposed to do anything fun without permission."

"Come again?"

She faked a bright smile. "I said I'm not supposed to do anything dangerous without permission."

"Don't think I didn't hear what you said first. Did you ask permission?"

"No." She wouldn't meet his gaze.

"No, what, Little girl?"

"No, Daddy," she answered.

Loosing his grip on her wrist, he cupped her jaw and ran his thumb gently across her cheek. "Do you know what it would do to me if you got hurt? Especially that far away? Getting to you would take me hours, and I would be worried sick."

Georgia's bratty manner disappeared. She flung herself at him and wrapped her arms around his neck. "I'm sorry, Daddy! I didn't think about it that way."

"I know, Peaches. But you were planning to do something dangerous. And you hid it because it was wrong. What should Daddy do about that?"

She sniffled. "I don't want to say, Daddy."

"I think a punishment is in order, don't you?"

Georgia stared at his thighs and nodded, then looked up, horrified. "You can't spank me here, Daddy. Someone might hear."

"You picked the place when you chose to misbehave. If you don't want people to hear, don't break the rules in public. Besides, not all punishments are spanking. Daddies have lots of ways to remind little girls to behave." He crossed to a cabinet that held supplies, taking out a disposable glove and a bottle of almond oil.

Georgia watched him walk back toward her, her expression confused and worried. Good. That was just where he wanted her.

He brought the desk chair with him, patting his leg once he sat down. "Over you go," he said.

Her shoulders slumped, but she dutifully placed herself over his lap.

"I thought you weren't going to spank me," she whined.

"Did you?" he asked. "I never said that."

He couldn't help but grin as she squirmed. Maybe he had more of a sadist in him than he thought. Without a word, he lifted her skirt and pulled her panties off.

"Spread your legs, Peaches."

She immediately stilled. "Why?" she asked, her tone worried.

His lips twitched at her sass, but still brought his palm down in a sharp swat to her rear. "Is that what I want to hear?" he asked.

"I meant, yes, Daddy!"

"That's my good girl," he said. "I'm not going to spank you. But you may still have to try hard to keep quiet." He pulled on the glove and snapped it against his wrist. Next, he opened the bottle of almond oil, coating his finger and dribbling enough on her bottom hole to make it nice and slick.

"What do you— oh!" Georgia gasped as he pushed her legs further apart and tapped her now quivering little pucker hole. "Daddy, stop!"

She tried to wiggle off his lap. He pressed harder at the small of her back and lowered his aim to her sopping pussy. His finger easily slid inside, and he worked it in and out, paying particular attention to that sensitive spot that sent her to the edge of her control every time.

"Oh, Daddy, I... I thought this was punishment. That feels good."

He should feel sorry for what he was about to do, but he didn't. She could not continue risking her health in the name of adventure.

"That's right, dirty girl. You like Daddy's finger, don't you?"

Her "Yes, Daddy" came out as more of a moan.

At the first slight quiver of her pussy's inner walls, he pulled his finger back.

She stiffened at the loss of his touch. "No, Daddy. That's mean."

He returned to her bottom and once again tapped on her sensitive hole. Her pussy tightened at his touch, and she tried to bring her legs together.

"Oh no, naughty girl. You leave those luscious legs where I put them."

"But Daddy, I need to, um...."

"I know what you need to do. Listen to Daddy while he plays with this pretty pucker." He continued to tap as he spoke. "Why didn't you tell me you planned to snowboard at night in Vermont?"

When she didn't answer, he pressed his finger more firmly and circled her anus. He didn't penetrate her hole. Not yet.

Her faint screech came close to a sob. "Daddy, don't!"

He didn't release the pressure on her hole, but he did pause. "Are you using your safeword, naughty girl?"

He waited for her answer. Finally, she said, "No, Daddy. I deserve a punishment. I just didn't ever think it would be something like this."

"Good girl," he said. "Now, why didn't you tell me your plans?"

"Because I knew you'd say no," she answered.

He was proud of her honesty, even if he disapproved of her decision. He pressed the tip of his finger into her dark hole. "And why would Daddy tell you no?"

"Oooh, because you don't want me to get hurt."

"That's right," he said, pushing in further and continuing to rock his finger, helping her muscles relax.

She was so tight. His cock throbbed, and his finger was barely inside. One day he'd bury his cock balls deep in her back channel.

"Any other reasons?" he asked.

She sobbed again as he pushed his finger to the first knuckle. He knew his little girl's cries. She was sorry and worried about what was next. But she was also turned on. Her arousal had already made a dark spot on his jeans.

"Yes, Daddy. Oh. Oh. Daddy, please," she moaned.

Her breathing sped up, and perspiration covered her lower back. "What else, little girl?"

"I shouldn't go without you." Her words were breathy and rushed. "Daddy, I need… I don't know what I need. But, please."

She begged so prettily. "That's right. Now, will you plan to do dangerous things without talking to Daddy ever again?"

"No, Daddy, no. I promise I won't! Oh god, Daddy!"

"I'm glad to hear it, little girl. Let's finish up your punishment. This lesson needs to be memorable."

As her muscles relaxed, he pushed his finger all the way in and fucked her, slowly at first, then gaining speed. Before long, she met his thrusts, pushing back against his hand.

And that was when he pulled out of her bottom.

"Noooo!" she wailed. "Daddy, I need to—"

"I know what you need, naughty girl. But you don't get rewarded for bad behavior. You are not to touch your pussy. This pussy," he said, giving her pussy a light smack, "is off limits."

She whimpered but answered, "Yes, Daddy."

He set her back on her feet. "Now you may pull your panties up." Once she set herself to rights, he said, "I have something special planned for us to do when we get home."

"What is it, Daddy?"

"It's a surprise, but we need to hurry."

She beamed at him as he took her hand and headed for his truck.

GEORGIA

The flickering lights floating around her in the meadow left her breathless. She had seen lightning bugs before, but she'd never given them much thought. She'd certainly never chased after them with a glass jar.

It was the most magical thing Georgia had ever experienced. Bucket lists, it turned out, could contain more than dangerous adventures. She would treasure this memory forever.

She had someone who loved her. Someone who would do anything to make her happy.

He hadn't just taken her to a meadow to catch fireflies. No, he'd taken her on an adventure to another world. She had somehow arrived in a fantasy world full of sprites and fairies.

He even bought her a silver hooded cloak he said made her invisible to the fairies. She chased after the little floating lights for over an hour, with him helping and encouraging her.

Then he built a campfire, spread out a blanket, and pulled out a thermos of hot chocolate. He even brought marshmallows with edible glitter that shimmered in the firelight.

He wove a story of fairies cursed by a wicked witch to look like fireflies until they granted a wish to a princess. She wished on her jar of glowing creatures and released them into the woods. Then they cuddled on the blanket beside the fire and talked for hours.

About their future together.

The life they'd share.

It was perfect.

He went to all that trouble just for her. Because he loved her. Which was good because she could no longer imagine her world without him.

CHAPTER 31

Georgia busied herself at work, prepping the kitchen for the day. She needed a few minutes to herself after the night before. The text she'd gotten from Jarrod last night had been nasty.

For the life of her, she couldn't understand why. She hadn't taken anything valuable with her when she'd left. True, the pictures she had were damning. But everyone at his law firm already knew he'd been sleeping around.

That's how she'd found out about it. She'd overheard two of the wives laughing about it in the ladies' room at a law firm Christmas party.

He had ruined her peace at Books-N-Brews with his little stunt at Halloween. She'd always felt safe there, especially after all the security Hutch had installed, until then.

"Hey, what did that coffee pot ever do to you?" Tazzy asked as she carried an overstuffed trash bag to the back alley. Georgia jumped as the back door slammed shut behind her friend.

Georgia glanced down at the carafe she held. She'd forgotten she was holding it. "Sorry," she told the large pot. "It's not your fault I'm so jittery."

Hutch was on high alert, along with all the guys at Sabre. It put her on edge. A sudden pounding on the back door almost made her drop the glass carafe.

"Georgia! Open the door!" Tazzy called out to her through the locked door. "Hurry!"

What in the world?

"Tazzy," she called back as she placed the pot beside the sink. "You almost gave me a heart attack!"

Another thump had her racing to open the door for her friend. Guess she wasn't the only one whose nerves were stretched thin.

"Hurry!" Tazzy sounded strained.

"Alright, I'm coming! Hold your horses." She didn't have her key, so she punched in the code and opened the door. "What is all the fuss about?"

Tazzy's pale face was rigid with fear. A man wearing a mask was holding a gun to her head. Before Georgia could react, the man grabbed her and pulled her to the side.

She immediately began kicking and screaming, losing her grip on the door. It slammed shut, locking both Tazzy and her out in the alley.

A shot rang out, deafening her, and smoke sparked from the outside keypad. Now no one could open the door without a key. Tazzy screamed and covered her ears, crouching to the ground.

The man pointed his gun straight in Tazzy's face. Georgia barely had time to scream, "Run, get Deke!" before a sweet-smelling rag closed over her nose and mouth. She fought to push the rag away, but the man who held her was too strong.

Tazzy did as Georgia said. Where was Deke? Probably inside the coffee shop, unaware anything was wrong.

Hutch! She needed Hutch. Her Daddy would keep this man from hurting her.

The burning in her lungs forced her to suck in a deep breath of the rag's fumes.

The world began to spin as she fought. A fist banging against the door rumbled through the alley. Deke cursed and yelled out her name.

All she wanted was Hutch. She tried to call out to him, but everything went black.

HUTCH

Hutch's gut clenched when Deke's name lit up his phone. He answered the call and demanded, "What's wrong?"

"Somebody grabbed Georgia," Deke answered.

"What the fuck do you mean someone grabbed Georgia?" Hutch gripped the steering wheel tighter and floored the gas pedal. "Who?" But he knew.

"Jemison. But he wore a mask. I don't even know what he was driving, man. He parked outside the range of the cameras again."

"How did he get to her?" Shit. Shit! That fuckwad had his little girl. Fuck!

He forced himself to listen to Deke.

"He used Tazzy. Grabbed her when she took some trash out and used her to get Georgia to open the door. The asshole shot the keypad and shorted out the door. By the time I reached the back, his truck was pulling out of the alley. He went right, but I couldn't get a plate number or shit-all else. The truck was black or dark blue. Damnit! That's all I got."

Fuck. Shit. Fuck!

He should never have left her at the shop. Not even with Deke.

Now that psycho had her, and Hutch had no idea where they were.

He gripped his phone and shouted, "Alert Sabre, the sheriff, and the state police. He might be trying to take her back to California.

Get someone on the airports, public and private. Someone needs to be searching the street cams." He took a breath. "We have to find her."

"We fucking will. Nothing is gonna happen to your little girl." Deke's voice didn't waiver.

A band of brothers, that was Sabre. They'd been in school together, enlisted together, and now took care of fuckers like Jemison together. Deke was right, they'd find her. They had to.

"Right," he said. Fuck.

He disconnected and called Georgia's phone. Hope flared in his chest when someone answered, only to crash when Tazzy said, "Hutch?"

He pushed back his rage long enough to get out a terse, "Yeah."

"Hutch," she said again, and he heard the tears in her voice.

"It's going to be alright, Taz. We'll find her." He needed to give her something to do, or she'd lose her mind worrying. "Keep Georgia's phone with you. If anyone calls, answer it. Write down who it is and what they say. Then you call me. You got that?"

"Okay, Hutch," she said. "Promise you'll find her?"

"Absolutely," he said. "I need to go, but I'll let you know when I have her back."

"Okay," she said again and then disconnected.

Shit. If Jemison did anything to his girl, the man would beg for death before Hutch finished with him. He was headed for the alley behind Books-N-Brews when Reid called.

"Anything?" he demanded.

"We got a direction from a city traffic cam," Reid said in a tight voice. "I think he's headed out to Graceview."

Hutch slammed on the brakes and turned toward Georgia's childhood home.

"I'll give you more when I have it." Reid broke the call before Hutch could answer.

Damn straight, they'd get her back. There was no other option. He had plans for his little girl that would take a lifetime.

He'd never hated living in the mountains before, but right now, he would give anything to live on the plains of the Midwest, where you could see miles in any direction.

Georgia's face was all he could see. Where the hell had Jemison taken her? Was she hurt? Scared? Did she know he was already looking for her? He'd save her if it was the last thing he did.

He had failed her. Had told her he would keep her safe and failed.

Fuck.

How had Jemison gotten so close?

His phone buzzed again. Deke.

"He drugged her," Deke said as soon as he answered the phone. "I found a cloth with chloroform a little way down the alley. There's no sign of a struggle except in front of the door. Only one set of prints in the alley."

Hutch tried to keep a handle on his rage. He was going to kill Jarrod Jemison when he found him. The ground would be red with the man's blood. He would never terrorize his little girl again.

Georgia

Georgia came to when she hit the floorboard of a truck. She winced but tried not to move. No sense alerting her captor.

"Jesus, be careful. Unless you plan to kill her before you get the information," a woman said.

Georgia froze. She might not know the man who took her, but she knew that voice.

Nevada.

What was Nevada doing here? If she'd been kidnapped, she'd be tied up in the back, too.

That meant Nevada was part of this. Whatever *this* was.

243

Georgia hadn't thought her sister could cause her any more pain. Turned out she was wrong. Betrayal ate its way through her.

"Don't go in the side entrance at Graceview," Nevada said. "Pull in the drive. We need to get Georgia into the manor house as quickly as possible. We don't want anyone to see her."

Georgia's heart sank. Graceview was the last place she wanted to go.

The driver took a sharp curve too fast and threw Georgia into the pickup's door. Jeez, she would look like a punching bag by the time she got out of the truck. They'd bound her hands with zip ties so she had no way to catch herself.

The driver slammed on the brakes to make the next curve, and Georgia again crashed into the back of the front seat, yelping in pain. So much for keeping them unaware she was awake.

Nevada peered down at her from the front seat, smirking. "You always were a klutz," she said. "And you," her sister added, turning on the driver. "You need to fire up one or two brain cells and figure a way out of this mess. Everyone in this freaking town loves Georgia. I don't know why. I told you to let me handle it."

"Just shut up. I know what I'm doing. If you'd handled it, I wouldn't be in the back hills of Tennessee," the man snarled. "Now shut the fuck up so I can think."

Georgia crawled onto the back seat. Something was wrong with the man's voice. It sounded strange, like he wore something to disguise it.

She looked at him and her heart stopped. She should have known. He wore that mask so she hadn't gotten a good look at him before. But she saw the scar on his wrist when he gripped the steering wheel.

Jarrod had surgery on his wrist that left a scar just like that. He thought it made him look tough.

Why had he grabbed her? Seriously, what could she have, other than those stupid pictures? Nothing that would be worth coming to Darling.

But whatever it was, Nevada was in on it.

She couldn't just sit back and let him do what he wanted to her. That was the old Georgia. Now she was a fearless adventurer.

A fearless adventurer who really, really wanted her Daddy.

"If you tell me what you want, I can help you. No one needs to get hurt," Georgia offered.

"You need to get hurt for all the trouble you've caused," Jarrod snarled. With that thing making his voice weird, he sounded like an angry frog.

Where was Hutch? Did he even know she had been kidnapped? If he did, he was already searching and wouldn't stop until he found her.

She pictured his handsome face, his strong hands, and how safe she was in his arms. She clung to the hope she would be back there soon.

When they got to Graceview, Jarrod skidded to a stop in front of the main house. Jumping out of the truck, he grabbed Georgia's arm tight enough to bruise. He ripped her from the back seat and shoved her toward the front door. "Get inside."

Black spots floated in her vision. She could hardly stand, much less walk.

"Hutch is going to kill you. You know that, right?" she told him.

"Not over a slut like you." He shoved at the small of her back, causing her to stumble. "No man will kill you but me. Now shut up and get inside." He grabbed her arm again and dragged her up the steps.

Pain lanced through her. "Stop it! You're hurting my arm!" she cried.

Jarrod shoved Georgia into a wingback chair beside the large stone fireplace.

Nevada barked out a humorless laugh. "I hear you like being

hurt. I know all about the men of Darling. Daddies, right? Perverts is more accurate. You love it when Hutch beats on you. You're as sick as the rest." Her voice grew more and more spiteful as she spoke.

Nevada warmed her hands by the fire. Unfortunately, she turned her back to Jarrod. Georgia could have told her. You never showed your back to a predator.

Jarrod prowled toward her sister and said, "I don't know. You could use a fat lip or two." Nevada turned back, but by then, it was too late. She must have seen something in Jarrod's eyes. She stepped back and held her arms out in front of her as if that would protect her.

Jarrod grabbed her by the shoulders. Nevada struggled against his hold, but Jarrod shook her so hard her chin almost hit her chest.

"You fucked up, and you want to blame me. All you had to do was get the fucking flash drive. How hard could it be? Georgia doesn't have the brains god gave a stump. Evidently, neither do you."

He shoved Nevada so hard she tripped. Georgia watched, help-less, as her sister fell, smacking her head against the stone fire-place. She landed on the floor and didn't move again.

Jarrod wasn't satisfied. He drew his gun and pointed it at Neva-da's chest.

"No!" Georgia screamed. "Don't shoot her!" She hated what Nevada had done. She wanted her to pay. But she didn't want her dead.

Jarrod faced Georgia, his smile serpentine. "Why should you care? She's done nothing but stab you in the back."

Blood pooled underneath Nevada's head. Georgia searched for any sign of life. A wave of relief washed over her when Nevada's hand twitched. At least she was alive. Now they just had to stay that way until Hutch found her.

CHAPTER 32

Georgia watched her sister bleeding, unconscious on the floor. She needed help for Nevada but couldn't exactly get up and leave. All she could do was stall for time until her Daddy arrived.

"I have a solution, Jarrod. Sign the divorce papers, leave, and never contact me again."

Jarrod gave her that condescending smile he always did when trying to worm his way back into her good graces. "You don't want that. If you did, you wouldn't have stolen the flash drive. You knew I'd come after it. You're just punishing me for that last hook-up. I get it. I should have met her at her place instead of bringing her to our home."

They'd never had a home. She'd walked in on him, banging away at his latest. It was the best moment of her marriage. She'd finally gotten the push she needed to leave. She should send that woman a freaking bouquet.

Jarrod lowered his gun. He was in lawyer mode now, giving his closing argument to seal the deal. "You know you loved it. The house. The parties. The power."

He didn't know her at all. She'd hated everything about their life together. Jarrod was a vile man who lived a disgusting life. She'd never go back to that. Never.

Her life now was so different. Hutch would be there soon to take her back to the life she loved. Back to their cabin with her bicycle and her playroom. They'd chase fireflies and toast marsh-mallows. And dance.

Hutch would rescue her from her crazy rich ex who wanted his stupid, cheap flash drive.

What the heck? She'd shuffled dozens of them when she'd grabbed the one at the back of Jarrod's desk drawer. She never even thought he'd miss it. Why he cared so much about those pictures, she couldn't guess.

Were some of the women famous? She didn't recognize any of them. Maybe they were married to clients he had represented. Who knew?

Jarrod grabbed the collar of her shirt, lifting her from the chair and twisting the cloth until it choked her. "I want the drive you stole, you stupid cow," he yelled in that mechanical voice. Spittle dotted her cheek as he waved the gun in her face.

He twisted her collar even tighter, catching her skin. The pinch to her delicate flesh was excruciating. Tears stung her eyes, but she refused to let them fall.

"Are you hearing anything I'm saying?" he shouted.

"It's hard not to when you're screaming. You're hurting my neck," she cried. "Why do you want the pictures back?"

A brief look of confusion flashed through his eyes before they narrowed. "What the fuck are you talking about? What pictures?"

Now she was confused. If he wasn't after the pictures, what was this about? Exactly what was on that flash drive?

Jarrod wasn't focused on her anymore. "If they find out I have a copy, I'm dead. You have no idea what they're capable of."

Not likely, since she didn't know who *they* were.

He dropped her collar and paced, running his hands through his hair and leaving it a tangled mess. He kept talking, but he wasn't talking to her anymore. He had forgotten her completely. "I have to get it back. I've been here too long. They are going to suspect something. If they do, they'll gut me like a fish."

She slid toward the door. Maybe she could make it out before he saw her. But her second step had his gaze swinging back to her. He strode toward her, gun raised, and fisted her hair. "I'll tell you this. I won't die before I kill you and that asshole you hooked up with. Now tell me where it is." He shoved her so hard she toppled to the floor, landing hard on her bottom.

She risked a glance out the window as she struggled to her feet. Hutch wasn't there. Not yet. She could keep Jarrod talking a little longer, but wasn't sure how much time was left. He was about to dive into the deep end of the crazy pool.

"Give me that fucking drive!"

"You keep saying that. Are you telling me all this is about the pictures I downloaded of you cheating on me? I only took them to prove my grounds for divorce. I'm not showing them to anyone. I'll return the drive when you sign the divorce papers."

How did he even know she had copied the pictures? She didn't know computers, but she didn't think that was something obvious.

"I don't care about the fucking pictures, Georgia. No one cares about the fucking pictures. Who'd expect me to be faithful to you? Look at you. You're a walking poster child for plastic surgery. That drive has important information on it about a lot of other powerful families. They will kill me and anyone else with access to that information. These people are brutal and relentless."

Georgia stared at Jarrod in horror. He'd been collecting information about his clients. Why? To steal from them? Blackmail them?

Her blood ran cold. What if those powerful families found out she had the drive? They would come after her. But not just her. They'd come for everyone she loved. Everyone was in danger because of her.

Jarrod's desperation rang as clear as a brass bell. "These people have powerful connections all over the world. I'm getting that drive back. And I'll kill whoever I have to in order to get it."

"What kind of people do you represent? I thought you handled movie stars and tech gurus."

"It doesn't matter." He pointed the gun right in her face. "What matters is that I get it back. I've looked everywhere," he said. "I searched here, that shop where you work, and your apartment. The only place left is Hutchinson's cabin."

That seemed to give him an idea. He yanked her toward him, forcing her head back so far she thought her neck would snap. "Give me your phone," he demanded. "Now!"

She didn't move fast enough, so he shook her and screamed, "NOW!"

The look in his eyes sent chills racing down her spine. Yep, he was swimming in crazy now.

"I can't," she gasped. "I dropped it when you grabbed me."

"Jesus," he said. "You're useless."

He let go of her and dug his knife from his pocket. When he sliced through the zip tie binding her wrists, arrows of icy hot pain shot through her hands. She couldn't move them at all.

He held out the phone and said, "Put in Hutchinson's number."

"No." She wasn't about to bring her Daddy into Jarrod's trap.

Jarrod dropped the knife, then slapped her so hard her head rocked to the side. Fire lanced over her battered cheek. He said something, but she couldn't hear over the ringing in her ears.

He fisted her hair again and twisted her back to face him. "I won't ask you again. Tell me his fucking number or Nevada is dead." She didn't doubt he was serious. With no other option, she called out her Daddy's number.

He punched in the number and held the phone to her. "Call Hutchinson."

She wanted her Daddy to rescue her and then carry her to safety. But that wasn't what would happen. If he came to Grace-view, Jarrod would kill him.

Jarrod didn't want her. He didn't even like her. But the thought of her being happy with anyone else drove him crazy. He would punish her by taking the man she loved.

"Hutch won't be able to find where I hid the drive even if I tell him. Let me get it. I'll come right back, I swear. Then you can take it and leave." And without hurting her Daddy, she added to herself.

He ground the gun into her temple. Hard.

"I'm not as stupid as you, Georgia. Unless you want me to shoot your sister, make the damn call!"

Having no other choice, she made the call. Her hands shook so badly she almost dropped it.

As soon as Hutch answered, the tears spilled from her eyes and traced down her cheeks. She had to warn him. "It's a trap, Daddy. Don't listen to him. He—" She broke off with a cry of pain when Jarrod swung the hand that held the gun and struck the side of her head.

The force of the blow drove her back into the chair. Her entire head throbbed with pain. Hutch screamed her name through the phone. She pressed her hand to her face and felt the wetness but didn't know if it was blood or tears. Jarrod leveled the gun at her and stared at her with vicious eyes as he spoke.

"Listen to me, Hutchinson. You will do exactly what I say, you wife-stealing motherfucker. I know who you are. I know all about your little saber tooth kitten crew. You think you know how to cause pain? You don't, but I do. I'll break every bone in Georgia's fucking body and make you watch. Then I'll start on you!"

Georgia heard Hutch cursing from the other end of the call.

"Shut up," Jarrod cut in. "You aren't going to do shit other than what I tell you to. You have one chance to keep Georgia alive. She took something of mine, and I want it back. She will tell you where it is, and you will bring it to me like a good little boy. She's already going to pay for warning you. The longer it takes you, the longer I have to play. When I have it, I disappear, and Georgia remains relatively unharmed. Understand?"

Jarrod put the phone on speaker in time for her to hear Hutch demand, "What the fuck do you want?"

Jarrod snorted. "Not so in control now, are you? Georgia, tell him where to find the drive," he said and shoved the phone in her face.

Her face ached so badly she wasn't sure she could talk. She tried to take a deep breath, but it hitched with her tears. She no longer cared that Jarrod was listening. If this was the last time she could talk to Hutch, she would make sure he knew what he meant to her. "D-daddy?"

"I'm right here, Peaches. I'm going to be there soon. It's going to be alright, I promise. Do you believe me?"

She nodded, then remembered he couldn't see her. "I believe you," she said. "I love you, Daddy. You are the best Daddy in the whole world. If anything happens, I wanted you to know–"

Hutch cut her off before she could say more. "You stop that right now, little girl. Tell me what you want me to know when we get home tonight. I'm coming, but I need to know what Jemison wants and where to find it."

When her Daddy used his stern voice, she knew he meant what he said. "Okay, Daddy. When I left Jarrod, I used a flash drive to download some pictures. He says there was important stuff on it, and he wants it back."

"You are doing so good, sweet girl. I'll get the drive. Where is it? Can you tell Daddy?"

She glanced past the gun Jarrod held near her face and saw

Nevada awake. Not that she could do anything helpful, but at least she wasn't dead.

"I hid it inside Penny's collar," she told him.

"That was a great hiding place, little girl. No wonder he couldn't find it. You outsmarted him. I'll get it, and be there soon. Can you hold on until Daddy gets there?"

Georgia nodded again before tacking on a wobbly, "Yes, Daddy."

"That's my brave girl," he said. "Is Jemison still close?"

"Yes, and Nevada is here, too. But he hurt her," she repeated. "You're still on speaker."

"Thank you, sweetness," he said gently. Georgia couldn't hold back a smile.

Then his tone changed. Badass Daddy was back. "You listen to me, you sack of shit. I'm going to make you wish you'd never been born. And if there is even one mark on her, you only think you know the meaning of pain. I will make your pain last for months before I let you die."

Jarrod paled. And with that parting shot, the call went dead.

CHAPTER 33

*H*utch might as well have been steering a wagon with how long it took to reach Graceview. He was driving through quicksand. At least, that was how it felt.

When Georgia called him, he had been on the road. He'd headed straight to his cabin after the flash drive. He couldn't believe it was hiding in her stuffed unicorn's collar all this time.

His mind kept playing through all she'd been through. Jemison had fucking drugged her. Kidnapped her. Hit her. He was a dead man walking.

He could let his rage have control once his little girl was safe at home in his bed where she belonged. When she was safe, Jarrod Jemison would pay for every second he had spent abusing his girl for the past eight years.

That Jarrod would be less than alive when he was done went without saying. It was just a matter of how long Hutch would draw it out. The terror that filled Georgia's voice on the phone ensured Jarrod would live in pain for a long, long time.

He'd almost lost the grip on his sanity when she started telling him how much she loved him. He always loved hearing that, but not when it was her saying goodbye. His heart nearly shattered at the fear and pain in her voice.

Reid called, and Hutch started right in before Reid could speak. "He has her. That fuckwad has Georgia. He wants some fucking flash drive back."

"Fuck," Reid said. "Jemison?"

"Of course, it's Jemison. He's wearing a vocal modulator, but it's him. I don't know what else is on that drive besides pictures, but it must be bad for him to take this big a risk. He told me to get it and bring it to him. Said he'd leave when he had it, and no one would get hurt."

"You don't believe that, right?"

"Fuck, no. He thinks I'm coming alone. He knows about Sabre. But I'll bet he doesn't know all the entrance points at Graceview. We need a plan." He took a breath. Even then, it was hard to keep his voice steady. "He hurt her, man. Punched her or something while I was on the fucking phone, and there was shit I could do to stop it."

"Fuck. Is she okay?"

She'd better be, or Jemison's life would be over much quicker than he deserved. Rage shot adrenaline through his system, making it hard for him to focus. He had to lock that shit down. Strategy now, wrath later. His little girl needed him.

"Hutch, is she okay?" Reid repeated.

"Fuck no," he snapped. "But she's trying to be strong. I want her safe, and I want him dead."

"He will be. The entire team is with me, armed and ready. We brought enough supplies to throw Jemison a real party," Reid said. "Now, let's nail down the plan."

Fifteen minutes later, Hutch pulled up at Graceview. He scanned the area but didn't see anyone.

That was good. If he couldn't see Sabre, knowing they were there, Jemison sure as shit wouldn't see them.

He palmed the flash drive, resisting the desire to crush it. This fucking piece of shit was the reason Jemison had put Georgia through hell.

Sawyer wanted him to give Jarrod a dummy drive so they could figure out what was important enough to lure Jarrod to Tennessee in person. No one believed it was a few compromising pictures.

But Georgia wasn't Sawyer's woman. Hutch had refused to swap the drive out. Jemison might try to verify it was the right one. Hutch wasn't putting Georgia in even more danger.

He'd met Sawyer on the way, allowing him five minutes to download the drive onto his laptop. Hutch's job was to keep Jemison occupied while Sabre got into position. Then they'd take him down.

Georgia

Georgia heard the squeal of tires out front and knew Hutch was there. She couldn't see him, but the knowledge settled her. She said a prayer to whoever might be listening to keep him safe.

Jarrod grabbed her arm when she raced toward the front door. He collared her throat in the crook of his arm, holding her in front of him like a shield. Pain stabbed her side when he jabbed his gun into her ribs.

"Don't try anything stupid," he said in that mechanical voice that would haunt her for years to come. If she had years to come, that was.

He forced her to the fireplace, where Nevada still lay on the floor. Her sister groaned but didn't move. At least Jarrod had allowed Georgia to put a pillow under her head.

The front door opened, and Hutch's footsteps echoed in the foyer. She stared at the archway opening he would walk through any second. Could she throw her elbow into Jarrod's stomach to give Hutch a chance to grab him? As if Jarrod read her mind, he squeezed his arm tighter around her neck, cutting off her air.

Hutch walked through the arch and his eyes went straight to her. His jaw clenched when he saw the hold Jarrod had around her neck.

"You make a habit of hiding behind women like a pussy, Jemison?"

"Only when the people in front of me want me dead," Jarrod answered, but he eased off the pressure enough for her to breathe.

Hutch looked straight at her. "You alright, little girl?" he asked her.

She tried to answer but couldn't force words past the arm choking her. She settled for nodding.

"It would almost be worth letting her breathe to hear her call you Daddy again," Jarrod said with a sneer. "Nevada was right. You are one sick fuck. Been into kids all your life? Or is it a recent thing?"

Hutch didn't rise to the bait. He merely held out the flash drive. "I have the flash drive. We can do an even swap. You give me Georgia. I'll give you the drive."

"Right," Jarrod said. "Because I was born yesterday. You toss the drive on that wingback chair. Once I verify it's the real deal, I'll give you my wife."

She could feel the vibration of his words against her back. She couldn't miss the emphasis he put on the words *my wife*. Her breath caught as he squeezed her throat tighter. She pushed against him for air, but it didn't help.

Hutch strode toward her, but froze when Jarrod shoved the gun into her ribs hard enough to make her yelp. She caught her lips between her teeth so she wouldn't distract her Daddy.

He was so calm, like he did this stuff all the time. She would have been impressed if she wasn't so scared.

"Same time then," Hutch offered. "We'll meet in the middle and exchange on three."

Jarrod hesitated but said, "Fine. I have the gun and the girl. Don't try anything stupid, and this will be over before you know it. You do try something, she dies."

Jarrod may be using something to disguise his voice, but she could still tell when he was nervous. He was also a dirty double-crosser, coiled like a snake about to strike. He'd shoot Hutch in a heartbeat if he knew it wouldn't damage the flash drive.

That couldn't happen.

She signaled her Daddy with her eyes, and he responded with a slight shake.

She mouthed, "I'm sorry."

Hutch broke into a run and yelled, "Now!" Hutch yelled toward the window, before adding, "Run, Peaches. Run!"

Everything happened at once.

A huge man dressed in camo kicked in the door to the dining room to their left. Two more crashed in through each window. Another raced through the archway and dropped a canister on the floor that started spinning around and shooting out smoke that stung her eyes.

Without pausing to think, she kicked back as hard as she could, connecting with Jarrod's knee. Jarrod screamed in pain and shoved her away. He raised the gun, aiming straight at Hutch's chest.

Georgia didn't think. She reacted. Leaping at Hutch, she crashed into him. Her momentum took them to the floor just like she'd planned. Sort of.

Shots glanced around the room as Hutch rolled on top of her. As he did, pain blazed through Georgia's ribs. Jeepers, he was heavy. She screamed into Hutch's neck.

He pinned her beneath his massive body, shielding her from the bullets streaking in all directions.

Then, as quickly as it had started, silence settled over the room.

Hutch pushed up on an elbow and scowled down at her. "Georgia, baby, you are in so much trouble, little girl," he said, his voice a low rumble of fury.

Hopefully, it wasn't aimed at her. She'd been saving him. Thank goodness Jarrod had missed. A wave of dizziness swept over her. She'd read about people in shock. This must be what it felt like.

"Are you alright?" Hutch repeated, cupping her face. His fury melted into concern. "I didn't hurt you when I landed on you, did I?"

That was sweet. She tried to smile at him, but her face was so tired. She was tired all over.

"No, Daddy," she said, but her words came out slurred. "I don't hurt at all. But I think the floor next to us got shot. I felt a piece hit my side. Isn't that silly?"

She ran her hand down her side to show her Daddy where the floor had hit her. Her arm wasn't cooperating too well. She gave up and reached up to touch his face. For some reason, there was red on her hand. She accidentally smeared some of it on his cheek.

And then she fainted.

Hutch

Hutch looked down at his girl, trying to shift his weight off her. She wasn't panicking, which was good. But she had an odd smile on her face.

"Georgia, baby," he said, cupping her face. "You are in so much trouble, little girl." He tried to scowl so she would know he was serious, but he was so damn relieved she was alright he didn't think he pulled it off.

He looked more closely at her eyes. They weren't quite focused. Had she hit her head? She was saying something, but he couldn't concentrate on her words. He was too busy watching her. Something about her movements was off. She was moving like she was underwater.

"Are you alright?" he asked, tilting her head to get a better look at her pupils. "I didn't hurt you when I landed on you, did I?"

She said something, but her words slurred together. He held up three fingers. "How many fingers am I holding up, little girl?"

She raised her hand and tried to grab his fingers but missed and grabbed his cheek. Had she even seen his fingers?

His heart kicked into high gear. Something wasn't right.

Realizing his cheek was wet, he wiped his hand across it. It came away red. He grabbed her hand, and blood covered it, too.

Her blood.

He shot up to his knees, scanning her body. Her right side was wet and bright red. So, so red.

"Georgia!" he shouted. He put a finger to her neck. She had a pulse, but it was faster than it should be. "Georgia, Peaches. Shit! Georgia's shot!"

Then things moved in slow motion. Men gathered around, stripping off her top and putting pressure on her wound. He could see the small wound across her ribs.

Nevada was yelling in the background, demanding to be released. He had not one fuck to give about Georgia's sister.

He bent down to his little girl's face and brushed her hair back. His heart was going to fucking detonate. It was good that he was already sitting down because his legs wouldn't have held him up.

"Fuck! Georgia, Peaches, hold on. Daddy's got you. It's going to be okay. Fuck, we have to get her to the hospital. She's losing blood."

He needed to calm down and focus on her. She didn't need him losing his shit. She needed his strength.

He pushed to his feet, lifting her with him. Her arms dangled down by her sides, and her head lolled back.

Shit! Fuck! Shit! He would reach down Jemison's throat and pull his balls out through his mouth.

Racing to his truck, he tried not to jostle her. Deke yanked open his door then ran to the driver's side. Hutch climbed in and held Georgia in his arms as Deke hauled ass to the hospital.

Why the fuck had he agreed to meet Jemison out at Graceview? He should have told that cocksucker to drive into town and meet him at Books-N-Brews. They were too far away from the hospital.

"Hurry up," he yelled at Deke.

Deke didn't take his eyes off the road. "It won't do her any good if I drive off the side of the mountain."

Hutch didn't have time for logic. "Just get us there."

Yeah, he was being an ass. He'd apologize later. Georgia was as pale as a ghost. A sheen of sweat coated her whole body.

He couldn't lose her. Not now. Not ever. His training told him she'd be okay. The bullet had sliced along her right side. She'd need some stitches and a lot of rest.

The Daddy in him did not give the first fuck about his training. His little girl was hurt. There was nothing he could do except hold her and get her to the hospital. "Does Doc know we're coming?"

"Yes," Deke said, his voice as tight as Hutch's. "Reid called him. He's already there."

She whimpered in his arms. "Hold on, Peaches," he said. "Daddy's here. Just hold on."

He'd never been this scared in his life. He yelled at Deke again. "Hurry the fuck up!"

CHAPTER 34

*S*omething was beeping, and voices spoke in soft hums. That was Georgia's first clue that something was different. And the smell. There was an antiseptic smell that stung her nose.

She should open her eyes, but she didn't want to. It sounded scary. Given her life recently, that could mean almost anything.

A smooth, gentle hand held hers. She could test the waters to see whose it was. She squeezed the hand to see what would happen and held her breath.

A new, higher-pitched beep sounded, and she dropped the hand.

"Breathe, sweet girl," a warm, familiar voice said. But not the one she wanted to hear.

Slowly, she blinked open her eyes and found she was in a hospital bed. The walls were painted pastel pink, and soft evening light filtered through a large window.

Turning her head, she attempted a smile. Vivi stood by her bed, a worried expression on her pale face. She reached out, and the older woman retook her hand. Warmth filled her at her fairy grandmother's presence. But as much as Georgia loved her, hers was not the face she wanted to see most.

A glance around the room caused her heart to sink. Her Daddy wasn't there.

She'd known that eventually, he'd realize she was too much trouble and find a Little who would always make the right choices. She didn't have the strength to stop the tears that traced their way down her cheeks. Her ribs hurt, and she missed Hutch already.

"There now," Vivi said. "None of that. You're going to be fine. You had a big scare, but it's over now. You were very brave, my precious girl. I'm proud of you. But you took ten years off my life, child. Don't ever do anything like that again."

"I won't," Georgia promised. She couldn't because she no longer had a Daddy. There was no one to save. The medicine was making her head feel funny.

"I'm fine now, Vivi. I just want to go home. Can you tell the nurse I want to leave?"

"She absolutely cannot," a deep voice stated.

Her breath caught in her throat. Hutch stood in the doorway, fists planted on his hips. His frown let her know just how he felt about her question.

"You're here," she said, stating the obvious.

Confusion crossed his face as he walked over to her bedside. "Of course, I'm here, little girl. Where else would I be?"

"I don't know. I woke up, and you weren't here." Even she heard the accusation in her voice. "I thought you decided I was too much trouble."

His brows shot up. "I'll never decide you are too much trouble." He leaned over, pressing a warm kiss to her forehead. Before he pulled away, he whispered in her ear. "I will, however, be having a discussion about little girls throwing themselves into the path of bullets as soon as you are better."

"Now that Hutch is back, I need to go check on the shop," Vivi said. "I am sorry to say all this drama has been good for business. The whole town wants to buy coffee and get the latest scoop."

Georgia smiled. "Well, at least something good came out of this mess."

Vivi scowled at her. "If I ever hear of such nonsense coming from your mouth again, I will wash it out with soap myself," she said.

"And then you will be standing in the corner with a very sore bottom," Hutch added. "You got me, naughty girl?"

Her eyes shot to Vivi, but she was only nodding in agreement.

Several sassy comebacks came to mind, but she said, "Sorry, Daddy. You're right."

Vivi patted her hand before heading to the door. "I'll be back as soon as I can. I was going to bring you a Samoa frappe, but after that comment, I'll have to think about it." With that parting shot, she left the room.

"I said I'm sorry," Georgia called to the slowly closing door. "Darn it! I love Samoa frappes."

"That's what happens to little girls who put themselves in dangerous situations," Hutch said. "How are you feeling?"

"Fine," she said automatically.

His eyes narrowed. "What is the rule about telling the truth? You're in the hospital, recovering from a gunshot wound. Do you want to try that answer again?"

She wanted to repeat that she was fine because she was. But one look at his face changed her mind. She could practically feel waves of worry and fatigue coming from him.

She placed her hand over his. "I know it's the meds they're pumping into me, but I'm not in pain. I'm sorry I worried you. I promise from now on to do whatever you say."

He stroked her cheek with the back of his fingers. "I love you, little girl. When you ran toward me as that dickwad was firing his

265

gun… Jesus, Peaches. The look on his face is going to give me nightmares the rest of my life."

"Jarrod shot me?" Holy moly! He'd shot her. That asshole!

"Yes, little one. Fucker. You don't remember getting shot?" he asked. When she shook her head, he prompted, "What do you remember?"

She tried to sit up, but a sharp pain cut through her side. "Ouch!" she yelped and stopped moving.

Hutch placed a hand on her shoulder and gently laid her back down. "Lie still, little one. You need to rest. If you move around, you'll reopen your wound."

She didn't want to do any of those things. Not lie back down. Not reopen her wound.

She wanted to go home and never leave again. If she had the energy, she would stomp her foot.

Apparently, getting shot made you grumpy.

She couldn't believe Jarrod had shot her. All she'd thought at that moment was not letting Jarrod hurt her Daddy. "Are you okay? Did he hurt you?"

She tried to push out of bed again to make sure he wasn't injured, but again the sharp pain in her side forced her to lie back down.

Hutch scowled down at her. "What did I just say, little girl? Lie still. Believe me, you do not want to add anything else to the things we will be discussing once you're better."

"I'm in trouble?" she asked as if she didn't know.

Of course, she was in trouble. She'd always known Jarrod was a jerkface. Now he'd gotten her in trouble with her Daddy. She should give him a piece of her mind.

"I'm going to stop those thoughts you're having right now. And yes, you're in trouble."

Tears stung her eyes. "I'm sorry, Daddy. I would never have

asked people to put themselves in danger. Especially you. I just never thought—mmph!"

Hutch cut her off with two fingers against her lips. "That's not why you're in trouble. The people here love you. You are in trouble because, instead of running when I told you to, you put yourself directly in the line of fire."

"But, Daddy, he was going to shoot you!" She couldn't just stand by and let that happen. Never in a million years.

She'd thought Jarrod wouldn't shoot if she were in the way. She should have known better.

"He might have tried, but he wouldn't have succeeded. And even if he had, I would rather he shoot me than harm you in any way. I love you. My job is dangerous at times. Your job is to stay safe so that I can do my job. Got me?"

Luckily, someone knocked on her door again. Deke walked into her room carrying *The Daily Nugget*. Thankful for a new topic of conversation, she asked, "What'cha got with you?"

Deke looked down at his hand as if he had forgotten he held anything. He frowned. "Nothing much. Just the latest edition of *The Daily Nugget*. Someone needs to talk to the woman that runs this rag. She spends way too much time in other people's business. Anyway, I came to make sure you're okay. This guy taking good care of you?" Deke asked, lifting his chin toward Hutch.

"I'm fi—." Hutch let out a low growl, so she quickly changed her answer to, "I mean, I'm better than I was."

A change of subject was definitely in order. "Did you catch Jarrod?" she asked Deke. "Is that why you're here? To tell us he's in jail?"

Deke didn't answer. Instead, he looked at Hutch.

Hutch took her hands in his. "He's not in jail, Georgia. But he will never threaten you again. When the smoke bombs went off, he tried to shoot his way out of the room." His eyes grew cold, and a strange look crossed his face when he told her, "He didn't survive the attempt."

His eyes searched hers as if he thought she would be upset at this news. Maybe she should be, but Jarrod had been an evil man. She suspected he was even worse than she knew.

Whatever was on that flash drive, he wanted back badly. She doubted it was anything good. And whatever it said about her, she was relieved she didn't have to worry about him showing up and hurting her or someone she loved ever again.

"Are you or the guys at Sabre Security in trouble?" she asked them.

The strained lines around his mouth and eyes relaxed at her question. "No, little girl. No one is in trouble except Nevada. She will have to face some tough questions about the part she played, but that's a worry for another day."

"Maybe if she has to face the consequences of her actions for once in her life, she will learn to be a better person," she said. She certainly hoped so.

There was a knock on the door, and a nurse came into the room. "We are seeing you too often, young lady," she said with a kind smile. She held up a small silver tray. "It's time for your medication," she said.

Georgia scrunched up her nose. "I don't want any medicine."

The nurse kept her smile as if she heard this all the time. "It will make you feel better."

"Don't care," she said. Boy, her Little wanted out. Big time. "It tastes yucky."

"We'll you're in luck. This medicine goes in your IV."

"Don't care," Georgia repeated. She crossed her arms so they would know she was serious.

"And that's my cue to leave," Deke said. "You be good, so you can get better. I won't have a good excuse to stay at Books-N-Brews all day until you get back to work." He grinned down at her, booped her nose, and lifted her chin toward Hutch. He slapped his thigh with his newspaper and said, "I think I'll go have a conversation with a certain nosy reporter." With that, he stalked out.

"He certainly knows how to make an exit," the nurse said, approaching Georgia's bedside. "Now, let's get your medicine taken care of."

"I don't want it," Georgia said again.

Hutch leaned close to her ear. "I'm sure the nurse can put that medicine in your bottom if you don't want to take it like a big girl."

Heat flushed Georgia's cheeks. Her Daddy looked down at her sternly.

Georgia darted a glance at the nurse and then shook her head.

"That's my good girl," Hutch said.

"It's gonna make me sleepy." She tried to keep the whine out of her voice. Tried and failed.

After she took her medicine, Hutch took both her hands in his. His touch sent a shiver of longing through her. She squirmed under the sheets. If only she were in her bed so there was something her Daddy could do about those feelings.

"Don't fight the medicine. You need plenty of rest to get better."

"I'm not tired," she said, but her eyelids were already growing heavy. Hutch smiled and shook his head.

"If you rest like a good girl, you should only have to stay here overnight," he told her.

Her heartbeat sped up, causing the monitor to beep faster. She hated hospitals. The thought of staying overnight by herself had her eyes burning again.

He'd told her many times to ask him for anything she needed. But he'd already done so much. Her stomach ached at the thought of the night stretching out before her.

Before she could stop herself, she blurted out, "Daddy, will you stay here with me?"

He smiled down at her. "Good girl asking for something you

need. You just let someone try to make me leave, little one. I already told the nurse I'm staying."

"I love you, Daddy," she said. The words weren't enough, but they were all she could come up with right then.

"I love you, too, Peaches. Tomorrow we'll go back to the cabin. I think you have earned some time in your playroom."

"That would be awesome," she said. She gave a huge yawn and blushed.

"Would you like me to read you a story?" he asked.

She nodded. "Here, Daddy." She patted the mattress beside her.

"I'm not sure that's a good idea, sweetie. But I'll pull my chair right next to the bed. How's that?"

She nodded again. He took a small book from a backpack someone had brought up earlier. The hum of his deep voice was hypnotic. She must have drifted off.

"You rest now," Hutch said, fingering her hair. "I'll be here when you wake up."

"Promise?"

He took her hand and hooked her little finger with his. "Pinky promise," he said. "I will always be here."

CHAPTER 35

*G*eorgia left the hospital with strict instructions to rest and take it slow until her follow-up appointment.

Hutch took the directives seriously. He didn't even let her walk from the truck to the cabin. No, he carried her bridal style to the playroom and laid her on the bed, insisting she remain there unless she had to go to the bathroom.

The first two days, he demanded she tell him so he could take her to the bathroom. He waited in the room for her to do her business and then carried her back to bed. She had never blushed so hard in her life.

On the third day, she earned lines for disrespect when she told him she didn't need his help in the bathroom. Actually, she pitched a fit. He still wanted to know when she needed to go. He walked with her, but stood outside the door at least after that.

Today was day five of her incarceration, as she'd labeled it the day before. If she didn't get out of this cabin, she would lose her ever-loving mind.

She stomped down the stairs in her warmest, footed pajamas,

boots, and hat. Hutch stood at the kitchen stove, cooking pancakes and bacon for breakfast. The aroma of fried bacon almost had her changing her mind about going outside.

Hutch frowned. "Where do you think you are going, little girl?"

"Just walking around the backyard for a few minutes," she said as if she did that every morning.

She headed for the door, only to be halted by a stern voice. "You are not going outside this early, Georgia Anne. Especially dressed like that. Now, if you eat your breakfast like a good girl, I'll take you outside when it warms up. We can walk, or you can play on the surprise I've been working on."

Momentarily distracted, she asked, "What kind of surprise?"

He smiled and said, "You'll see, but only if you're a good girl."

That reminded her of her quest for freedom.

"Please, Daddy. Just a short walk. I won't leave the yard. I need to get out of the cabin." She closed her eyes to pray for patience. "There isn't enough air in here. I'm suffocating!" She clutched at her throat and gasped for air.

She cracked one eye to see his reaction. Instead of convinced, he looked amused.

She tried bargaining. "Only for a few minutes. Pleeeeaaase???" She wasn't above begging.

He shook his head again. "Breakfast first. I made chocolate pancakes with chocolate chips. I even made peanut butter syrup. Once it warms up, we will go outside. Now go wash your hands and come sit in your chair."

Hmm. She did love pancakes. But she needed to get outside. "I'm not hungry."

Of course, her stomach picked that moment to growl like a bear coming out of hibernation. Hutch appeared not to have heard. She blew out a sigh of relief.

"I bet you'll change your mind when you see them on your plate. Now wash your hands and have a seat."

"Fine," she snapped and stomped toward the bathroom next to the backdoor.

"One of us is about to fix that attitude, young lady. It will be more comfortable for your bottom if it's you. But if you don't, Daddy will."

"Yes, Daddy," she said. At least, that was what her mouth said. Her brain was saying he was a giant overprotective grouch.

She told her hand to reach for the bathroom door. She really did. But her hand didn't listen. It wanted to be naughty and grabbed the backdoor instead.

One glance told her Hutch was busy plating the pancakes and bacon. She'd step right outside the backdoor for just a second. Her Daddy wouldn't even miss her. She'd take a couple of deep breaths, and then she'd feel better.

And if she accidentally got a peak at the surprise Daddy had for her, that wouldn't be her fault.

Quietly, she cracked open the door and slipped outside. The sun was just above the tips of the trees, skirting the edge of the backyard. She pulled in a breath and shivered.

Maybe she should have listened to Daddy. It was a little chilly. Freezing, actually. Her warmest pajamas weren't as warm as she thought.

Goosebumps prickled her body. Daddy's advice was looking better and better. She would sneak back inside and come out later when it warmed up. She turned around and ran smack into a hard chest.

She would have bounced off and landed on her bottom if her Daddy hadn't had such quick reflexes. She gripped his arms to hold herself in place. Then she peeked up at his face.

"Uh-oh."

"That about sums it up," Hutch said.

"Um... Hutch... I mean, Daddy. I was just coming back inside.

My hands didn't mind. I told them to open the bathroom door, and they decided to open the backdoor instead."

"I see." He covered one ear with his palm. "What do you know, now my hand has something to say. It says to smack your bottom until your hands get the message."

With that, he bent down and lifted her bridal style, carrying her back into the kitchen. He stopped at the ceramic crock beside the stove and picked out the largest wooden spoon.

"Daddy, you don't need that. I'll be a good girl from now on. I promise!" Her bottom was already clenching at the thought of that awful spoon.

"Yes, I imagine you will," he said. He pulled the cushion from one of the straight-back chairs and placed it on the table's edge. "You are still recovering, naughty girl, so use your safeword if this hurts your ribs. Prop up on your elbows to keep the pressure off your wound," he said.

He placed her tummy down on the cushion, making sure her feet could still reach the floor.

"I bought these drop-seated pajamas for situations just like this," he said. He unzipped the seat, and her bottom was exposed.

He planted his hand firmly on her lower back. No wriggling or kicking would get her out of her punishment.

He rubbed her bottom, making small circles with his large hand. The cool air on her exposed backside wasn't the only thing causing shivers to skitter across her bottom.

"Tell me, naughty girl, did you or did you not ask me if you could go outside before breakfast?"

"I don't think I specified before breakfast, Daddy—"

Smack!

His palm landed on the center of her right cheek.

"Owie! But that is what you meant. So, yes, Daddy. Um… what are you doing, Daddy?"

She stilled when his fingertips trailed lightly across her upper thighs. She liked that, and so did her pussy. It began to pulse and squeeze.

"I'll be asking the questions, little girl. When you asked to go outside, what did Daddy say?"

She was finding it hard to focus. "You, um… you said to wait until later. But, Daddy, I haven't been outside in forever!"

Smack! Smack!

"How long?" His wicked fingers returned to her thighs. With each pass, they traced closer to her princess parts.

"Well, it feels like forever. But maybe a week." Her voice was breathy, and if he didn't stop touching her like that, she would spontaneously combust.

He didn't stop. He moved even higher up her thigh. Soon he'd be touching her pussy. Her soaking wet pussy. She closed her eyes and tried to control her breathing.

"And why did Daddy tell you to stay inside?"

"You said it is too— eep!"

His finger brushed between the cheeks of her stinging bottom. She had to strain not to push her pussy into the pillow when his finger dipped between her thighs and brushed the opening to her core.

Her breath came in gasps and pants. She pushed her legs further apart, allowing him better access. As he stroked up and down her slit, a moan escaped her.

She had never experienced anything like this before. She raised her butt higher, meeting his fingers.

The hard cock against her thigh told her he was affected, too. God, this was so hot.

"Outside is too what, Peaches?" he asked. His voice was deep and rough. Oh yes, he was definitely affected, too.

"Too cold, Daddy," she said. "You said it was too cold."

"That's right, little girl. I did."

"Oh," she cried out when Hutch plunged one finger deep into her pussy. She pushed back against his hand, but he smacked her bottom hard, twice on each side.

"Be still, naughty girl. Daddy is in control now. You take what he gives you."

He was going to drive her crazy. His fingers were wicked. He pushed two of them deep inside her. Slowly. And drew them out just as slowly before plunging them back in a second time.

"Daddy," she moaned. "Daddy, please." She couldn't have told him please what.

She had no thoughts. All she could do was feel. He stopped and smacked her bottom every time she pushed back to meet his thrusts. The heat from each swat only drove her desire higher.

"Now, naughty girl, Daddy can't let you think disobeying him is acceptable. I think ten smacks should do the trick."

He pulled her thighs further apart.

"Daddy, what are you doing?" she asked and then screamed as he brought the wooden spoon down right on her pussy. "Oh, God!" she cried as he brought the spoon down again.

He set her pussy on fire. Not hard enough to harm, but hard enough to get her attention. Pain flared briefly with each smack, then morphed into pure heat.

Her pussy was sopping wet by the time he finished her punishment. Without a word, he shoved down his pants and drove deep inside her in one powerful thrust.

"You may not come without permission," he said, his voice all command.

He filled her completely, and his hips pressing against her hot ass only sent her higher. He pounded into her over and over until she was on the brink of coming apart.

"Daddy, I need to come," she said.

"Was that a question, little girl?" he answered.

"Please, Daddy. Please, can I come?"

"Not yet," he said, shifting to something inside her that felt so good she thought she might not be able to stop herself from falling over the edge. "Let's see if you've learned a lesson in obedience."

She begged and pleaded as he fucked her so hard she saw stars.

Just when she thought she couldn't hold on another second, he ground out, "Now, Peaches. Come for Daddy now."

And the world exploded.

She came so hard her knees would have buckled if he hadn't pressed his hips into her backside and held them there. She would have slipped, but his firm grasp held her in place.

It was mind-numbingly spectacular.

He threw his head back and cried out his release. It was the hottest thing she had ever heard. She wanted to come all over again.

"That was amazing, little girl," he said. "Hold still and let Daddy clean you up." He ran warm water over a cloth at the sink. When she was clean, he carried her up to the bedroom. She lay on the bed, tucked into his side, with his arms wrapped around her waist. She nestled into him and closed her eyes, utterly exhausted.

"I love you, Daddy," she whispered. "That was the most incredible thing ever."

She snuggled deeper into him, content to rest in his arms.

"Better than your bucket list?" he teased.

"Much better," she said.

"Good to know. I guess we'll have chocolate pancakes for lunch."

She should feel guilty. But what they did instead had been too fantastic. "I can help, Daddy," she offered.

"You sure can," he answered, then added, "Peaches, I want to make something perfectly clear."

Uh-oh. That was his ultra-serious tone of voice.

"Yes, Daddy?"

"The next time you intentionally disobey Daddy, the result will not be nearly as pleasant. Do you understand?"

Yikes!

"Yes, Daddy," she assured him. "There won't be a next time. I promise."

He smiled and kissed the tip of her nose. "Good."

CHAPTER 36

our weeks later...

Hutch sat over to the side and watched Georgia, bent over the counter in Books-N-Brews, concentrate on her latest attempt at latte art. It was nearing time for the Christmas menu, and she was trying to create a Santa hat.

Unlike Reid, who leaned over her shoulder, Hutch had the smarts to stay on the other side of the bar.

As if she read his mind, Georgia beamed at Reid and asked, "What do you think?"

Hutch almost spit his coffee all over the counter at the terrified expression on his friend's face. Reid threw him a deer in the head-lights look. Hutch just grinned and lifted an eyebrow.

Reid gazed into the cup Georgia held up to him. "That's... um... well, I don't have words. It's something else." His phone rang, and Hutch couldn't hold back a bark of laughter at the relief on Reid's face. He held up his phone to Georgia. "Sorry, gotta take this." Then he all but ran to the other side of the room.

"No worries," she called out after him, then skipped behind the counter. "I knew if I kept trying, I'd figure it out. Now I can help make lattes at the ThanksGathering next week."

Hutch's heart warmed. She got so much joy out of the simple things. When he could keep her mind off her bucket list, that was.

She had spent ten minutes standing bare-assed in the corner last night, sniffling and sporting a bright red bottom. He'd pulled her from a spring-fed swimming hole on the coldest day of the year, shivering and almost blue. Something about training for a polar bear swim in January. He'd been too angry to speak as he drove them back to the cabin, where he'd thawed out her ass with her wooden hairbrush.

Hopefully, he wouldn't have to deal with bucket list items for at least a few weeks.

"Hutch," Reid called from the fireplace and lifted his chin. His expression was ominous.

Reid wasted no time once Hutch got to his side. "That was Sawyer. We need to head over to Lowell's Garage. Somebody offed Billy Evans last night. Winnie found him just a little while ago. Ezra Harper caught the case, so we have an in with the Darling police."

Billy Evans was no one's favorite person. He was mean as a snake and cagey as fuck. Sabre swung by Lowell's whenever they could to check on Winnie.

"I told Sawyer to let Ezra know we wanted to check out the scene, too."

"Right," Hutch said. "Give me a sec to tell Georgia."

She leaned over the counter, concentrating on another cup. It gave him a spectacular view of her luscious ass. He grabbed her by her hips just to hear her squeal.

"I have to go, Peaches. There's trouble at Lowell's garage. I'll probably be gone a while."

Concern immediately filled her eyes. "Is Winnie okay? She

came by this morning for her usual Sugar Cookie Latte with Sprinkles. Tell her to call me if she needs anything."

Hutch nodded. "I'll do that."

His girl cared about everyone in her town. The shop depended on her more and more, which was good since Vivi wanted to move closer to her sister.

"I'll call you as soon as possible," he said. "We'll pick up takeout on the way home. This weekend we can go to That's Italian."

She hopped up and down and clapped her hands. It was still her favorite restaurant.

"Winnie was excited about finishing up a restoration she's been working on forever. She is so talented. Make sure to tell her to call me."

He gave her a chin lift as he left.

Winnie had been working every spare minute she had for him. She had done a total restoration on Georgia's truck. Oh, it was still neon pink with flowers. But now it had seat belts, airbags, mirrors, and everything else it needed to be safe. It also had heat and air conditioning, soft leather seats, and a charging port for her phone.

Hutch couldn't wait to give it to her. It was the perfect ride for his perfect girl.

It was also the perfect wedding gift. Hutch had bought a ring months ago. Then she'd been kidnapped and needed time for life to settle back down.

But he was ready to make her officially his. They could wait as long as she wanted for the wedding, but he wanted it known she was off the market.

His heart warmed as he pictured a life with her by his side. There was nothing he wanted more.

Reid was waiting outside. "Someone finally had enough of Billy and his shit. He was found dead this morning at the garage."

"Fuck. Who found him?" He was pretty sure he already knew the answer.

"Winona," Reid said, tension radiating off him in waves.

"Fuck!" Hutch swore again.

"On the ride out, we can talk about Jemison."

Hutch did not like the grim look on Reid's face.

"Sawyer didn't know how Winnie was doing," Reid said as if he couldn't hold the words in.

There was something in his tone that made Hutch glance at his friend. "I'd imagine she's pretty shaken up," he said. "Sawyer say how he died?"

Reid grunted. "Said somebody bludgeoned him to death."

"Fuck! And Winnie found him like that?"

Reid nodded. He stared out the window and changed the subject. "Sawyer finally cracked the encryptions on the flash drive. Jemison was one sick fucker. The women in the encrypted files were young. They were legal, but barely. But that's not the worst of it. The drive held several lists labeled as vendors, customers, and merchandise. The *merchandise* was girls. And I do mean girls, not women. This is seriously dark shit. We haven't sorted out the vendors and customers, but it makes sense they were sellers and buyers. But get this. Mara Donnelley's name was on the list."

Hutch clenched his jaw to hold his anger in check. "Which one?"

"Vendor. And before you ask, Jemison's name was on the vendor and customer lists. If it's what I think it is, things are about to get seriously ugly."

Reid had seen a lot. For him to say something was seriously dark did not bode well.

"So, if Georgia's mother was on the list, that means whatever this was, it was happening in Darling and California."

"Not was, brother. Is. Jemison was involved in human trafficking, which is sick enough. But if it's what we think, these women aren't being snatched off the streets. Their parents are selling them."

"You're shitting me," Hutch said. How could a parent do something so horrific to their own flesh and blood?

"Wish I was. It kills me to say this, but I think Georgia's mother was up to her ass in this mess. And I don't think Mara's disappearance was by accident. I think Jemison decided she was a liability. Maybe he threatened Nevada with the same thing."

It was all Hutch could do to keep his truck on the road. At least Georgia didn't know what her mother had done. Not yet, anyway. He was going to have to tell her at some point. Especially if her sister was a victim. He'd wait and see how their investigation into Nevada played out.

"You got the list of these assholes? These *vendors*?"

"Working on it. It's all encrypted. Sawyer will break it. You'll know as soon as we do."

Hutch didn't have time to ask more questions because they pulled up to Lowell's Garage. Yellow tape barriers were up around the whole area. Sabre and several law enforcement vehicles were already there.

Once he pulled a stop, Reid headed straight for Winona. He pulled her close, and she let him. Interesting. Reid put his arm around her shoulders and led her to the other side of the building.

Hutch found Ezra and got the go-ahead to look at the scene. It was gruesome, just like he'd expected. Whoever attacked Billy had done so with a vengeance.

He took pictures of everything and listened in when Reid questioned Winnie. She couldn't give them much. Once he'd done all he could do, Hutch headed back into town to pick up Georgia.

Reid stayed at the garage to 'collect more information.' The knowing glances exchanged between the other Sabre team told Hutch they hadn't bought that, either.

Georgia opened the door to her apartment before he even knocked. "Did you make sure it was me?" he demanded. The scene he'd just left was too fresh. His protective instincts were in overdrive.

"Of course, Daddy. I watched you walk across the shop and up the stairs on the security cameras." Georgia scanned his face. It must have given away more than he would have liked. "Are you alright?" she asked, worry clouding her eyes.

"I am now, little girl." With his hands on her shoulders, he backed her into the apartment.

Georgia wasn't ready to let it go. "What happened at the garage? Is Winnie okay?"

"Later. Right now, I want a kiss."

She smiled, and the beauty of it chased away some of the darkness of the past few hours.

He lowered his mouth to hers, kissing gently, then deepening it when she parted her lips for him. She tasted as sweet as silken honey. He rocked toward her, pressing his hard cock against her softness.

She pressed back and held him closer. He loved how she lit up for him when they made love, and her flames burned hot. He ran his hand under her shirt and cupped her breast, tweaking her nipple until it pebbled hard against his palm.

As much as he didn't want to, he pulled back. She hadn't eaten yet. He needed to feed his girl. He consoled himself with the knowledge it would give her energy for later.

His girl. She was everything he wanted. Everything he needed. Everything he ever would.

Pulling back, he asked, "Ready to go? We'll grab something to eat on the way home."

She stared at him for a moment, lips swollen from his kiss and eyes glazed with desire, then nodded. Her eyes glowed with happiness as she took his hand. "I never knew what home was until you," she said. "I love you so much, Daddy."

"I love you, too, Peaches," he said. He kissed her one last time and, pulling her toward the door, said, "Let's go home."

ABOUT THE AUTHOR

Cami Carlisle has always loved reading romances of all kinds. Now, she loves writing stories of playful, sassy heroines and the strong, dominant Daddies who love them, whether that means a trip to the toy store or a trip over their knee. Married to her own alpha Daddy, she loves creating worlds where everyone gets their happily ever after with 'a Little sweet' and 'a Little heat.' Make sure to follow her on social media and visit her website www.camicarlisle.com!

KEEP UP WITH CAMI!

Use the QR code below to sign up for my newsletter to keep up with the latest news and receive exclusive snippets, insights, cover reveals, updates, and much more!

BOOKS BY CAMI CARLISLE

Sabre Security Daddies

Hutch

Reid

Gage

Deke

PLEASE LEAVE A REVIEW!

It would mean so much to me if you would take a brief moment to leave a rating and/or a review on this book. It helps other readers find me. Thank you for your support!

-Cami